GHOSTS AND GRUDGES

A REVERSE HAREM URBAN FANTASY

JASMINE WALT
J.A. CIPRIANO

DYNAMO PRESS

IMPORTANT NOTE FROM THE AUTHORS

Dear Reader,

Thank you so much for picking up Ghosts and Grudges! This book is a reverse harem urban fantasy, featuring Japanese-American characters, and Japanese mythology. Japan's mythology is rich and unique, but we realize that you may not be familiar with it, so we have enabled Amazon X-Ray for your convenience. This means that when you click or press any of the italicized Japanese words in this book, the definition will pop up immediately, so you do not have to hunt through the internet to find it.

There is also a short, spoiler-free glossary in the back of the book, which you are free to refer to, or read ahead of time if you'd prefer to familiarize yourself with the mythology beforehand.

A lot of research and care was put into this book, including Jasmine taking a two-week trip to Japan, where she visited many amazing temples and shrines, and drove the locals crazy with her incessant questions. ;) We sincerely hope you enjoy the fruits of our labor, and have fun following Aika and her men on this wild adventure!

Love,

Jasmine and J.A.

1

The day my life turned to absolute hell started out just like any other. I woke up to the sound of birds chirping outside my window, the sensation of a paperback novel digging into my cheek...and the horrible, horrible realization that my alarm clock never went off.

"Shit!" The digital readout on my alarm clock flashed repeatedly —3:00 a.m., which definitely did *not* line up with the amount of sunlight streaming through my gauzy red curtains. The power must have gone out. Again.

Throwing off my bed sheets, I dashed across the room to where my phone was plugged in and found it completely dead, which explained why my backup alarm system hadn't gone off either. Dammit. I hastily fiddled with the charger while powering it on to see that it was at a whopping four percent charge. My heart sank into my toes as the screen finished booting and loaded the time.

11:00 a.m.

I was *so* late.

"Aika?" my mom called sleepily from her room as I rushed down the hallway, making a beeline for the bathroom. "Why are you still here?"

"Overslept!" I shouted, slamming the bathroom door shut. I jumped into the shower and stifled a shriek when ice-cold spray hit me full in the face. I hated cold showers with a passion, but there was nothing for it—in this old place, it took a good five minutes for the water to warm up, and I didn't have time to wait.

I stumbled out of the shower a few minutes later, shivering from head to toe. We tended to keep the heat on low in order to save on the gas bill, so the bathroom was nearly as freezing as the water had been. I toweled off as fast as I could, then rushed back down the hall and leapt into my clothes before my extremities iced over.

Yeah, so maybe I was exaggerating. So what? I hate the cold. You would too, if you weighed ninety pounds and had almost no body fat. The curse of being Asian, I guess—we are slim and trim as a general rule, which is great in the summer when I can wear sundresses and bikinis. Not so great in the fall and winter, when I have to wear two pairs of socks and a big puffy parka that has the added function of making sure I don't get blown away by a stiff wind.

I'm a real badass, I know.

After doing a quick check to make sure my clothes were wrinkle-free, I twisted my long black hair into a knot, secured it with a pair of faux-jade chopsticks, and wrapped myself up in the aforementioned puffy coat before I rushed out the door.

Then I rushed back in and grabbed the monkey charm bracelet on my nightstand. It was a tiny red and white monkey, made of silk and stuffed with cotton, that hung on a leather band. I never left home without it. My father had given it to me when I was a baby, too small to remember. My mother told me it was a protective charm, and that my father had made her promise to never let me leave home without it.

If I was being honest, I really didn't believe in protective charms, or any of the other *Shinto* stuff that my mom swore by, but this was the only thing I had from my father, so I clasped it onto my left wrist before heading back out the door. The part of me that hated being late urged me to hurry down the stairs and out the door, but I ignored it and raced to the room at the end of the hall instead.

"Aika?" my mom asked as I shoved the door open. She pushed herself up in bed, her thin limbs trembling a little under the strain. I picked up her glasses from the bedside table before she had a chance to reach for them. A smile twitched across my lips as I gently perched them on her nose. She smiled back, and as she did, the wrap she wore on her head slipped sideways a little, revealing her bare scalp. Without thinking, I adjusted it so she wouldn't lose any of her body heat.

"Your color is up," I told her as I sat down on the edge of the bed next to her. I took her frail hand in mine. "How are you feeling?"

"Much better," she said. "I think that chicken soup you gave me yesterday did the trick."

She squeezed my hand, and I felt a zing of *ki* dart into me. She did seem to be more energetic than yesterday...but there was still pain in her, I realized as I examined the tiny bit of life energy she'd unwittingly sent into me.

"Lie down," I said, easing her onto her back. "I'll give you a quick healing before I go."

"There's no need," she began to protest. "You're going to be late."

"Hush." I placed my hands directly over her chest, just beneath her collarbones, and closed my eyes. Taking in a slow breath, I envisioned my own *ki* gathering in my chest, a soft ball of light. A friend of mine had dragged me to a *reiki* class forever ago, and although at first I'd been skeptical, I'd quickly found I had a natural aptitude for it. The *reiki* master had agreed, and had taken me on as his student for a little while. Using *reiki* to heal was what had inspired me to go to medical school in the first place—I enjoyed healing people, but even *reiki* had its limitations on what it could do. Proper medical care was still important.

Gently, I sent a stream of healing energy flowing into my mother's body. She sighed, her body relaxing beneath my hands, and I smiled. I might not be able to cure my mother's leukemia, but the healings augmented her treatment and had helped beat back the cancer before. I kept it up for a minute longer, flowing more energy into her, until I felt her pain ease.

"Thank you," my mother said as I opened my eyes. "I didn't realize how much I needed that."

"You're welcome." I leaned in and kissed her cheek, then reluctantly stepped back. "Please take it easy today, Mom. If you need help with anything, just call. I'm not that far away."

"Don't you worry about me," she said, shooing me away impatiently. "I'm a grown woman, and you've your own life to live. I'll be fine."

I grabbed her hand again, and her chin stiffened in the same way mine did whenever I was about to dig my heels in. The healing I'd just done had obviously given her a boost if she was already being this obstinate.

"Promise me you'll call if you need anything," I pleaded. "*Please.*"

The desperate note in my voice worked—she softened, her shoulders relaxing again. "I promise," she agreed, "if only so that you'll get out of here. Now shoo! You're late already. And tell Sanji I said hello."

She didn't have to tell me twice.

———

SHABU SHABU HOUSE, the hot pot restaurant my mom owned, was only a twenty-minute bike ride across town, but as I pumped the pedals as hard as I could, it was the longest twenty minutes of my life. The Presidio golf course flashed by as I zipped down Lake Street, and the late morning sun glittered off the San Francisco Bay beyond the stretch of green. The briny breeze beckoned, practically daring me to change direction and go lounge on the beach.

But my days of being a carefree girl were long over. They'd died the day my mother had been diagnosed.

I liked to split my life into two epochs—Before Cancer, and After Cancer. Before Cancer, I'd been a cheerful college student, working in my mom's restaurant part time while I took pre-med classes, and hanging out with friends during my spare time.

The last time I'd gone to the beach with my friends had been over a year ago. Before Cancer. Before my mom had received the terrible diagnosis that changed our lives forever.

By the time the doctors identified the leukemia, it had already progressed to Stage III. She'd originally gone in thinking she had anemia. I knew I should have forced her to go sooner—she'd been suffering from fatigue for months, and had grown far too thin. But my mother had always been a workaholic, and she'd refused to listen to me until the day she collapsed and nearly spilled a tea tray on a customer.

That was truly the day that After Cancer began, before we even really knew what was going on. While Mom had been on bed rest, in and out of the hospital as they tried to figure out what was going on, I'd switched to online classes and taken over running the restaurant. She'd already groomed me for it—I'd been by her side from the day she'd first opened it when I was four years old. I knew how to handle the books, how to deal with the vendors and manage the employees.

I just hadn't expected to be doing it for quite this long.

"Aika!" Janet, one of our waitresses, exclaimed in relief as I entered the restaurant. She was Japanese, like me, but smaller, and her fine black hair was dyed a honey brown and styled into corkscrew curls that bounced around her heart-shaped face. "Thank goodness you're here. I thought something had happened to you!"

"Just a case of dead alarm clock," I said, glancing at the clock—twenty minutes until opening time. "Sorry I left you hanging. Where are the others?"

"Sanji and Matthew are in the kitchen, as usual," Janet said, referring to our chefs. "Mihoko called in sick."

"Damn." Being down one waitress on a Saturday was *not* a good thing. "Guess I know what I'm doing today," I said, stalking to the closet behind the counter. I shucked off my jacket and hung it up, then grabbed a spare apron and tied it around my waist. "Let's finish getting set up."

Janet and I hurried around the orange-colored tables, testing the hot pot burners to make sure they were working and putting out silverware and condiments. Once I was certain she had that in hand, I went into the kitchen to check on Sanji and Matthew.

"You are late," Sanji said, not bothering to look up from his workstation. He was cutting a loin of Kobe beef into very thin slices, while Matthew chopped up vegetables. Matthew was a culinary student who worked part time, and Sanji had worked for us for close to fifteen years. He was close to fifty, with silver threaded through the goatee jutting from his chin and faint lines creeping in on his thin face.

"*Sumanai*," I apologized, biting my tongue at the thinly veiled belligerence in Sanji's tone. He had a lot of respect for my mom —me, not so much. Not since the day I told her, nearly four years ago, that I had no intention of continuing the family business. "My mother needed a little extra help this morning." A white lie, but I didn't need to give Sanji yet another reason to doubt me.

Sanji's face softened a little—he and my mother had become good friends over the years. "Is she doing any better?" he asked as I went to taste the pork stock that was keeping warm on one of the burners. "I was very worried when I went to visit her in the hospital last week."

Mom had given us all a very nasty scare recently. The leukemia had gone into remission for a while, and she'd even been spending more time in the restaurant, giving me more time to hit the books and even relax a bit. But last week, she'd collapsed in the middle of making dinner. I'd come home to see her lying on the kitchen floor with a knife clutched in her hand and a pot of soba noodles burning on the stove. Chills of horror still raced through me every time I thought about how close a call that had been—if she'd landed on her knife, or if the place had caught on fire, she could have died.

"She seemed stronger this morning," I told Sanji, not wanting him to worry. "I think she'll be starting chemo again soon." I hated the idea of her going through that again, but dying was far worse.

"Good." Sanji nodded decisively. "I will go to the shrine and pray for her this afternoon. The *kami* have smiled down on Hamako before—surely they will do so again. It is not her time to pass yet."

I nodded as a sudden lump settled in my throat. I didn't believe in the old gods, but Sanji did, and there was no point in telling him otherwise, especially since he meant well.

Swallowing back my tears, I pasted a smile on my face and went to unlock the front door for the lunch crowd. There was already a small crowd of people out front—Shabu Shabu House was a popular spot in Japantown, known for our cook-it-yourself Japanese hot pot dishes. Within minutes, the place was packed, and I was too caught up in the hustle and bustle to think about my troubles. Taking a deep breath, I stationed myself behind the counter and focused on greeting customers and getting them seated.

A good three hours passed before the crowd finally began to die out, tourists and regulars filtering out to go about their business or continue touring Japantown. Exhausted, I leaned against the bar counter for a minute to catch my breath. Maybe I could even sneak into the back and grab a glass of water.

"Hey, Aika." A familiar voice, smooth and with just the slightest hint of mischief, snagged my attention just as I was sending a couple off to their table. My pulse quickened and my nerve endings tingled as I turned to see a man saunter through the front door. He was tall and lean, close to six feet, dressed in a white chef's coat, black jeans, and high top sneakers. He swept his wind-tossed, shaggy caramel hair out of his almond-shaped eyes and grinned at me. "Still serving the same old stuff around here, huh?"

"Better than your second-rate sushi!" Janet retorted, instantly appearing by my side. She leveled a scowl at the intruder even as she struggled not to eye the black box in his hand. "You're not welcome here, Mr. Hayasaka."

"Is that any way to talk to a customer?" Shota Hayasaka pressed a hand to his heart in mock offense. "I'm amazed you keep the doors open with such a rude waitress," he said to me in a loud stage whisper.

Janet gave him the evil eye. "You're not a real customer. You're just a money-grubbing, second-rate chef trying to steal our business!"

I rolled my eyes. "Enough," I said, putting a hand on Janet's shoulder. "I don't need the two of you clawing each other's eyes out in front of the customers. Go do your job, Janet."

Huffing, Janet flounced off toward the tables. Shota watched her go, an odd look in his eyes that gave me pause. I'd seen him looking at Janet like that before, and it wasn't the way a man looked at a woman when he was attracted to her. It was more like the way you looked at someone when there was something off about them. Like their eyes were set a bit too far apart, or there was something funny about the way they walked. Except that didn't make sense, because Janet was flawless. She got more than her fair share of male attention, and went out on dates *all the time.*

If only I had some of her mojo.

"Don't you have fish to fillet?" I asked, drawing Shota's attention back to me.

"My junior chef can stand to be away from me for a minute or two." Shota leaned against the counter as if he had all the time in the world. He placed the box on the countertop, drawing my attention to his muscular forearm. His sleeve was rolled up to the elbow, and I caught a glimpse of a *kanji* tattoo on his inner wrist. "You're a lot more interesting to look at than he is," he teased, his dark eyes gleaming.

"If you think that bringing me lunch is going to convince me to accept your business proposal, you're dead wrong," I said, even as I fought to keep the blush out of my cheeks. Shota had this kind of magnetism about him—an air of carefree confidence that drew me to him like a moth to a flame. The only problem was, I was smarter than a moth. And I had no intention of going down in flames for the sake of a pretty face.

"Oh, come on, Aika." Shota lowered his voice, leaning in a little. This close, I could smell his aftershave—something spicy with undertones of cinnamon. "We both know your life would be so much easier if you sold this place to me. My offer is more than generous; your mother will never have to work another day in her life, and you'll be free to focus on your own future."

I sighed, pushing away the treacherously seductive picture his words painted. The sincere concern in his tone made it hard for me to be angry with him, but I couldn't give in. "You know my mother will never sell this place to you." I'd already discussed it with her in the past, and she'd dug in her heels. *Over my dead body,* she'd said.

I had a feeling she meant that literally.

"How about lunch, then?" Shota countered. "*Real* lunch," he added when I opened my mouth to make a smartass comment. "As much as I enjoy wowing you with my superior culinary talent"—he gestured to the black box on the table—"it might be a nice change of pace for us to go some place neither of us own. Neutral ground, if you will."

I snorted. "Are you asking me out on a date or a negotiation?"

"It can't be both?"

Typical. "I don't have time for your games," I said, shooing him out of the way so I could help the customers who had just walked in. "Come back when you're serious."

"I am serious." Shota's gaze bored into mine as he shifted, blocking my view of the front door. He covered my hand with his own, and a tingle shot up my arm. "I know you're interested, Aika. You can try to hide it, but I can see it in your eyes." His thumb skimmed over my skin, sending a tendril of heat through me. My breath hitched in my throat.

"I don't know what you're talking about," I said, my voice remarkably even considering I couldn't breathe.

"Sure you do." His eyes twinkled as he pulled away, leaving me feeling strangely bereft. "But there's no rush. You know where to find me when you're ready. Enjoy the food."

He walked away, leaving me to stare after him. It took me a second to realize my eyes were glued to his tight ass—did he really have to wear such well-fitted jeans?—while the couple who had just walked in was still waiting. My face flamed, and I quickly apologized, then took care of them. God, what was *wrong* with me? Was I really that hard up for some action? Sure, it had been over a year since I'd last taken a man to bed, but I'd been so wrapped up with work and school it hadn't occurred to me that I was missing anything.

My gaze fell on the black box, and my stomach chose that moment to growl. Loudly. Giving in, I flipped open the lid, then groaned at the sight of the sushi spread within. Shrimp, salmon, tuna, roe, eel, yellowtail—

"You've got to stop encouraging him, Aika," Janet said, appearing at my elbow as if by magic. "Every time you eat his food instead of sending him away with it, you're sending a message that you want more."

"You're one to talk!" I exclaimed as Janet snatched up three sushi rolls. She shoved them into her mouth before I could grab her wrist. "I don't understand how you can eat so much at once," I muttered as I watched her swallow them down. Janet had a voracious appetite and was eating constantly. She claimed she had a crazy-fast metabolism and that if she didn't eat every hour she'd get dizzy and weak. Considering how trim her figure was, I was inclined to believe her about the metabolism part. I'd have to roll myself down the stairs every morning if I ate like she did.

"Practice," she said, reaching for another sushi roll. I smacked her hand away, but she simply used her other one, snatching up an eel roll. "I'm going to take my break now," she said around a mouthful of fish and rice. "Cover me for a minute, would you?"

"Sure, no problem," I said sarcastically to her retreating back. It wasn't as if I was the boss or anything, right? Shaking my head, I picked up one of the shrimp rolls and popped it into my mouth. My eyes nearly rolled back into my head as the flavors burst onto my tongue. As usual. *So. Freaking. Good.*

If Shota's that good at making sushi, what else can he do with those hands?

Pushing that dirty thought out of my head, I grabbed the notepad Janet had left on the counter and quickly reviewed it to make sure there weren't any outstanding orders. All of her tables looked to be taken care of, but as I glanced around the room, I noticed there was a man sitting in the corner by the circular window who hadn't been served. Hell, he didn't even have any water or anything. Weird. Janet was usually on top of her customers.

Hating to keep a customer waiting, I went over to help him, but as I approached, alarm bells began to go off in my head. The guy had long silver-gray hair that he pulled back into a high pony-tail, and instead of normal clothing, he wore a black and silver *haori* and *hakama*—a kind of Japanese-style coat and pants. I half-expected him to be carrying a *katana*, but instead he held a sketchpad and paper, and his wizened old eyes were trained out the window, as if he was sketching the view.

"*Konnichiwa,*" I greeted him, defaulting to Japanese. "Would you like to see a menu?"

The man started, then twisted around in his seat to face me, faster than I would have expected for someone his age. "You can see me?" he asked, astonishment filling his voice as he looked me up and down.

"Umm. Yes. Why wouldn't I?" Now that the man was facing me, I was struck by the odd color of his eyes. He was Japanese, like me, and normally we weren't very creative in the eye color department. But instead of dark or light brown, his eyes were a brilliant vermillion—the exact same shade that we always painted the *torii* gates outside our shrines and temples.

The man beamed at me, and a curious sensation enveloped my body as I stared into them. It was almost as if his smile had parted the clouds, and the sun was shining directly onto my body. Except that didn't make sense, because I was inside.

"You are the one I've been searching for." He set his pad and pencil down, then leaned back in his booth as though he'd just eaten a very satisfying meal. "I can return to the Heavens now, knowing my duties are done."

"What are you talking ab—" I began, but the man was already out of his chair and across the room. How the hell had he moved so fast? I was about to shrug it off, but then I noticed he'd left his pad and pencil behind. Snatching them up, I raced out of the café as fast as I could, hoping I could catch up with him in time.

"Mister!" I shouted as I burst through the door, whipping my head left and right. I caught sight of him halfway across the street and rushed to the corner. "Mister! You forgot your stuff!"

He turned toward the sound of my voice, and that was when the bus plowed straight into him.

2

"**M**ister!" I screamed as I watched the bus plow into the man. Holy crap, the driver hadn't so much as tapped on his brakes! My heart in my throat, I leapt forward, fully intending on using my petite frame to stop traffic. Someone had to make sure he was okay—

Except there was no body in the street. The old man was gone.

"Guh..." I sputtered, trying to process what I'd just seen. How was that possible? The old man had been standing *right there*. He'd turned his head to look at me right before he'd been run over.

And yet there was no body on the asphalt. Not so much as a single finger. It was as if he'd never been there.

As traffic continued on like nothing had happened, I became vaguely aware that I was clutching something in my hand. Frowning, I looked down to see that I was still holding the man's art supplies. Ha! Proof! He was totally real. The pencil in my left hand was solid, and the sketchpad in my right...

"What the..." I mumbled, my eyes going wide as I stared at it. I brought the cream paper closer to my face, certain that the light was playing a trick on me. But no.

The sketch was of a Japanese woman in an elaborate *kimono* embroidered with large *sakura* blossoms, her hair done up in an elaborate style that even a *geisha* would be envious of. That wouldn't have been weird, except her face was a carbon copy of mine—my long-lashed, almond-shaped eyes, my small, slightly rounded nose, my wide cheekbones and square-shaped face.

Hell, even the tiny beauty mark at the corner of her left eye was identical to mine. Had this man been sketching me the whole time? But then why had he been looking out the window?

"Aika!" Janet's high voice startled me out of my state of muddled confusion, and I turned to see her hurrying down the front steps of the café toward me. Her face was the picture of concern. "Are you okay? What happened?"

"I..." A glib response sprang to my lips, but it died instantly as Janet's form flickered before my eyes. Instead of a young woman in her twenties, I was looking at a creature with sunken lips and eyes, leathery skin that looked like it belonged on a mummy, and an enormous distended belly that threatened to burst her orange uniform dress open. My mouth dropped open, and the image flickered away, replaced by Janet's normal, pretty face.

"What are you staring at?" Her eyes narrowed, and a chill ran down my spine. If I didn't know better, I'd say she was looking at me with suspicion.

"Nothing." I pressed a hand against my stomach as nausea roiled in my gut. Why was I hallucinating? "I... I guess I don't feel well."

Janet's expression softened. "Of course. You've been super stressed. Go home and spend some time with your mom," she said, and her face changed again, back to the leathery mummy. I choked down a scream as she reached out with an impossibly long, narrow arm and patted my shoulder with a stubby, four-fingered hand. "Make sure to get plenty of rest. We need you back tomorrow!"

"Y-yeah, sure," I stammered. Janet turned around to go back in, and I swallowed at the sight of her long neck and bulbous head. Had I eaten something strange today? Had Shota put something weird in the sushi? A chill ran down my spine at the thought. What if he'd drugged me?

Don't be ridiculous, I scolded myself. Shota wasn't that kind of guy. Sure, we didn't know each other that well, but I was a decent judge of character. Shota might want to buy my mom's business, but that didn't mean he'd resort to dirty tricks like this to get it. Besides, I hadn't noticed anything off about the food he'd given me.

Shaking my head, I went back inside, grabbed my stuff from the closet behind the bar, and headed out. Maybe Janet was right, and the stress was finally getting to me. A cup of tea and a good night's sleep were all I needed, I assured myself firmly as I hopped onto my bicycle.

But as I pedaled up the narrow streets toward the apartment I shared with my mother, I couldn't shake the feeling that something significant had happened to me this afternoon. And that the universe wasn't quite done doling out surprises for me yet.

3
_____

"This can't be real," I muttered as I stared at a cat-woman chatting on her cell phone across the street. No, not the Halle Berry Catwoman. That wouldn't have been weird, not in SFO. This fine lady was dressed in a cardigan and jeans like a normal Jane, but she had the head of a calico cat and a matching tail waving behind her.

Did Halloween come early? I wondered. I supposed she could be wearing some kind of mask that covered her whole head, but I couldn't figure out the waving tail thing. Was it animatronic?

Blue eyes with cat-like pupils met mine from across the street as we both waited for the light to change. I gave her a weak smile, but her eyes narrowed in suspicion, just like Janet's had earlier. Swallowing, I looked away, my heart hammering in my chest. What was going on?

Oh crap, I thought as the light changed. _You're gonna have to pass her in the street._

Gripping my handlebars tight, I pedaled into the street and forced myself to look at the woman. I almost toppled off the bike as our gazes met again—her blue eyes were perfectly normal now, and there was no sign of a cat's head or tail. My heart rate ratcheted up, and I pumped harder, wanting to get away before she changed back into a cat.

A block and a half later, I forced myself to a stop.

What is wrong with you? I scolded myself, leaning against a wall. My lungs burned like I'd run a marathon, even though I'd pedaled maybe three blocks total. My heart was trying to pummel its way out of my chest, my skin was clammy with sweat, and I felt faint.

You're not feeling well, I told myself firmly. *You're obviously hallucinating. Maybe you've caught some kind of weird bug.* Yeah. That was it. Cat people didn't exist, and neither did goblins, or whatever I'd seen when I'd looked at Janet. I was gonna go home and sleep off whatever this was so I could resume my life tomorrow.

And if it turned out that Shota had given me a bad case of food poisoning, I was gonna rip him a new one the next time I saw him.

Decided, I resumed the rest of the journey on foot, walking my bike alongside me. If I really *was* hallucinating, I had no business steering any kind of vehicle.

"You don't want to do this," a low male voice said, and I froze. Something about it was familiar, tugging at my chest like a long-lost ghost from the past. Turning to my left, I saw a tall, athletically built guy standing in the alleyway. He was confronting a masked girl in a *kimono*, who was clutching a *katana*. For a moment I wondered if maybe she was a *kabuki* performer— Japanese theater performers were traditionally men, but times were changing—except that *katana* looked wicked sharp. The sliver of sunlight that managed to filter in through the alley glinted off the edge of the blade, making the folded steel shimmer.

That's definitely not a production blade.

The woman let out a high-pitched giggle that caused the hair on my arms to rise. "Am I pretty?" she asked coyly in Japanese, canting her masked head to the side.

The man's broad shoulders stiffened. "There's no need to go down this route—"

"Am I pretty?" the girl asked again, her voice harsh this time. Her pale hand tightened around the hilt of the *katana*, and I gulped. Oh my God, she was gonna kill him!

"Yes," the man said tightly, and I wondered why the hell he wasn't hightailing it out of there. Why was he even talking to this crazy woman? He should be calling the cops! I had reached for my cell phone to do just that when the woman slowly lifted her mask.

"Ahhhhh!" I screamed, stumbling back at the sight of her face. It was absolutely horrific—someone had slashed her mouth from ear to ear, exposing the bloody insides of her cheeks and her rows of back teeth. The loose skin flapped as she whipped her head around to face me, and bile rose in my throat as glowing blue eyes met mine.

A memory flickered in my mind of an old Japanese folktale, but before I could catch it, the gruesome woman raised her *katana* and charged me with a scream of pure rage.

"Dammit, no!" the man shouted, chasing after her. The crazy woman slashed at my face with her sword, but I somehow managed to duck. Unfortunately, grace and I aren't exactly best buddies, and I landed on my ass on the sidewalk.

The woman raised her sword again to strike, but before she could bring the blade down, a glowing piece of paper smacked into the side of her face. Howling, she dropped the sword, clutching at the paper—an *ofuda*, I realized, staring at the Japanese characters scrolled across the vertical slip of paper. Shocked, I turned toward the man, who already had another one in his hand. I thought he was going to throw it at her, but instead, he grabbed my hand and hauled me to my feet.

"It won't hold her for long," he shouted. "Run!"

"My bike!" I cried as he pulled me down the street, but there was nothing for it. Looking back, I saw the monster-woman writhing in the street, clawing at the thing on her face. A chill shot down my spine, and somehow, I knew deep down that she would get it off soon enough, and then she'd be after us.

"Come on!" the man yelled impatiently, yanking on my hand. I could see him more clearly in the street now—he was Japanese, with tanned skin and long, dark hair pulled back into a ponytail. Good-looking, and that strange *something* tugged in my chest again, making me want to slow down and study him some more. But there was no time, so I turned around and pumped my legs hard, running as fast as I could. Even so, I tripped and stumbled on cracks in the sidewalk—the man's legs were much longer, and I couldn't keep up with his breakneck pace.

A furious shriek echoed down the street, and I looked back to see the monster-woman running after us. Cursing, my...savior? Kidnapper? New best friend? Anyway, he knocked a food cart over, scattering dango and onigiri across the sidewalk.

The vendor swore, shaking his fist at us, but my companion didn't bother with so much as an apology. Instead, he knocked down two sandwich board signs and a table, then dragged me into an alley and shoved us through a metal door.

"What the hell is going on?" I yelled as we stumbled into the kitchen of a ramen shop. The heavenly smells of pork bone broth and boiling noodles would normally have made my mouth water, but at the moment my stomach was flip-flopping around in my abdomen like a dying fish. "Who *was* that woman?"

"I think the more important question," the man growled, hauling me away from the gawking kitchen workers, "is who the hell are *you*?"

"Umm, excuse me," the chef said, appearing at the man's elbow, "but this isn't really the place for—"

The man slapped a fifty-dollar bill on the metal counter. "Leave us alone."

The chef scowled, but apparently fifty bucks was his price,

because he slipped the money into his apron and slunk back off to his workstation.

"Do I get one of those too?" I asked, raising an eyebrow. "You know, since I saved you from that psycho-lady?"

The man scowled. "You didn't *save* me from anything," he snapped. "I was *working*, and you screwed everything up by screaming like a little girl!"

"*You* would have screamed too if someone who had their face slashed open smiled at you!" I protested.

"Except I didn't." The man smirked. That stupid curve of his lips made my heart flutter, and a weird sense of déjà vu rippled through me. Slowly, I took him in, trying to figure out who I was dealing with.

A modern version of Sessue Hayakawa, I thought as I looked him up and down. He had the same intense stare, strong jaw, and sensual lips that had made Hayakawa one of the first male heart-throbs in Hollywood during the silent film era. But unlike Hayakawa, he had shoulder-length hair that he pulled back into a ponytail at the nape of his neck, he dressed in modern clothes, and his eyes were a bit larger.

Those eyes were magnetic—they were the kind of eyes that could hold a woman's attention whether they sparkled with laughter or darkened with brooding anger. The kind of eyes that pulled you right in and made you feel as if he could see every inch of your soul.

And so what if he looks like a celebrity hottie? I scolded my fluttering heart. *That doesn't mean he has the right to manhandle you.*

Depends on what kind of manhandling we're talking about, a wicked voice in my head said. I shoved that voice back into the dark depths from whence it had come and finished my perusal.

He stood a good six inches taller than me and was dressed in a black button-down that strained against his broad shoulders, jeans that hinted at powerful thighs, and a pair of black boots that looked like they could do some serious ass-kicking. A clunky-looking keychain hung from a lanyard attached to his belt loops, and though I was curious about that, it wasn't nearly as interesting as the rest of him.

"Are you done staring yet?" the man asked, a hint of dry humor in his voice.

I frowned at him. "What's your name, anyway? The least you could do after almost getting me killed is tell me who the hell you are."

"Getting you killed?" he sputtered. "Why, you—" He stopped himself, clearing his throat. "You're getting us off track."

"Didn't realize we had an agenda." I folded my arms across my chest and leaned my hips against the table behind me.

"Fine. My name is Raiden Takaoka, of the Takaoka Shaman Clan." His eyes narrowed. "We're the only shaman clan in America, or so I thought. Which clan are you from?"

"Shaman clan?" I echoed. "Is that some kind of joke? I'm not from any clan."

Raiden rolled his eyes. "Everyone of Japanese descent is from some kind of clan. What's your name?" A suspicious glint entered his eyes. "You look familiar for some reason."

"Aika Fujiwara." *You look familiar too,* I thought, but I didn't say it out loud. Frowning, I mulled over his words. Sure, maybe back hundreds of years ago Fujiwara had been a clan, but I didn't know much about my family history. As far as I knew, I'd been born and raised here in America.

My father had died when I was little, and my mother had never remarried, so she'd raised me on her own. An unexpected pang of sadness hit me as I remembered how, when I was little, my mom had always stared at the picture of the two of them she'd kept by her bed before she turned in for the night.

She prayed for his soul every night, hoping that he had found peace in the afterlife. And I could tell from the look in her eyes whenever she talked about him that she was still deeply in love with him. She often said that if the cancer did take her, at least she would get to see him again.

"Are you all right?" Raiden asked, as my eyes began to sting. His gaze softened with concern, ruining my preconceived notion about him being an overbearing asshole.

"I'm fine." Embarrassed, I tried to blink the tears back, but one slipped down my cheek. Angry, I swiped at it. "Why are you asking me about my family anyway?" And why was I getting so emotional? Was the recent incident with my mother bringing all these feelings back to the surface again?

"Because I wanted to know if you were from a shaman clan,

since it's obvious you can see spirits," Raiden said matter-of-factly, as if crazy talk weren't spewing out of his mouth. He leaned against the back of a steel refrigerator, studying me with eyes so dark they were nearly black. "I'm not familiar with the Fujiwara name, but it's possible you could be from some obscure shaman clan that died out somewhere."

My skin went ice-cold. "Spirits?" I echoed. "You're trying to tell me that thing was a ghost?"

Raiden nodded. "The *Kuchisake-onna*," he said. "I didn't expect to see her around here, but I guess she migrated over somehow. I had hoped to capture her, but you screwed it up by screaming your head off when she took off the mask."

I glared, about to protest, when suddenly the memory that had been niggling me earlier burst forward. I'd read about the *Kuchisake-onna* in a Japanese fairy tale book my mother had given me when I was ten—far too young, to be honest, because some of the tales were pretty gruesome.

The *Kuchisake-onna* was a woman whose face had been slashed open by her husband after he found out that she'd cheated on him, and she'd returned as a vengeful spirit to torment him. She carried a *katana*, and always either wore a mask over her face or covered it with a fan or scarf. The tale went that when she came across a man, she would ask him whether or not she was pretty. If the man said yes, she would take off her mask and ask him again. If he answered no, or screamed, she'd slash him from ear to ear so that he'd resemble her. If he said yes, she'd walk away... only to follow her victim home and brutally murder him that same night.

A win-win situation.

"How exactly were you planning on subduing her?" I asked. "Since the *Kuchisake-onna* kills regardless of your answer?"

"Ah, so you are familiar with the tale." Raiden's eyes glinted with something like approval. "There are ways to get around it by giving confusing answers that are either yes or no. The plan was to catch her off guard and use one of my own spirits to help subdue her. But I hadn't gotten to that part yet." His lips thinned. "She'll probably kill someone else tonight."

Guilt swamped me at the idea that the crazy, sword-wielding woman was still out there because of something I had done. "I just don't understand how she can be a ghost," I protested. "Aren't ghosts non-corporeal?"

Raiden shrugged. "Some of them are, which is why shamans have to join with them in order to use their powers. But a ghost with a grudge is a powerful thing. Killing her own husband didn't bring the *Kuchisake-onna* peace—it only corrupted her heart further, which is why she can't pass on. It is the duty of a shaman to purify these souls so they can move on to the afterlife."

I pressed the heel of my hand against one of my throbbing temples. So many questions were swirling through my head, questions I could spend all night asking. But foremost in my mind was the desire to shut myself in my room, crawl under the covers, and pretend like this had never happened. I had no room in my life for ghosts. I might be a *reiki* practitioner, but I was pragmatic. I didn't believe in ghosts.

"Look, I'm sorry I screwed up your...purification ritual...or whatever it was you were trying to do," I said. "But I don't really have time for all this. I have to get home to my mother."

"Are you telling me you've never seen a ghost before today?" Raiden's eyes widened.

I shook my head. "Nope. And I don't plan on seeing one ever again." I pushed myself upright, then made to move past him. "Nice meeting you, Raiden."

Raiden slapped a hand against the opposite wall, nearly clotheslining me. "Oww!" I complained as my chest slammed into his rock-hard forearm. He had some serious muscles hiding underneath that shirt and jacket. "What is your problem?"

"You can't just walk away from this," he said. "Once you gain the Sight, you have it for life, Aika. It's not something you can wish away."

I scowled. "Well I'm damn well going to try," I snapped, shoving at his arm. Unfortunately, my attempts to move it were about as effective as shoving at a brick wall. "Are you going to let me go? You can't hold me hostage in a restaurant all night. Fifty bucks can only buy you so much time." I slid my gaze sideways, toward the chef, who was watching us again. I knew that if things got violent he would step in—it wasn't in his best interests to have a fight break out in his kitchen.

Raiden sighed. "At least let me take you home," he said. "It'll be dark soon, and you've lost your bike."

I cursed. "I have to go back and get it," I said, ducking under his arm. "It's my only mode of transportation!"

Raiden snagged my wrist, pulling me to a stop yet again. An electric current shot through the veins in my inner arm at the skin-on-skin contact, and I jerked, startled. His eyes flashed, as if he'd felt the same thing, and suddenly there wasn't enough air in my lungs. He was way too close.

"Don't worry about it," he said gruffly, to my surprise. "I'll pay for you to replace it. It's not safe for you to be wandering around, especially now that you can see the ghosts. They don't like knowing that others can see them for who they really are, and if you don't know how to defend yourself you can get killed."

An icy chill rippled down my spine at the dire note in his voice. As much as I didn't want to believe Raiden, I also didn't want to get myself killed by my closed-mindedness. Better to be safe than sorry, right?

"Fine," I said. "I live in the Richmond district."

"All right." Raiden finally let me go. "We'll call a cab, then."

We went back to the main street, and I blinked—the sun was already setting, bathing the tops of the buildings with gilded light. Just how long had he and I been arguing? Raiden flagged down a cab, then held the door open for me so I could get in first.

Pretty gentlemanly behavior, I thought as I slid along the faux-leather seats, *considering he was yelling at me before.*

"So," he said casually as the cab eased into traffic. "You work at Shabu Shabu House?"

I nodded—he must have recognized my uniform. "My mom and I run the restaurant together." I didn't see any reason to tell him that, right now, *I* was the only one running the place. I winced as I remembered all the paperwork I'd skipped—I would be having a *very* full day tomorrow.

"I see. And you've never noticed anything...odd, about any of your employees?"

I was about to shake my head when I remembered how Janet had changed from her normal appearance to a weird, monstrous, *mummy* thing. My stomach turned as the memory of her yellowed, sunken eyes and skeletal arms filled my head.

"I see that you have," Raiden observed quietly, switching to Japanese so we wouldn't be overheard by the driver. *"She's a gaki."*

My mouth dropped open. *"How...how do you know that?"* Was this guy friends with Janet? Surely I would have noticed if she was hanging around a hunk like this.

"I'm a shaman. It's the family business to know which yokai are hanging about town, and Janet has a file. She's actually been working at the café since the day it opened, under different guises."

"Well that explains why she's always eating," I muttered, trying to wrap my head around it. I couldn't deny that the hallucination I'd seen looked pretty much exactly like a *gaki*. *Gakis* were tormented spirits who were constantly hungry and thirsty, but

no matter how often they ate, they could never satisfy themselves. And Janet had a constant habit of taking frequent food breaks. She always brought in a huge bag filled with snacks to tide her over on every shift.

"So, if you know that Janet is a yokai, how come you've left her alone?" I asked warily. *"Or do you not hunt down every yokai that you find?"*

Raiden shrugged. *"She does no harm, so we leave her be,"* he said. *"The reason she is so attached to your café is because it once belonged to an ancestor of hers."*

"Oh." Sadness swept through me—what must it be like to be tied to a spot for all eternity, simply because you couldn't bear to part with something that had belonged to a loved one? But I shook it off—I couldn't let myself be swept into all this stuff. I needed to focus on my medical degree and keep the shop running at the same time. I hoped to start working in cancer research, and if my mom went back into remission, that might buy enough time for me to help find a real cure for her.

A slim hope, but one I clung to daily.

"You need to come by my family's shrine," Raiden said, breaking my train of thought. *"I get that you don't want to be a shaman, but since you obviously are one, you need to learn the basics of how to defend yourself."*

I scowled. *"Just because I can see ghosts doesn't mean I'm a shaman,"* I argued. *"Maybe I'm just clairvoyant. Ever think about that?"*

Raiden threw back his head and laughed, flashing perfect white teeth. The sound raised the hairs on my arms, and I couldn't figure out if I was annoyed or turned on, which really pissed me off. Why did he have to be so damn attractive?

"Denial doesn't suit you well," he finally said, his gaze hard again. *"You're a walking statistic right now, Aika, and as a shaman, I can't just stand aside and watch you get killed. You need to learn what you're dealing with."*

A walking statistic? I drew myself upright, indignant, and prepared to give him an earful.

"The archaeological dig between the coast and Mount Koya has taken an unsettling turn," a female voice on the radio said, distracting me before I could give Raiden a piece of my mind. I leaned forward to listen—my mother had been following news of the dig intently. She hadn't been home to Japan in years, but she was still very loyal to the country, and the idea that an important piece of history might be uncovered was exciting to her. *"The archaeologists found a tomb halfway up the mountain, hidden in a forest cave that has never been explored until now. Several team members went into the newly excavated tomb yesterday but did not return. Tremors have been shaking Mount Koya since then, and some of the more superstitious residents even say—"*

A loud *crack* rent the air outside, followed by a sizzle. I jumped in my seat as all the street lights went out, including the traffic lights. The radio hissed, turning to static, and the driver, an Arab wearing a brightly colored Hawaiian shirt, swore.

"Must be a power outage," he grumbled. "I was listening to that, too!"

"That doesn't sound good," Raiden murmured in English, his eyes narrowing on the radio. "I wonder what those archaeologists found at *Koya-san*."

Dread settled in my gut like a lump of greasy tofu, and I swallowed back a wave of nausea.

"Looks like this is my stop," I said as we pulled up in front of my dingy apartment building. I opened the door. "Thanks for the ride," I said to Raiden, looking back at him. His dark eyes met mine, and even though he'd just pissed me off, I was suddenly reluctant to walk away from him. That tug in my chest grew stronger.

"Maybe I will come and visit the shrine," I said hesitantly. There was a connection between us, and I wanted to know what it was. Besides, what's the worst that could happen?

Raiden's lips curved into a smile that made my nerve cells do what I was pretty sure was the neurological equivalent of a mating dance. "I'd like that." His voice was dark and just a little bit husky, and suddenly I was no longer quite sure what he wanted from me.

Could it be that he felt the same pull I did?

I opened my mouth, feeling like I should say something. But he looked past me, breaking the moment, and his face tightened with worry.

"I'll walk you up," he said, scooting forward. "It's too dark out for you to be on the street by yourself."

"It's only a few feet away," I protested as he got out of the cab, but my words were half-hearted. I'd seen some freaky stuff today, and it was nice to have someone at my back who looked like he could actually beat someone in a fight. I was a mean volleyball server, and I'd excelled in dance competitions back in high school. But put a pair of boxing gloves on me, and suddenly I was all thumbs.

Good thing I don't have any samurai in my family tree, I thought as I climbed the stairs. *And that I'm not a man.* I'd be a real disappointment.

"Don't be too long," the cabbie called as Raiden slammed the door behind us. "I can't sit here forever, you know!"

Raiden ignored the driver as he followed me up the steps. I turned around, and stifled a gasp when I nearly smooshed my nose into his chest. "W-what are you doing?" I asked as he came to a stop. He was so close I could feel his body heat, and I was struck by the desire to lean in and wrap him around me like a fur coat.

That doesn't sound creepy at all.

Cheeks flaming, I backed up against the door. "I appreciate your concern, but you don't need to come in with me."

"Yes, I do." Raiden's gaze darkened as he lifted his head. A bad feeling settled into my chest as his eyes zeroed in on the second-floor window of my apartment. "There's a strong *yoki* presence in this place. And it's coming from that room."

4

"*Yoki?*" I echoed in disbelief. "You're trying to tell me there's a monster in my apartment?" *Yoki* was the Japanese word for the dark energy generated by monsters—known as *yokai*. *Ki* was the Japanese word for energy. Hence, *yoki*.

"That's your place?" Raiden's eyes widened. "Is anyone home?"

"My mother!" Fear slammed into my chest as I flung the door open. I dashed down the hall to the front door of our two-story home, Raiden on my heels, and skidded to a stop in front of my apartment door.

"*Okaa-san!*" I called, fumbling with my key ring. "Mom, are you there?"

I managed to get the key into the lock on the second try and shouldered the door open. The stench of something awful, like swamp rot, filled my lungs, and I gagged. Some kind of faint, smoky rainbow haze hung in the air, and I instantly began to feel lightheaded. I clutched at the wall as the room started swaying even though I wasn't moving.

"Here." Raiden slapped a kitchen towel into my hand—one of my own, I dimly realized. "Breathe through this."

I did as he asked, and the sensation lessened almost immediately. A weird croaking sound echoed from upstairs, and the hair on my arms stood straight up. "What the hell is that?"

"Stay behind me," Raiden ordered, stepping past me. I followed him up the stairs, my heart pounding with every step. The stairway was narrow, and there was no banister up to the upper floor, so I had no idea what was waiting for us.

Raiden reached the upper landing and immediately began to swear. That croaking sound echoed against the walls, and I dashed forward despite my better judgment. My eyes bugged out at the sight of a gigantic toad with a *naginata* clutched in its... hand? Paw? Webbing? I didn't know, but it was insane. The thing stood on two legs and was dressed in a white Japanese-style coat and pants, with a tall matching hat perched on its slimy, brownish-green head.

"An *ogama!*" Raiden cried, flinging an arm out to block my way. "Get back, Aika!" He unhooked his keychain from one of his belt loops and held up a tiny stone tablet the size of my index finger. But before he could do anything with it, the toad *yokai* opened his mouth wide and belched out a cloud of rainbow smoke.

"Gah!" I ducked my head, pressing the cloth firmly against my face. But the rainbow smoke—which smelled like rotten eggs, a decidedly *un*-rainbow-like stench—engulfed us.

The cotton rag Raiden had given me was flimsy protection against the *ogama's* rainbow burp. Even with it clutched over my nose and mouth, my head began to spin, and I stumbled backward, landing hard on the carpet. Raiden swayed on his feet, shouting something I should have been able to hear. Except his voice was warped, and suddenly I was seeing three of him...

"Whoa," I mumbled as the walls around me turned purple and began to melt. Red and white spotted mushrooms with bulging, veiny eyes burst out of the walls, and I screamed as they leapt on me, crawling all over my body while giggling maniacally. I tried to fight them off, but they stuck to my arms and legs, and began multiplying, burying me in a mountain of sticky, icky shrooms...

"Aika!" Raiden shouted, sounding very far away. "It's just an illusion! Fight it!"

That's easy for you to say! I wanted to shout, but a mushroom was stuck to my mouth, and I couldn't do more than squeak. I lifted my hand to try and pry it off, but my fingers were covered in tiny versions of the bastards, and I couldn't get a grip.

They are not real, a voice murmured in my head, and I stilled. *Calm yourself, child. And stop breathing so hard. You are only drawing more of the poison smoke into yourself.*

I didn't know where the voice came from, but I nodded. Warmth stole through me, like someone had injected a ray of sunlight straight into my veins. The mushrooms vanished, the walls stopped melting, and suddenly I could see Raiden again. He was facing off against the giant toad, a broomstick in his hand. It would have looked silly, except that he was dodging the toad's strikes with inhuman speed, and there was a strange, fiery aura around him. A strange feeling washed through me, and suddenly the aura coalesced into the silhouette of a samurai.

The toad croaked in anger as Raiden dodged one of his strikes, then landed, cat-footed, on the spear's handle. He brought the broomstick down hard in an overhead swing, smashing it into the top of the toad's head with a sickening *squelch* that flattened its hat. The toad's yellow eyes bulged, and it let out a horrible sound as it stumbled sideways.

"*Filthy yokai,*" Raiden spat in Japanese, jumping off the spear before it clattered to the ground. His voice was deeper, more guttural than normal, and his eyes blazed with the same fire as his aura. He snatched up the spear and pointed it at the toad's head.

"No!" I sprang forward, closing my fingers around his forearm. "Don't!"

Those fiery eyes met mine. "*Back away, foolish girl,*" he growled, and I was gripped by an intense urge to obey his command. But the flames flickered away for just a moment, and Raiden's dark eyes locked with mine.

"*Why don't you want me to kill it?*" he asked in his normal voice, though he still spoke Japanese.

"I..." I didn't know, I realized, dismayed. I should have wanted to kill it. It was a monster, after all, and it had invaded my home. But some instinct had moved me to defend the creature. "We need to question it," I insisted. "Find out what it's doing here."

The flames rushed back into Raiden's eyes. *"No questioning. Kill it now."*

"No!" I yanked Raiden's arm, and the spear flew out of his hand, embedding itself into the wall across the room. "We need to check on my mother. *Please.*"

"Relax, Katsu," Raiden murmured, and the flames died away. *"Sorry about that,"* he said gruffly, lowering his arm. *"Katsu's a bossy spirit. He used to be a daimyo."*

"I am still *a daimyo,"* that deep, guttural voice thundered. *"Even in death."* The flaming aura separated from Raiden, coalescing into the form of a Japanese man in his thirties sporting a thin mustache. He wore a badass *kabuto* helmet with golden antlers and plates of metal that curled back from the sides of his head in a kind of bowl, and a full suit of samurai armor. A *wakizashi* and *katana* were strapped to his waist, and though the handles and scabbards were of fine make, and fancy-looking, I knew the weapons were more than just for show.

"Yes, we know," Raiden said, with barely concealed impatience. He stepped past me, heading down the hall. "Which room is your mom's?" he asked me, switching to English.

"The one at the end of the hall." I pointed with an unsteady finger. Fear seized my throat as we approached my mom's room —the door was closed, something she almost never did. Had the toad *yokai*—the *ogama*—killed her? Would we open the door to see her slashed open by that wicked *naginata*? Oh God. Bile coated my tongue, and I swallowed it back down. But it came right back up again as I heard pained moans coming from the room.

"Mom!" I shoved past Raiden as he slowly opened the door. "Mom, what's wrong?" She was thrashing around in the bed, the sheets tangled around her thin limbs. I grabbed her hand, squeezing it hard, the sweat from her palm soaking into my skin. I reached for her *ki*, then winced—her spiritual energy was throbbing, like a live wire, and scorching hot. I tried to send a flow of healing energy into her, but it was instantly repelled, and I recoiled as it slammed back into me.

"What the hell?" I stared at my hands, which were smoking faintly. That had *never* happened to me before.

"She's hallucinating," Raiden said tightly. "The *ogama* must have hit her with its smoke, and she reacted more strongly to it. Do you have any *matcha* in the house?"

"Of course we do," I said. What self-respecting Japanese household didn't have green tea? "Do you think it'll help?"

"It'll help drive the toxins out of her more quickly," Raiden said, scowling at my mom. "Does your mother have any kind of illness? The hallucinogenic effects don't usually last this long."

"She has cancer," I said shortly, stepping away. "Stay with her while I go get the tea."

I ran downstairs and grabbed the canister of *matcha* powder from the closet. There was a Japanese tea set in one of the cupboards, and I grabbed the whisk and the tea bowl, not bothering with the other stuff—there was no time for ceremony. I plunked a regular old kettle onto the stove, filled it with water, and had it whistling in no time flat. Fast as I could, I poured the boiling water into the pot, added the tea, and whisked it together until it was frothy and thick.

On my way back up the stairs, I glanced toward the toad, still unconscious on the floor. Rage filled me, and suddenly I was tempted to pick up the spear Raiden had left on the ground and stab the *ogama* with it. What if that smoke had somehow accelerated my mother's condition? What if she died? My hands trembled with outrage, and some green tea sloshed over my fingers.

"Oww!" I hissed as the hot liquid scalded me. Taking a deep breath, I wrenched my thoughts away from the toad and continued down the hall. There was no point in dwelling on the past. And besides, I did want to question the creature, if it was even possible. Could the *ogama* speak human words? I seemed to remember from the old tales that some *yokai* spoke, while others didn't.

Guess I'll find out soon enough.

"Good, you're back," Raiden said when I stepped inside. My mother was still shaking, but I noticed it was a little less. "Let's get her to drink."

Raiden slid his arms beneath my mother, pulling her up into a sitting position. Her eyes were squeezed shut, her hands fisted, and she moaned in pain.

"Come on, Fujiwara-san," he murmured soothingly into her ear as he eased her jaw open a bit. *"You can do this. Be strong."*

Tears pricked at my eyes as I gently poured some of the rapidly cooling tea into her mouth. Most of it dribbled straight out of the corners of her mouth, but her throat bobbed, so I knew she swallowed some. I tried again, and this time she got more of it down.

My mom was one of the strongest people I knew. She'd raised me on my own, in one of the most expensive cities in the world, and prided herself on her independence. It hurt me, like a knife to the gut, every time she was brought low like this, because I knew it tore at her, too. She hated being so feeble, so bedridden, even though she hid it behind cheerful smiles and reassurances not to worry about her. To live my own life.

But how could I, when my mom's life was slipping away, day by day?

I managed to get half the bowl of tea down my mom's throat, and to my relief, the tremors began to lessen. She sagged against Raiden's chest with a sigh, and I dabbed some of the green tea from her chin.

"How is it that you weren't affected by the smoke?" I asked, my tone just this side of accusatory.

"Protective charm," Raiden said. "I would have given you one if I'd had extras, but since I had to fight off the *ogama*..." He shrugged a shoulder. "I figured I needed it more."

"Aika?" My mom's eyes opened, saving me from having to respond. Her voice was a little thick, probably from the remnants of the toxin, but her eyes were clear. "What's going on?"

"Mom." I gripped her hand again. "How are you feeling?"

"A little woozy, but all right." She sat up a little straighter, and her eyes widened as she seemed to realize there was a man holding onto her. Tilting her delicate chin back, she looked up at Raiden. "And who is this young man?" she asked, sounding both surprised and pleased.

Raiden immediately backed away, dipping into a bow. *"My name is Takaoka Raiden,"* he said in Japanese, his voice low and respectful. *"I apologize for the intrusion, but you seemed to be in danger."*

My mother's smile widened. *"Handsome* and *well-mannered."* She turned to me. "You should marry this one," she said, in English.

"Mom!" Heat exploded across my cheeks. My mother was always telling me to date—it was her fondest hope that I settle down with a nice Japanese boy. "We only just met. Besides, don't you think we have more important things to talk about? You were just attacked!"

My mother's face pinched. "Ah, yes. The *ogama.*" She gripped my forearm, hard, right over the bracelet from my father. "He was looking for you, Aika."

My mouth dropped open as shock hit me like a freight train. "For *me*? Why?"

My mom shook her head. "I don't know. He said something about a prophecy, and that a man named Kai is looking for you. He was sent here to find you."

"Kai?" Raiden frowned. "That doesn't make any sense."

"Do you know this Kai?" my mother demanded. She shot Raiden a look that would have made me wither on the spot. "Who is he, and why is he after my daughter?"

"He's a shaman who lived and died nearly two thousand years ago," Raiden said, a puzzled frown on his handsome face. "A famous one to anybody who knows shaman lore. But Kai was a spirit shaman—he couldn't control *yokai*. So even if he was somehow alive, that wouldn't make any—"

A puff of purple smoke exploded behind Raiden before he could finish. "Raiden, watch out!" I cried as the *ogama* burst out of the smoke. A *tanto* blade flashed in its webbed hand, and he flung it just as Raiden spun around, instinctively dodging the attack as he brought his hands up to face the toad. The blade sliced through the spot where Raiden had been, and a bolt of fear hit me as I realized it was headed straight for my chest. I tried to move out of the way, but I didn't have Raiden's ninja-like reflexes, and the *tanto* sank into my chest, right above my heart.

I screamed as burning pain sliced into me.

"Aika!" Raiden shouted as my knees buckled, and I hit the floor. Blood gushed from the wound, fast and furious, ruining my outfit. My mom cried out as I slapped my hand against the bed to hold myself upright, her hand outstretched toward me. I reached for the knife in my chest, but before my fingers could connect with the hilt, the charm bracelet on my wrist flared, blinding me.

Suddenly, I was no longer in the room. I was kneeling in a bamboo forest that smelled of rain and fresh dirt. The sounds of a stream burbling nearby and birds twittering in the air were a refreshing change from the croaking frog *yokai* and the swamp stench it had brought along with it. The knife was gone from my chest, and I didn't hurt anymore.

"What is this?" I asked aloud, my voice trembling. "Am I dead?"

"You would be, if not for me." The bamboo rustled, and a creature stepped from the shoots into the clearing. My mouth dropped open—it was some kind of strange monkey, with red eyes and a black leopard pattern on its fuzzy fur. Kind of like the love child of a baboon and a jaguar.

"I am a furi," the monkey answered in response to my unspoken question. *"A kind of monkey yokai. Your father bound my spirit to the charm you wear."*

"Oh," I said dumbly, having absolutely no clue what I was supposed to say to that. After a second, I added, *"Umm, sorry. I didn't know."*

The monkey smiled, showing a set of wicked-looking fangs I was certain I didn't want to get up close and personal with. *"No apology necessary. I have been able to live a life of relative freedom, as your father rarely called upon me."* The smile faded. *"I hope you are not planning on jumping in front of blades often, or that will change."*

I frowned. *"I don't understand. What did you do for my father?"*

"I have the power to absorb a fatal blow in your stead," the *furi* said, as if it were no big deal. *"That is what I am about to do now, before your life blood is gone. But I can only do this once per sunrise,"* the monkey warned. *"If you are stabbed again before the*

next, I will not be able to keep your soul from crossing over to the Reikai."

"*Is that where we are now?*" I asked as the monkey padded toward me on all fours. *Reikai* was the Japanese word for the afterlife. Normally, I would have backed away if an animal with glowing red eyes began to approach, but the sense of calmness in this clearing flowed over me. Somehow, I was at peace here, and I instinctively knew I was safe. "*Are we in the Reikai?*"

The monkey made a hacking sound, and I realized it was laughing. "*In a way,*" he said, placing a black, leathery palm against my chest. "*You could say we are at the border between the human world and the spirit world. My duty is to push you back to the side where you belong.*"

Light exploded from his palm, and I cried out as pain knifed through me. The monkey shoved me, and I landed flat on my back...on the carpet. Raiden was kneeling next to me, his face hovering over mine.

"Aika!" he exclaimed, his dark eyes widening with surprise and relief. "You... where did the knife go?"

I glanced down at my chest, frowning. The knife was gone, and though there was a hole in my shirt, the skin beneath it was smooth and pink, as if it had never been touched. "I...I don't know," I said faintly, still in shock. "I guess the *furi* must have made it disappear."

"*Furi?*" Raiden's eyes narrowed. "What *furi?*"

I shoved myself upright, ignoring him as reality came rushing back. "Where's the *ogama*?" I demanded, my heart rate spiking as I saw my mom's bed was empty. "Where's my mother?"

"I'm sorry, Aika," Raiden said. My heart plummeted at the tone of his voice, and I turned to see his face had twisted into an expression of guilt and sympathy. "I couldn't stop the *ogama* in time. She's gone."

5

"No!" I shot to my feet, blood pumping wildly in my veins. "No, this can't be happening!" I ripped apart the bed as though my mom might be hiding somewhere in the sheets. Nothing. Shoving past Raiden, I ran out into the hall, calling her.

"Okaa-san!" I yelled, flinging open the bathroom door. My bedroom. Rushing down the stairs into the kitchen. God, where *was* she?

"Aika, she's not here!" Raiden hurried down the stairs after me. "The *ogama* took her!"

"But *why*?" I whirled around to face him, tears blurring my vision. Grief and anger warred in my heart, and I had to fight against the urge to lash out at him physically. "Why weren't you able to stop him?"

"Believe me, I tried," Raiden growled. "The bastard was too fast for me. He jumped right over me and grabbed your mother, then poofed out in a puff of purple smoke. There was no way for me to follow—I don't even know where he went."

"Well we need to figure that out," I said, clenching my hands into fists. "We need to track him down, we need to..."

But how? How the hell were we supposed to track down a magical toad? A wave of hopelessness filled me, and suddenly, the anger fell away, replaced by agonizing grief as I realized a terrible truth.

This was all my fault.

"This isn't fair," I choked, tears spilling down my cheeks. "My mother doesn't deserve this. She's already dying of cancer. Why did this have to happen? Why didn't he take me instead, like he was supposed to?"

"Shhh." Raiden gently enfolded me in his arms, pressing my cheek against his strong chest. I was briefly struck by the urge to push him away, but my need for comfort won out, and I buried my face in his T-shirt and cried. This day had been beyond stressful, and the dawning fact that I was the one responsible for my mother's kidnapping was the straw that broke the camel's back.

"It's all right," Raiden said roughly, stroking my back. His big hands gliding down my tense muscles eased some of my pain, and as I sucked in breath after shuddering breath, I took in his scent. It was some kind of incense, mixed with his inherently masculine scent, and it calmed me enough that I finally drew away.

"Sorry about your shirt," I muttered, swiping at the big wet stain on the front of it.

Raiden shrugged. "Shirts are replaceable," he said, slipping a hand beneath my chin. He tilted my face up to meet his. "You're not, Aika, and it's obvious that someone thinks you're valuable enough to kidnap. We need to find out who, and why."

"My mom specifically mentioned Kai," I said as I wiped at my face with my sleeve.

"That doesn't make any sense." Raiden raked a hand through his long hair, inadvertently yanking it from its ponytail. It swung free around his angular face, lending an edge of wildness to his otherwise stoic appearance. "Kai has been sealed away for thousands of years. The only way he could have come back is if..."

"If what?" I asked. My stomach sank as an expression of dawning horror crept over Raiden's face. "Raiden, what is it?"

"That archaeology excavation we heard on the radio..." Raiden swallowed. "I think they might have been digging where Kai's tomb was located."

"Shit." It was my turn to rake my hand through my hair. "Just who is Kai, anyway? If he was buried in some kind of tomb, how is he still alive? Was it recent?"

"Recent?" Raiden laughed hollowly. "The last time Kai was seen alive was nearly two thousand years ago. He was imprisoned for using dark magic to kill the son of his clan's leader *and* the woman he was engaged to marry."

"Two thousand years ago?" I squeaked, my mind struggling to

process that. "That doesn't make sense. How can he still be alive in that tomb two thousand years later?"

Raiden reached for the kitchen towel hanging from the refrigerator door and handed it to me. "It's a long story, but he'd been joined with a powerful evil spirit when he was sealed away, so that spirit might have kept him alive all this time," he said as I mopped my face. "Powerful spells were placed on that tomb so that humans would never find it. I don't understand how these archaeologists managed to dig it up."

"Maybe Kai figured out a way to weaken the spell," I suggested. I couldn't even believe I was saying these things, thinking in these terms. But as they said, when in Rome...

"We need to go and talk to my parents," Raiden said firmly. "There's no point in standing around here speculating. My entire family are shamans, and they know more about the legend of Kai than I do."

I nodded. "Let me grab some stuff first." There was no point in fighting Raiden on this any longer—his parents were the only people who could tell me who Kai was and help me find my mother.

"Okay. But hurry up. We don't have a lot of time."

I dashed up the stairs to my room, then exchanged my backpack for a cross-body purse and stuffed my wallet, keys, a small canister of pepper spray, and lipstick inside. I didn't know if pepper spray was going to have any effect on *yokai* or ghosts, but it was the only weapon I owned, and I damn well wasn't going to leave without it.

The lipstick wasn't going to do anything either, but my mom had taught me to never leave the house without makeup. *You never know when you might need it,* she'd always cautioned me. *What if you run into Mr. Right? Or your dream employer?*

Tears stung at my eyes at the thought of my mother. I'd pray to any god I had to if it meant getting her back safe and sound. Sniffing back the tears, I shrugged on a denim hoodie, then ran down the stairs to meet Raiden.

"I got us another cab. It's outside," Raiden said, standing by the front door. He looked me up and down, and whatever he saw must have reached past his tough exterior, because his gaze softened a little. "Are you ready?"

I pulled in a long breath. "Yeah. Let's just get this over with."

I locked up the house and got into the cab with Raiden. As I was putting my seatbelt on, Raiden leaned forward to talk to the driver. "Takaoka Investigations, please."

My eyes nearly bugged out. "Wait a minute," I said as the car rolled into traffic. "Your family owns that huge building in the Financial District?"

"Yeah, for three generations now. Our particular set of...talents lends us well to the private investigations industry."

"Huh." I chewed on that for a moment—I could see how being able to talk to ghosts could help someone track down missing people or belongings, or even find a murderer. How different would my life be if I'd known I had the ability to see ghosts from the beginning? Would I have chosen a different career path that complemented this particular skill set? "Guess you guys do pretty well."

"You could say that." Raiden smirked a little, and my face flamed as I became all too aware of the disparity between us. He was a rich kid from a hugely successful company, while I was a struggling college student trying to manage my mother's business. We couldn't be more different.

My heart clenched unexpectedly at the realization. There was no way I had any kind of connection, déjà vu or not, with a guy like Raiden. I must have been reading into something that wasn't there.

I wanted to ask Raiden more questions about what had happened, but the cab driver was Japanese, and I didn't want him overhearing us. Instead, I gazed out the window, curious to see if I could spot any ghosts from the car. At first, I didn't see anything odd—just the usual foot traffic crowding the sidewalks, heading to and from work, or disappearing into bars and restaurants to wind down after a long day.

But as we slowed down outside a hotel, I caught sight of a bellhop loading up a luggage cart. He was a short, round man with male pattern baldness, but he managed to handle the large suitcases without issue. Our eyes locked, and his form flickered, revealing marbled blue skin, stringy hair, and a ring of stubble around his mouth. His yellowish-red eyes widened, and I choked back a scream when he hissed at me, exposing a set of curved fangs. For a moment I thought he was going to jump at me, but the car lurched forward, and we rolled out of range.

"Another *yokai*," Raiden murmured from behind me, his voice pitched too low for the driver to hear. I turned away from the window to meet his intense gaze. "We're seeing more and more of them."

"What does it mean?" I asked, and I hated the way my voice trembled. I'd been shaken more by that brief encounter than I wanted to admit. "Why am I suddenly seeing these things everywhere?"

Raiden shook his head. "Later," he said, glancing toward the cabbie.

I lapsed into a resentful silence for the rest of the cab ride. I hated that I was so completely out of my element. My life was organized around a very strict routine of studying, working, and caring for my mother. It kept me sane, allowing me to focus on the important things while not leaving me room to worry about the future.

Now, my entire routine had been shattered, and all the worries were crawling back into my brain, threatening to eat me alive. I needed to know more about this situation, so I could figure my way out of it, but so far Raiden hadn't been very forthcoming.

He isn't the only one who isn't telling you things, I thought as I glanced down at my charm bracelet. The tiny silk and cotton monkey was still there, and a shiver went down my spine as I remembered what the *furi* had said. He'd served my father before being passed down to me. What did that mean? That my father had been a shaman? Did my mother know about this?

She had to have known. How can you marry someone and not know about such a huge part of them?

But if she did know, why hadn't she told me? My mom had always believed in the Old Gods, or *kami*, as they were called, and we had a small shrine in our living room she used for prayer. She'd told me plenty of stories about the *kami* when I was little, but as I'd grown up and become more interested in science, I'd forgotten them. And she'd never pushed me.

Maybe she just wanted you to live a normal life. One free of ghosts and monsters.

Well, so much for that, I thought as we pulled up to a black, twelve-story building just a few blocks from the Transamerica building. I didn't know what had happened today that had changed my life, but I knew one thing: there was no going back. I could see the ghosts and monsters now, and until my mother was safe and sound, I wasn't going to stick my head in the sand and pretend they didn't exist.

6

R aiden paid the cabbie, then led me toward the huge black skyscraper his family owned. As we walked toward the glass doors, a tingling feeling spread over me from head to toe. It was as if I'd passed through some kind of electrical field. Shivering, I rubbed my arms—they were covered, but I could feel the hairs on them prickling.

"Sorry," Raiden said, noticing my discomfort. "We've got wards around the perimeter to keep *yurei* out," he explained, using the Japanese term for "ghost."

"Do they keep out *yokai* too?" I asked, glancing back toward the street. After what I'd seen today, I wouldn't be surprised to see more *yokai* and *yurei* watching us from outside. But there were only humans walking around, which was perfectly normal. After all, they couldn't all be monsters, right?

"Yeah, though we haven't gotten many of those," Raiden said, reaching for the keychain on his belt loop. "We really don't get a lot of *yokai* out here. They don't usually wander very far from Japan."

I opened my mouth to ask him to elaborate, but before I could, a guard rushed forward to open the door before Raiden could use his key.

"Good evening, Mr. Takaoka," he said, holding the door wide. "And to you, Miss."

"Are my parents in, Goro?" Raiden asked as we stepped into the lobby. It was a huge space, with green and white marble tile and huge clay pots with bamboo shoots for decoration. There were two groupings of furniture on opposite sides of the room where visitors could sit and talk, and in the center was a vacant reception desk. The lights were all down low, since the building was closed for the evening.

"I'm afraid not," the guard said, locking the door behind us. "They left for Japan not too long ago."

"What?" Raiden's eyes crackled with annoyance. "Why didn't anyone tell me? I didn't get any phone calls." He pulled a cell phone out of his pocket and swiped at the screen. "Not even a text message."

Goro cleared his throat. "You should ask Mamoru," he said, sounding decidedly uncomfortable. *I just work here,* his body language screamed. "I wasn't given the details."

"Fine. Thanks." Glowering, Raiden stalked toward the bank of elevators on the opposite side of the room. I smiled hastily at the guard in thanks, then hurried after Raiden before he left me in the dust.

"Who's Mamoru?" I asked as Raiden pressed the button for the eleventh floor.

"He's a cranky old man," Raiden said crossly. "And also our oldest shaman—although officially we're called 'investigators.'" He scoffed. "Americans wouldn't hire us if they knew we relied on spirits to help solve our cases."

"No, I guess not." I wouldn't have, not before today.

The elevator doors swished open, and we stepped out into a huge room that was something like a cross between a Buddhist temple and a library. *Tatami* mats covered the floor, and the walls were lined with lacquered oak bookshelves. More bookshelves filled half the space in rows, while the other half was filled with low wooden tables and seat cushions. Half of these had reading lamps on them, like study desks in a library, while the other half had computers.

Sitting at one of these desks was a wizened man with a bald head and a thin mustache. He wore a pair of linen pants and a red silk shirt, and a pair of silver-rimmed spectacles perched on his long, thin nose. I wondered if he'd ever considered transplanting the tufts of hair sprouting from his ears onto the top of his head, then pushed away the mean-spirited thought. It wasn't his fault he suffered from male pattern baldness.

"Raiden," the old man said in a quavering voice, turning to meet us. "Where have you been? I have been waiting for you to return."

"Hunting *yurei*," Raiden said. "Aika, this is Date Mamoru." He pronounced the old man's surname *dah-tay,* introducing him last name first, as was traditional. "Mamoru, this is my friend, Fujiwara Aika. She's a shaman, although she doesn't seem to realize it." He shot me a look as if to say *I* was the crazy one for not believing.

Mamoru's eyes narrowed, and he slowly got to his feet. There was a slight hunch in his back, but even so, he only stood a few inches shorter than Raiden. "Is that so?" he asked, padding toward me on bare feet. My face flamed as I suddenly realized I was still wearing my converses, and I quickly toed them off, shoving them toward the space next to the door. "The Fujiwara name is very old, but I have not met a shaman from that line. Who was your father?"

"Fujiwara Hidetada," I blurted, without thinking. If my father had been a shaman, wouldn't one this old have recognized my family name?

Mamoru shook his head. "Never heard of him. But you have the Sight," he went on, studying me with sharp eyes. "That much I can tell just by looking at you. Do you know anything about how to use your powers?"

"I didn't know anything about this until tonight." I glanced sideways at Raiden, who'd also taken a second to remove his shoes. His expression was blank as he watched us, and I wished I knew what he was thinking. "I was walking home when I saw Raiden talking to the *Kuchisake-onna* in an alleyway, and I thought I'd lost my mind."

"The *Kuchisake-onna*?" Mamoru's bushy eyebrows flew up his bare forehead as he turned to Raiden. "Did you capture her?"

Raiden shook his head. "Aika screamed when she saw her, and the *Kuchisake-onna* attacked. I had to choose between the ghost and the girl." A faint smile curved his lips, and I relaxed a little as I realized he wasn't angry about it anymore.

"Harrumph!" Mamoru folded his arms. "And you say this is the first time you've seen a *yurei*?" he prodded, giving me the stink eye.

I opened my mouth to say *yes*, then remembered what had happened in the café. "Actually, I might have seen one a bit earlier. A guy wearing old-timey Japanese clothes was sitting in my café, and when I approached him to ask what he wanted, he seemed surprised that I could see him."

I told them about the strange encounter, right down to him disappearing when he was hit by that bus. "And when I looked at the piece of paper he'd been drawing on, I saw that it was a picture of me, dressed in a really fancy *kimono*. Like an ancient Japanese princess."

"Fascinating!" Mamoru's eyes gleamed. "You very well may have been visited by a *kami*," he said, his voice brimming with excitement. "It sounds like he opened your Sight."

"It sure does." I sighed, resisting the urge to scrub a hand through my hair. "I don't suppose there's any way to close it?"

Mamoru scowled. "And why would you want to do that, child? Your Sight is a gift from the gods, not something to be shunned!"

I bit back the snarky retort that sprang to my lips and bowed my head. My mother would bend me over her knee if she heard me speaking rudely to an elder.

"I didn't ask for any of this," I said quietly. "I just want my mother back." My hands trembled, and I clenched them into fists, trying to steady myself. I'd already broken down once, in front of a stranger, no less—I wasn't going to let it happen again.

"Your mother?" Mamoru's voice changed, and when I looked up, his expression had softened into sympathy. "What happened to her?" He seemed to realize that I'd been through an ordeal, and gestured to the seat cushions. "Come sit, and tell me your story."

Biting back a sigh, I did as he asked, sitting Japanese-style on the red silk cushions. Raiden joined me, and though his expression was still blank, I could sense his impatience. He probably wanted to ask about his parents but was polite enough to address my needs before his.

The tips of my ears turned hot, and I turned back to Mamoru, who was pouring tea from a clay pot that had already been sitting on the table. He handed us two round clay cups with no handles, and I cradled mine carefully between my palms, blowing across the top to cool the liquid before I took a sip.

"After Raiden and I got away from the *Kuchisake-onna*, he took me back to my apartment," I said. "When we arrived, we found an *ogama* on the second floor and had to fight it. My mother had been affected by its smoke, but when we revived her, she told us that the *ogama* had come here looking for me, and that it had been sent by a man named Kai."

"Kai!" Mamoru's eyes widened. "Are you certain?"

"Yes," Raiden affirmed. "She definitely said Kai. We meant to question the *ogama* about it, but it took Aika's mother and disappeared before we got the chance." A frustrated look crossed his face. "We don't know where he took her, or what he wants."

Mamoru scowled. "If he was sent on Kai's orders to kidnap Aika-san, the *ogama* might have decided to take her mother as a hostage instead." He rubbed his chin thoughtfully. "Your parents were called back to Japan, along with most of our high-level shamans, to deal with that archaeological disaster, Raiden. We suspect those foolish people found the shrine Kai was sealed away in, and in their ignorance, they may have released him."

Raiden paled, and my chest tightened, making it hard to breathe. "So...are you saying that a centuries-old evil shaman is after me, and that he's kidnapped my mother in an effort to get to me?" I choked out.

"It does appear that way," Mamoru said ruefully, "though I cannot fathom why Kai would want an inexperienced shaman like you." His gaze grew thoughtful. "Are you sure you have *never* used your powers?"

"She healed herself when the *ogama* stabbed her," Raiden said suddenly, his eyes glittering with suspicion. "I meant to ask about it, but there was too much going on. One moment she had a knife sticking out of her chest, and the next thing she was fine. How did you do that?" he demanded.

I swallowed as both men stared intently at me, my skin crawling with nerves. "I...a *yokai* saved me." Slowly, I lifted my wrist, showing them the charm hanging from my bracelet. "A *furi* took me to this bamboo forest and told me he was a gift from my father. He was assigned to protect me."

Mamoru's eyes looked like they were about to fall into his lap. "You...your father bound a *furi* to that monkey charm?" he asked, pointing to my wrist with a trembling finger.

"No..." Raiden breathed, staring at me in a kind of dazed shock. "It can't be. It *can't*."

"It's the only explanation," Mamoru declared, his voice vibrating with excitement. "And it explains why I've never heard of her clan."

"But no one has seen them for centuries!" Raiden protested. "Not since...not since..."

"Not since Kai was sealed away," Mamoru finished for him. "Which explains why he is after Aika-san, now that he is awake."

"Is someone going to explain to me what the hell is going on?" I finally exploded, my anxiety overriding my manners. "What are you talking about?"

"*You*, Aika-san, are a *yokai* shaman," Mamoru said, fixing me with a penetrating stare that cut straight into my soul. "A shaman who controls monsters instead of spirits. No one has seen a *yokai* shaman in centuries, so you may very well be the only one around. And if that is the case, your life is in grave danger. Because if Kai needs a *yokai* shaman for whatever he is planning, and you are the only one available, he will hunt you until the end of time."

7

"I ...what?" I gaped at the old man, who had clearly lost his mind. "What do you mean, I'm a *yokai* shaman? I thought shamans used spirits!" Not that I knew a lot about shamanism, but that was what Raiden had told me.

"Yes, most shamans do," Mamoru said, adopting a lecturing tone. "But there was a rare group of shamans who broke away from the traditional methods. They learned to harness the souls of *yokai* and bind them to charms. Much like the one you are wearing." He pointed at the monkey charm on my bracelet. "Himiko, the ancient Japanese queen who ruled from her seat in Yamatai nearly two thousand years ago, was a *yokai* shaman. She was very powerful, and she could control the elements. But *yokai* and *yurei* shamans have always been at odds with each other, because many shamans consider the use of *yokai* to be a kind of black magic."

I swallowed, looking down at the monkey charm. "It does seem like slavery," I admitted, shifting uneasily. "Does that mean I shouldn't use my powers?"

Mamoru shrugged. "From what little I know of *yokai* shamans, it seems that they are just as capable of good or evil as their *yurei* counterparts." A wry smile curved his thin lips, causing his mustache to twitch. "The *yokai* shamans believed that harnessing spirits to do one's bidding was, in itself, a kind of evil, as those spirits should be guided to the *Reikai* and not forced to do a shaman's bidding in the human world."

I frowned. "Is that what all *yurei* shamans do? Force ghosts into servitude?" If that was the case, how was it any better than what *yokai* shamans did? One could argue that *yokai* shamans were more justified, because many *yokai* were evil and caused great damage when left to their own devices.

"Of course not," Raiden scoffed. He folded his arms across his chest, his dark eyes sparking with irritation. "We do our best to guide all souls to the afterlife, but sometimes we find one that would rather stay, like Katsu." He fingered the little stone tablet on his key ring. "We form a partnership with those spirits, until they are ready to move on. And even when they move on, we can call them back when we've need of them. A fully trained shaman can summon any spirit they need, regardless of whether or not they reside in the *Reikai* or the human world."

"And just what is that supposed to mean?" I bristled, suddenly feeling the need to defend myself. "You sound like you think *yurei* shamans are better than *yokai* shamans."

Raiden stiffened. "I didn't say that. I'm just defending our ways from *yokai* shaman prejudices."

"Now, now," Mamoru said before I could fire off a retort. "Let's not argue. This is a momentous occasion, Raiden," he said sternly, "and it should be treated like such. Aika-san's talent could be very useful to us."

"I didn't come here to work for you," I protested. "I came here to find out what happened to my mother."

"And so you have," Mamoru said, spreading his hands. "But how do you expect to rescue her from Kai if you don't know how to use your powers?"

I blew out a frustrated breath. "I'm not sure how that's possible, unless you can teach me how to be a shaman overnight. Kai has my mom right now. I don't have time to sit around here for months or years." I took a deep breath, trying to calm myself. "And how are you going to teach me when you aren't even the same type of shaman?"

"The type of magic is similar," Mamoru said, sounding unconcerned. He waved at Raiden. "Take her to the training room, Raiden, and get her started."

Raiden stared. "You want *me* to train her? I'm not a *yokai* shaman!"

"Who else?" Mamoru spread his hands wide. "There are no *yokai* shamans here, Raiden. And since you are the one who brought her here, she is your responsibility!"

"I'm not denying that," Raiden said stiffly. "But you know more about *yokai* magic than I do, and I have to get to Tokyo. My parents need me!"

"Your parents have ordered you to stay behind," Mamoru growled. "And until I hear otherwise, those orders stand."

Raiden's jaw clenched. "But I can be of use—"

"Are you questioning my authority?" Mamoru asked, raising an eyebrow.

Raiden looked as though he very much wanted to continue doing just that, but he pressed his lips together and glowered instead.

"Good. Then you will stay here, and you will train Aika-san. You found her, and that makes her your responsibility. End of discussion."

"*Fine.*" Raiden stood up, then stuck his hand out toward me, almost as if he were jabbing me with it. "Come on, we may as well start now."

I stared at his outstretched arm. "Isn't there anyone else who can train me?" I blurted out, a little desperately. I couldn't bear the idea of being forced to learn from someone who didn't want to teach me. Especially someone I'd developed an insta-crush on. I couldn't believe how much Raiden's sudden rejection stung, even though I understood his need to get to his parents. After all, that's what I was doing, wasn't it?

Mamoru shook his head. "All our other high-level shamans were called away. Raiden is the best we have, and usually, he acts like it." He gave Raiden a look. "Don't forget to take the charm box with you."

Raiden froze. "The charm box? You don't mean *that* charm box, do you?" he asked warily.

Mamoru scowled. "What other charm box would I be talking about?" he demanded imperiously. "Do you want to stand here all night arguing, or do you want to train? Neither of you are leaving this building until she has *some* idea of what to do with her powers," he added, his voice growing low and threatening. The air shifted, growing charged with power, and the hair on my arms stood on end as Mamoru began to glow.

Raiden's spine went ramrod straight. "Very well," he said tightly. Not looking at me, he stalked toward the back of the room, disappearing between the shelves.

"Don't mind him," Mamoru said, refilling my cup of tea. I noticed the shelves weren't just lined with books—there were ancient artifacts as well, though I couldn't identify them from where I sat. "Raiden thinks he knows everything, but he is still young, and growing up in America has shielded him in many ways. The old gods do not visit here often." His wizened face grew sad.

"The old gods?" I asked. "What do you mean?"

Before Mamoru could answer, Raiden returned with a lacquered wooden box inlaid with *kanji* symbols. An *ofuda* charm had been slapped across the latch, and I noticed the box was glowing faintly.

I frowned. "What's that glow?"

"The *yoki*," Raiden said. He still sounded irritated, but he was glancing curiously at me now. "I guess you're able to see it now, unlike before?"

I blinked. "Is that why you said you could sense the *ogama* when we were outside the apartment? Because you saw a glow?"

"Yes." He gestured for me to get up. "Come on. Let's head to the training room."

I stood up, then bowed to Mamoru. "Thank you for the tea," I said, "and the conversation."

Mamoru huffed. "No need for thanks," he said, waving us away. "Now get going. I have work to do!"

Raiden and I grabbed our shoes, then got back into the elevator. "What a strange guy," I muttered as we began to go down. "He's nice one moment, grumpy the next."

Raiden shrugged, and some of his annoyance seemed to dissipate with the motion. "Mamoru is an elder, so he's allowed his mood swings." The hint of derision in his voice told me exactly what Raiden thought of that, but to his credit he didn't say anything disparaging about the old man. An awkward silence fell between us, and we both looked away.

Finally, Raiden exhaled. "I'm sorry if I came off too harsh earlier," he said. "It isn't that I consider you a burden. Really, you're not." He turned toward me, and the sincerity in his voice soothed some of the sting from earlier. "It's just that I really wasn't expecting any of this." Frustration bubbled in his voice.

"That makes two of us," I said, raising my eyebrows. I held his gaze for several seconds before I added, "But I was rude to you too, for the same reason. We're both shaken up tonight." I gave him a small smile. "I guess you could say this makes us even."

Raiden chuckled. "That's not the answer I was expecting, but I'll take it."

The doors opened into another room with *tatami* mat flooring. The tang of old sweat mixed with the fragrance of jasmine flowers made my nose wrinkle, and I looked around to see that this was a kind of dojo. There was a sitting area toward the front with cubbies, where you could store your shoes and hang your coats, and two walled off changing areas. A hallway cut through the center of the room, which was subdivided into various smaller rooms by drywall. Some of the rooms had windows that you could look into, while others were completely closed off.

"I thought we were here to do shaman training?" I asked as Raiden led me into the biggest room, toward the back. The walls were lined with every weapon imaginable, as well as boxing pads of varying shapes and sizes. There were gym mats stacked in a corner, and a huge wire basket filled with sparring gear.

"We are," Raiden said, sitting cross-legged on the floor. His thigh muscles strained against his jeans as he settled, and I had to force myself not to stare. "Shamans are required to train both our bodies and our minds," he continued as I sat down in front of him, as far away as I possibly could without being obvious. "The stronger our bodies are, the better our spirits are able to use them. There's little point in merging with a samurai spirit if your body is too weak to wield a sword."

"Makes sense," I admitted, scanning the weapons on the walls again. "Do you know how to use all of those?"

"Most of them." Raiden set the lacquered box down between us. "Open it."

My stomach fluttered, this time with nerves, as I stared down at the box. Hesitantly, I reached for the *ofuda* and pulled it off. The paper withered to ash in my hand, and the box immediately began to glow brighter, no longer hampered by the *ofuda's* magic. Holding my breath, I flipped up the gold clasp and opened the box, bracing myself for a *yokai* to come rushing out.

"Relax," Raiden said, sounding amused. I met his gaze, and glared at the mirth I found in his eyes. "They're just charms. They won't bite...yet."

"Whatever," I muttered, tearing my eyes away from him so I could focus on the contents of the box. Sure enough, it was filled with tiny charms of all shapes and sizes—a turtle carved out of jade, a metal ball covered in *sakura* blossoms, a tiny *ofuda* in a silk drawstring pouch. They were all the kind of charms you'd find at a *Shinto* shrine or Buddhist temple... except they were old, the colors faded and the paint chipped on many of them. The stone ones were shiny and smooth, and some of the carving details had worn away, as if by repeated touching.

"So all of these can summon a *yokai*?" I asked, pulling out a shiny yen coin attached to a jewelry fob with two tiny bells. The charm flared, nearly blinding me, and I shrieked, dropping it back into the box.

"Whoa!" Raiden said as I scrambled back, his eyes wide. "I've never seen them do that before."

I pressed a hand to my hammering chest as I stared at him. "Is that a good thing or a bad thing?"

"A good thing." Raiden picked up the same charm I'd dropped. It had gone back to its faint glow from before, and what's more, it didn't react to his touch. "The fact that the charm responded to you means that you really *are* a *yokai* shaman. No one in the Takaoka Clan has ever been able to harness the power inside these charms. You'll be the first to use them in at least two thousand years."

There was an odd note in his voice—almost as if he was both amazed and disappointed. But my mind latched onto something else he'd said, and my mouth dropped open in shock. "Doesn't that make these ancient artifacts? They should be in museums!"

"Some of them were," Raiden said darkly. "Our family has been recovering them over the centuries. You don't think we could leave such powerful objects in the hands of normal humans, could you? That's just a recipe for disaster."

"But I thought humans can't use these?" I asked, confused. "What's the harm?"

"Yeah, but funny things tend to happen when you leave objects like these around. That's why they were kept locked up." He tapped on the box. "Pick a charm. Whichever one calls you the most. We're going to summon your first *yokai*."

Sweat broke out on the small of my back. "I don't think I'm ready for this."

Raiden sighed. "Like Mamoru said, the concept isn't going to be very different from what a normal shaman does." He unhooked his keychain from his belt and held it up. "These are tiny mortuary tablets," he said, holding up three tiny rectangular stone pieces with Japanese characters carved on them. They instantly began to glow brighter in his hand—not quite as bright as the *yokai* charm, but close. "This one here," he said, picking up the middle stone, "is the one Katsu sleeps in when I'm not using it. The other two have different spirits."

I frowned. "So you're saying that the spirits sleep in them?"

Raiden nodded. "They need a place to relax when I'm not using them and when they're not wandering around. That would usually be their graves, but since those are far away, we use the mortuary tablets." He tapped the side of Katsu's tablet. "*Mezame,*" he intoned.

The tablet flashed, and Katsu appeared, sword in hand. "*Where is the danger?*" he demanded, sweeping the room with a penetrating glare. His eyes narrowed as he saw me, and he raised his sword. "*Is it her?*"

"*No!*" Raiden jumped to his feet. "*Calm down, Katsu. Aika isn't an enemy. We're training.*"

"*Oh.*" Katsu lowered his sword, looking disappointed. It would have been comical if I wasn't in such a bad mood. "*So what do you want me to do?*"

"What you do best, of course." Smirking, Raiden crossed the room. He took a heavy wooden *bokken* from its mount on the wall and gave it a few experimental swings.

Katsu huffed. *"Your form is terrible."*

"Well excuse me for not being a thousands-year-old samurai." Raiden tucked the sword into his belt, then clasped his hands together. *"Maji,"* he commanded, power beginning to glow from his body. His ponytail began to swing, even though there was no wind, and the ends of his button-down shirt rustled. *Merge,* he'd said.

Katsu's form swirled into a fiery ball and shot across the room to Raiden's waiting palm. He grabbed the ghost, and I gasped as he slammed it into the center of his chest. Dark red *ki* flared around him as he absorbed the spirit. His eyes snapped open, blazing with the same orange fire as before.

"A paltry weapon," Katsu said, his deep voice coming out of Raiden's throat as he drew the *bokken* from Raiden's belt. *"But it is better than the broom handle."* He turned his imperious gaze to me. *"Bring that flimsy punching bag to the center of the room."*

Swallowing, I did as the ghost asked. Even though he was in Raiden's body, he was still intimidating as hell—his presence was immensely powerful, which I guess was only to be expected for someone who had been a *daimyo*. A row of freestanding punching bags were lined up against the wall, and I picked the smallest one, which looked like it was the easiest to carry.

"Not that one," Katsu scoffed as I began to roll it. *"Do I look like a weakling to you?"*

"No, but I am." Finding my courage, I met the samurai's gaze steadily. "If you want a bigger one, get it yourself."

Katsu/Raiden's nostril's flared at the insolent tone in my voice. *"If you were a servant, I would have you whipped for that."*

"It's a good thing you're *the servant, then, instead of the master,"* I said lightly, standing the punching bag up. I stepped away, giving him plenty of space. "Now are you going to hit it, or are you all talk?"

Katsu laughed, a deep, surprisingly warm sound that threw me off. *"I like you,"* he said, raising his sword. *"There is fire in your soul."*

He moved then, a blur of motion my eyes barely followed. One moment he was standing ten feet from the bag, and then he was right next to it, his sword plowing into the faux leather with a loud *crack*. The bag tore open, cotton gushing everywhere as Katsu sliced almost completely through it.

"Hmph." Katsu withdrew the sword and slid it back into Raiden's belt in one smooth motion. *"We should have used the katana."* He gestured to one of the sheathed swords hanging on the wall.

"I'll take that under advisement," Raiden said, taking control. *"San-shutsu,"* he ordered, placing a hand against his chest. *Yield.*

Raiden's chest flared bright red as Katsu was expelled in a burning ball of light. It hovered there for a moment before reforming into the ancient samurai.

"I am retiring for the evening," Katsu declared imperiously. "Do not call on me again unless there is real danger."

He disappeared back into the mortuary tablet with another flash of light.

"Well that was...interesting." I stared at the ruined punching bag again before glancing at Raiden. "Are you sure you have control of him? He's awfully bossy."

Raiden rolled his eyes. "Trust me, Katsu just likes to sound like he's in charge. He isn't powerful enough to take over my body completely, though he *is* powerful enough to resist my commands if he doesn't want to carry them out." Sighing, he sat down on the ground again. "That's the thing about being a shaman—you have to be in harmony with your spirit in order to operate at max potential. If the two of you can't fully become one, then you're going to have problems harnessing your spirit's abilities, and your spirit is going to have a hard time controlling your body." He glanced at me, admiration in his eyes. "You didn't back down when he was trying to intimidate you."

My skin tingled beneath Raiden's warm regard and I forced myself to break his gaze. Glancing down at my bracelet, I changed the subject. "I didn't merge with my *furi*. It just touched me and healed me. Does that mean my magic is different from yours?"

"I don't really know. I've never seen a *yokai* shaman perform magic. None of us have." He shrugged. "Even Mamoru, with all his years of wisdom, doesn't know much about it."

"That's not exactly making me feel better," I said as I sat down in front of him, the charm box between us. "But I'll try it anyway." It wasn't like I had room to be picky. My mom was missing, and I needed to learn how to use my powers if I was going to rescue her from an evil shaman.

I reached for the box, but before I could take a charm, Raiden grabbed my hand. "Take a breath," he said. "Focus on what you're doing. Drive the fear from your mind. The last thing you need is for the *yokai* to sense that you're afraid."

He squeezed my hand, a gesture that I was sure was meant to be comforting. But the motion sent sparks skipping up the inside of my arm, and I was suddenly aware of how small my hand was in his. While his fingers were long and somewhat elegant, like a pianist's, calluses brushed against my skin, and there was hidden strength in them. A strength that had allowed him to grip that wooden sword and smash it clear through that punching bag. Absolutely nothing like my own delicate hands... and under normal circumstances, I might have been intimidated. Instead, I found myself wanting to squeeze his hand back, to lift it and run my fingers along the ridges and tendons.

Flustered, I snatched my hand away from his. A hurt look flickered in Raiden's eyes again, but then they hardened, and he leaned back. Giving me my space.

Knowing I was never going to be able to concentrate if I kept looking at him, I closed my eyes and drew in a long breath to calm myself. Unfortunately, Raiden's incense-and-hot-guy scent filled my nose, and the butterflies in my stomach went haywire again.

Get a grip, Aika! I scolded myself. *You don't have time to be mooning over a guy when your mom's being held hostage by a psycho shaman!*

The thought of my mom suffering in some dark prison, alone and afraid, was like a cold bucket of water being dumped on my head. Determination filled me as I forced all thoughts from my head and focused on breathing. In, two, three...out, two, three... in, two, three...

It took a minute, but finally the emotions swirling in my gut began to drain away with each breath, loosening the tightness in my chest and shoulders. With no worrisome thoughts or fears chasing themselves around in my head, it was easy to let go of that emotion, to smooth my frazzled nerves and center myself. As I did, I became aware of my *ki* inside me, a warm, glowing ball of energy that had tiny trickles of energy bleeding off it. Those trickles flowed through channels in my body like a nervous system all their own. I was all too familiar with how this worked—I channeled my *ki* all the time when I was performing *reiki* healings.

Did yokai power flow through these channels as well? I wondered as I grabbed hold of the energy and studied it. *Was this how I harnessed yoki?*

There was only one way to find out.

I opened my eyes, rock steady now. Raiden blinked as I reached for the box. Part of me wondered what he saw that surprised him, but I didn't ask. My fingers closed around a tiny wooden carving of a fox, worn smooth and glossy by time and skin oil. Like the yen coin, the fox flared brightly in my hand, and this time I felt its power ripple across my flesh. For a second, I could have sworn something furry rubbed against my arm. But that had to be my imagination...

"Maji," I commanded, using the same word Raiden had used to summon Katsu. I latched onto that trickle of power and tugged on it mentally as I said the words, summoning it forth.

Sapphire light burst from the fox charm like a firecracker that swirled overhead in a vortex of blue fire. Scorching hot flames licked the moisture from my face and hands. Raiden stumbled backward in shock, but I realized I wasn't scared of the fire. Sure, it was hot, and it could burn me to a crisp, but for some reason, I knew it wouldn't.

At least not yet.

Raising my chin, I stared straight into the vortex of flame. Glowing yellow eyes blinked at me from within the swirling sapphire flame as it solidified into a seven-foot-tall fox with luxurious crimson fur and nine long, bushy tails waving behind it.

"A *kyuubi!*" Raiden exclaimed, his apprehension lost as excitement took over. "I've always wanted to meet one!"

The *kyuubi* turned its nose up at Raiden, pointedly turning away from him. It regarded me thoughtfully. "It has been a long time since a shaman has dared to summon me," she hissed in Japanese, exposing long, white canines. "Who are you to command me?"

A large part of me wanted to shrink back from the *yokai's* yellow gaze and beg her forgiveness before she ripped my throat out with her teeth. But something else inside me, something ancient and primal, forced me to stand firm. I would not back down.

"I am Aika of the Fujiwara Clan," I replied, gathering my power around me. It flowed freely from the center of my chest, enveloping me in a golden glow, and the *kyuubi's* eyes widened. "*I* summoned you by the power of this charm."

The *yokai* growled at the sight of the fox charm dangling in my fingers. She jerked forward, as if she was going to lunge at me, then stopped. Part of me wanted to flinch, but I ignored her threat, meeting her gaze squarely. "I cannot kill you while you wield that charm, or I myself will perish," she spat. "But that does not mean I will agree to do your bidding. You are not worthy."

I bristled at that. "What do you mean, I'm not worthy? I summoned you, didn't I?"

The *kyuubi* laughed. "Any shaman can do that. But you are a weakling, untested, not like the shaman who bound me." Her gaze turned sinister. "I eat weaklings."

"Aika," Raiden murmured, putting a hand on my shoulder. I wasn't sure when he'd sidled up to me, but the worry in his voice concerned me. "Just let it go. There are other charms."

He was right. And yet, as I looked into the *yokai's* eyes, I was seized by the need to dominate. To show it who was boss. Shrugging off Raiden's hand, I took a step forward. "Give me a test," I challenged her. "I'll prove to you that I'm worthy."

"Is that so, little shaman?" the *kyuubi* mocked, her face twisting into a feral smile. "And what happens when you fail? What happens then?"

"I won't fail."

"Then you won't mind wagering my freedom on it, eh?" she asked.

"Aika..." Raiden warned.

"I agree to your terms," I said coolly, ignoring Raiden. I *needed* to do this.

Evil, feminine laughter echoed throughout the room. "Very well," the *kyuubi* said, eyes sparkling with mischief. Her tails beat the air behind us, whipping up a tornado of flame. "You shall have your test."

And with those words, the world all around us exploded into sapphire flame.

8

Heat unlike anything I'd ever felt before tore a scream from my lungs. The sapphire flame rippling out from the *kyuubi* melted the ground into slag, and the smell of burning wood and plastic filled my nose as thick black smoke made my eyes water. The room was so hot I swore my blood was boiling. I'd turn into an Aika-kebab any second now.

Maybe this wasn't such a good idea.

"What's the matter, little shaman?" the *kyuubi* mocked. She watched me through glimmering eyes, clearly unaffected by the fire swirling around us. "Can't you take the heat?"

"I'm fine," I gasped, doing my best to ignore the rivers of sweat coursing down my body. My lips were chapped, and my mouth was so dry I could barely speak.. But I refused to buckle beneath the *kyuubi's* power. Yes, it was hot, but I wasn't actually dying. I knew the *kyuubi* couldn't kill me, not so long as I still held possession of the charm I'd used to summon her.

"Are you going to stand here and stall, or are you going to give me the test?" I managed to say.

"Very well," the *kyuubi* said. She flicked her tails, and ash rained down all around us. "All you have to do is take the charm from my paw."

She extended a paw, and I gasped at the sight of my fox charm sitting there. How the hell had she gotten it from me? Panic surged through my veins—if she had the charm, that meant she could kill me with impunity. I was entirely at her mercy.

Do not allow such thoughts to poison your resolve, a cool voice in my head said, and I froze. *You are far too powerful to be easily overcome.*

Who are you? I asked, looking around. I'd heard the voice before, back in my house when I was being buried by those mushrooms. But the voice didn't answer, and there was nobody here but me and the *kyuubi.*

Whoever it was that kept speaking to me clearly wasn't going to give me instructions. I was on my own in this.

"So that's it, huh?" I asked through gritted teeth. "Just take the charm?"

The *kyuubi's* grin widened. "If you can, little shaman."

You can do this. I reached down inside myself and gathered up my courage. Then I extended a hand toward the *kyuubi's* outstretched paw, where the fox charm sat innocuously.

But before I could grab the charm, the *kyuubi* flicked her tails, and a wave of fire rose up over her. Fear slammed into me, and I threw myself back seconds before the flames crashed down over us in a whirling tornado of fire.

"Dammit!" I cried as waves of heat scalded me. My entire body felt like it was on fire, and I was half-certain that if I looked in the mirror, my face would be a cracked, bleeding mess. How the hell was I supposed to reach the charm if the *kyuubi's* fire was going to attack me every time?

"Pathetic," the *kyuubi* sneered, looking down her snout at me. "You'll never be able to master me, little shaman, if you're so easily frightened by a little flame."

The derision in her voice reached past my fear and ignited the outrage that had been simmering in the bottom of my heart ever since I'd learned my mother had been taken.

"You don't know anything about me," I spat, getting to my feet. "You have no idea what I'm capable of."

"You're a puny little human, barely an adult," the *kyuubi* scoffed. "You don't think I notice how your little body trembles with fear and pain before me? A real shaman would have already had me subdued."

"I am a real shaman," I growled, taking a step toward her. "Shaman blood flows through my veins."

The *kyuubi* flicked her tails, whipping more fire up around us. Scalding air blasted me, searing my flesh, and suddenly it hit me. The *kyuubi* was a master of illusion. If these flames were real, and this heat was real, I would already be dead. There was no way the human body could withstand these temperatures for as long as we'd already been in this place. The heat, the flames, the pain...they were all in my head.

Or at least I sincerely hope so.

"Enough games," I growled, gathering my courage again. The *kyuubi's* eyes narrowed, and she whipped another wall of flame up as I stepped within range. But this time, I ignored the wave of sapphire fire and reached for the fox charm winking in her palm.

The flames crashed down on me just as my fingers touched the charm, and a scream ripped from my lips. But the scream was reflexive...because the flames never touched me. White light burst from the charm, enveloping me in a harsh glow. The flames burst into nothingness on contact with the pure energy, and a flood of power rushed through me, chasing away all the pain and uncertainty.

Grinning, I closed my fist around the charm and met the *kyuubi's* shocked gaze. "You're *mine*."

The *kyuubi* snapped her jaws, her tails flashing wildly. But the flames gushing about her slapped uselessly against the field of energy surrounding me. The illusionary magic no longer had any effect on it, and in fact, as I stared at it, the flames began to melt away.

"Hmph." Recognizing defeat, the *kyuubi* sat back on her haunches. The flames disappeared, leaving only a vast expanse of darkness around us. "Maybe you are strong enough to command me, little shaman. But it will take more than one little test to earn my respect."

She swished her tails one more time, then disappeared in a ball of fire.

"Aika!" Raiden cried as the dojo reappeared around me. He grabbed me by the shoulders. "Are you all right?"

"Yeah." Relief rushed through me—for a split second, I'd been worried that the *kyuubi* was going to leave me stranded in whatever realm she'd taken me to. "The test was easier than I thought."

"Thank the gods you're safe." Raiden pulled me against his chest. I stiffened in surprise as he wrapped his strong arms around me. "You scared the hell out of me."

"Sorry," I squeaked, trying to come to terms with the conflicting feelings I was experiencing. The warmth from Raiden's body curled around me like a blanket, both soothing and arousing all at once. Heat bloomed in my core, sending tingles racing through me, and I had the strangest feeling that we'd done this before.

But that was impossible. I'd never met Raiden before today. There's no way I would have forgotten about him.

"Umm," I finally said after several seconds had passed. "Do you think you could let me go? It's getting a little hard to breathe."

"Oh." Raiden quickly let me go. "Sorry," he said, scratching the back of his neck as he looked away. His cheeks were stained red with embarrassment, which I found kind of adorable considering how stern and imposing he normally was. "Er, why don't you tell me what happened when the *kyuubi* took you away? How did you defeat her?"

I sat down on the floor with Raiden and told him all about what had happened. As I talked, I fiddled with the fox charm. It continued to emit a soft glow, and it felt a bit hotter to the touch than it had in the beginning. I wondered if that was because the *kyuubi* was still pushing her boundaries.

Well, that was going to have to change. It would take time, but eventually I would show her who was boss.

"Wow." Raiden blew out a breath when I was finished. He stared at me as if he wasn't quite sure what to think. "I didn't know if you were going to be able to handle that one, Aika. Pretty sure you picked the strongest *yokai* in the box."

"Did I?" I looked away, not wanting to read too much into the impressed look in his eyes, and fastened the fox charm to my bracelet. When I was finished, it dangled a few chain links away from the silk monkey. "You mean the other *yokai* aren't necessarily going to be like that?"

Raiden shook his head. "I doubt it. You're strong, Aika, strong enough that the average *yokai* wouldn't even try to challenge you."

"I don't get it." I scrubbed a hand across my face. "If I really have this much power, how has it stayed dormant for so long? Why did I need to see that *kami* in order to activate it? Is that how all shamans find their powers?"

"No," Raiden said, sounding just as puzzled as I felt. "We usually come into our powers by around five or six. But my parents have been using their abilities around me all my life, whereas yours haven't. If your father really was a shaman, and he'd stayed around, you might have discovered your abilities earlier. What happened to him, anyway?"

"He's dead." I broke Raiden's gaze, looking down at the charm around my wrist. "I don't have any memories of him."

"I'm sorry," Raiden said, his voice quiet. Seconds passed in silence, and I was grateful that he didn't offer further sentiments. I didn't have any kind of emotional connection with my father, but after everything that had happened today, I couldn't help but feel sadness and resentment toward him. Why did he have to leave us so soon? Would things have turned out differently if he'd stayed? Would Kai still have come after us?

"Let's call it a day," Raiden said gently, taking my hand. I looked up at him as he pulled me to my feet, and the compassion in his steady gaze warmed me. "I can see that you're tired. We'll come back to this in the morning."

"Thanks," I said, grateful for the reprieve. I followed him to the elevator, my hand still in his. There was something comforting about Raiden—he was a rock steady presence, the kind of guy a girl could lean on when she needed support. And right now, with my thoughts and feelings in such turmoil, with all these new experiences and ideas to sort through, I could sorely use a shoulder.

"Wait a second," I protested as Raiden pushed the button for number seven instead of the lobby. "Where are we going now? I'm not up for any more training tonight—I want to go to bed."

"You are. I'm showing you to a room for the evening."

"I'm not staying here," I said as we began to go down. "I didn't bring a change of clothes or anything!"

"It's too dangerous for you to go back to the house," Raiden said. "If Kai really is looking for you, he'll have your place watched. This entire building is warded—he can't get to you as long as you stay in here. Besides," he added as the elevator doors opened, "we have toothbrushes and pajamas here. We're not barbarians."

I pressed my lips together and glared at Raiden. I didn't really have an argument against this—surely there was no harm in spending the night. But when the elevator doors opened again, the reality of what Raiden was saying hit me in the chest. "Are you saying that I have to stay inside here? That I can't leave?"

"Yes, for now," Raiden said. "You need to have a little more practice defending yourself before you can just go out on your own again."

"And how long is that going to take again?" I asked as we stepped into the dark hallway. Impatience brewed inside me, chasing away the exhaustion. I knew I couldn't just rush outside again—I didn't even have the first clue of where to go, beyond Mount Koya. And it wasn't like I had the money to jump on a plane anyway. But I hated feeling helpless, and being told I had to hide inside this tower like a damsel in distress was really chafing at me. No, I wasn't a superhero, but I was still used to taking care of myself. I didn't like being told what to do.

"Considering your aptitude, it should only take you a couple of days to get a grasp on the basics," Raiden said. "But knowing Mamoru, he'll want to keep you longer. It takes years of training to become truly proficient."

My stomach dropped. "I don't have years," I said as the elevator doors opened again. "My mom is kidnapped now. Even if she had the best medical care ever in Kai's custody, which I highly doubt, she might not have years. Who knows what Kai is doing to her!"

"I get it, Aika. Really, I do." Raiden gripped my shoulders and pinned me with that steady gaze. "Do you think I want to be holed up in here while my parents are across the Pacific Ocean, possibly fighting off the greatest evil the shaman world has seen in centuries? I *know* they left me in the dark because they didn't want to get me involved," he growled, the planes of his face tight with anger now. "I'm their only heir, and they don't want me hurt in case something goes wrong. But it's not in my nature to sit back while others put themselves in danger. If they die..." His voice cracked a little, and he looked away. "I'd never be able to forgive myself."

That little crack in his armor, that moment of vulnerability, soothed my ire, and my anger finally slipped away.

"I understand," I whispered, placing my hand on top of his. His fingers, which were digging into my shoulder, loosened a little.

"I'm sorry, Raiden. I guess I didn't think you'd be worried about your parents, since they're trained shamans."

The anger slid from his face, leaving a heavy, exhausted look in his eyes.

"They can take care of themselves," he said, sticking his hand between the elevator doors as they tried to close on us. He stepped into the hallway, and I followed. "But if it really is Kai who's escaped, this is a level of threat that none of us have ever dealt with before." He paused, then added, "I know we're both worried, but we should really try to get some sleep. You need to be well-rested for your training tomorrow."

I nodded, following silently as Raiden led me down the hall. The plum-colored walls were lined with faux paper lanterns set on low, their dim lights casting a faint glow on the hardwood floor. Instead of doorways, the rooms were separated by *shoji* —room dividers made of Japanese paper and wood. As we passed one, I caught the faint sound of someone snoring.

"There are other people staying here?" I asked in a hushed voice.

"Yeah. These aren't permanent residences, just lodgings for visiting shamans, mostly." Raiden came to a stop in front of one of the rooms and slid the *shoji* aside. "This is your room."

I peeked inside. Directly beyond the door was a room with a low, Japanese-style table and two seat cushions, where one could have tea or enjoy a meal. The walls were papered in *matcha*-green, the floors covered in *tatami* mats. There was another room to the left, out of view, where I assumed the bedroom was.

"You'll find pajamas and a toothbrush in the closet," Raiden said, "and the bathroom is back up the hall. Go on," he said, nudging me. "There aren't any *mokumokuren* hiding here."

I shivered at the idea—*mokumokuren* were ghosts that lived inside torn *shoji* or beneath *tatami* mats. "Thanks for that thought," I said as I stepped inside, glaring over my shoulder. "You really know how to make a girl feel safe."

I blinked in surprise as his face lit up in an unexpected grin. "I'll be right across the hall if you get scared. Sleep tight. Don't let the *tatami* mats bite."

He slid the door shut before I could throw one of the pillows at him. Huffing, I listened as the door across the hall slid open, then shut. What a cheeky bastard. Still, it was reassuring to know that Raiden was just a few steps away if I needed him. Not that I really thought there were any ghosts lurking in the walls or floors when the whole building was warded...but after the day I'd had, it was nice to know I wasn't alone.

Pulling out my phone for the first time in hours, I was surprised to see it was nearly ten o'clock at night. Where had all the time gone today? I scrolled through my notifications, half-hoping I'd see some text or missed voicemail from my mom. Anything to let me know she was okay. But she hadn't had her phone on her when the *ogama* took her, and even if she had, I doubt her captors would have let her keep it.

Then again, if Kai really was nearly two centuries old, he wouldn't know anything about cell phones. I wondered if that was an advantage we could somehow use against him. Just how powerful was he? And why exactly had he been sealed away? There was a lot I didn't know about this shadowy enemy of mine, I realized.

Maybe you can ask Mamoru tomorrow, I told myself as I explored the rest of my little suite. There was a bedroom beyond the sitting area, with a futon and bedding laid out on the floor, and a metal rack that could be used for hanging up a *kimono.*

In the closet I found extra pillows, a set of white pajamas that fit me well enough, a soft robe, and cloth slippers. I took two of the towels into the bathroom down the hall, which I was pleased to find had a sizable bathing area separated off from the toilet and sink. These rooms were *way* bigger than I'd anticipated. It was almost like staying in a *ryokan*—Japanese-style inns with hot spring baths.

Excited, I stripped off, then scrubbed myself down before getting into the tub for a long, hot soak.

Enjoy it while it lasts, a sinister voice whispered in the back of my mind. Goosebumps prickled across my skin, and I jerked upright, looking around the bathtub. But there was nothing in here but the curling steam and shampoo bottles. Nothing here but the sound of my harsh breathing.

You're just hearing things, I told myself, sinking back into the bath-water. But I was wary for the rest of the night, and when I finally tucked myself into the covers, it took a long, long time before I could work up the courage to close my eyes and give myself over to sleep.

9

I awoke at six in the morning to the sound of voices arguing outside my door.

"You are *not* going to ask her about this right now," Raiden growled. "She just got here."

"Come *on*," a male voice whined. It sounded about an octave higher than Raiden's, and oddly familiar. I scrubbed at my face, trying to banish the heavy exhaustion that still clung to me after a fitful night of sleep. Who was Raiden talking to? Was it another shaman? "She's the only one who can help me with this. You *have* to let me talk to her."

"Mamoru isn't going to be happy about this," Raiden warned, and that, more than anything else, piqued my curiosity. Pushing off the covers, I sat up and stretched, then shrugged on my robe and slippers before padding over to the door.

"What are you two arguing about?" I asked, sliding open the

shoji screen. The two men froze, mid-argument, and turned to look at me.

"*Shota?*" My eyes nearly popped out of my head as I got a good look at the man standing next to Raiden. He wore a black button-up shirt with tiny cranes embroidered on it and tight, salmon-colored pants instead of his usual chef's coat and jeans, but I'd recognize that shaggy J-pop band haircut and that face anywhere.

Relief flooded through me at the sight of a familiar face, and I threw my arms around him. "Oh my god, it really is you!"

"Aika?" Shota stiffened beneath my embrace, his voice faint with shock. Slowly, he wrapped his arms around me, returning the embrace, but his reception was far colder than I'd anticipated. "I...I wasn't expecting to see you."

The strained note in his voice had me pulling back, and my heart sank a little. The blood had drained from his face, and he was looking at me as if he'd seen a ghost. "Are you all right?" I asked, feeling deflated. I thought he'd be happy to see me, but...

"Do the two of you know each other?" Raiden asked, looking back and forth between us. His eyes were narrowed, and lines of displeasure bracketed his mouth.

"Yeah, she runs the shabu shabu place just around the corner from my sushi restaurant." Shota cast me a wary glance. "You didn't say *she* was the one," he said in a meaningful voice.

"I had no idea the two of you already knew each other," Raiden said, sounding pained. An awkward silence passed between them. "Is this going to be a problem?"

I folded my arms across my chest. "Would one of you *please* tell me what's going on here?" I felt like I was only hearing half the conversation and that there was a whole level of subtext I was missing.

Raiden cleared his throat. "Sorry. This is Shota Hayakawa, my cousin. He's a shaman too, but recently he's decided to forego the family business and pursue the culinary arts instead." His tone was colored with disapproval. "But then, you already know about that last part, from what I understand."

I shook my head. "I can't believe you're a shaman, Shota," I said, still trying to wrap my head around that. When I'd seen him standing in the hall, my brain had short-circuited, and all I'd thought was that it was so nice to see a familiar face. But of course he was a shaman. Why else would he be here?

Shota gave me a lopsided smile. "It's not exactly like I'm a walking advertisement for one. I'm sorry I reacted so badly. It's just...I'm surprised to see you here. They told me your first name, but I figured it couldn't be you, because I'd already ruled you out as a shaman."

"Wait a second." I pinched the bridge of my nose, trying to relieve the tension headache brewing. Glancing back and forth between him and Raiden, who was still dressed in his pajamas and looking a bit rumpled, I could see the familial resemblance in the angle of their jaws and the shape of their noses. Was that why Raiden had looked familiar to me when I'd first run into him? Because of his relation to Shota?

But that didn't explain the connection I felt. With *both* of them.

"What do you mean, you already ruled me out as a shaman?" I asked. For some reason, that line had stung, even though I was still struggling with the idea myself. "Did you, like, test me or something?"

"No, but you have a *gaki* working in your shop." Shota shrugged. "You didn't seem to have any idea of what she was, and she didn't know what you were either or she wouldn't have been so nice to you. Why do you think she hated me so much even though I was always bringing by food?"

"Oh." I bit my lip, thinking it over. "I thought she just hated you out of loyalty to my mother."

"And yet you didn't?" Shota raised an eyebrow.

"Who's to say I don't?" I stuck out my tongue at him.

He grinned. "There's no way you hate me. My food is far too spectacular."

My breath hitched in my throat at his familiar, teasing smile, and for a moment, the rest of the world fell away. There was no mistaking it—Shota and I definitely had a connection. And yet... I'd felt the same thing with Raiden when I'd first met him. How was that possible? Was I really crushing on two different guys?

"Shota," Raiden said, his voice full of warning.

"Sorry." Shota looked away and scratched the back of his neck. "This is all just...surreal to me."

"You don't have anything to apologize for," I said, scowling at Raiden. What was his problem? If I didn't know better, I'd say he was telling Shota to back off, which didn't sit well with me. After all, I'd known Raiden all of five minutes. And yeah, maybe there was some kind of pull between us, but that didn't mean he owned me. I'd known Shota a *lot* longer.

"So, what was that thing you came to talk to me about?" I asked, trying to engage Shota again, who seemed to be looking at everything *but* me. "You were saying that you needed something and that I was the only one who could help you."

"Right!" Shota brightened up again. He unhooked a keychain from his belt, which was laden with those little mortuary tablets, just like Raiden's. How had I never noticed he'd been carrying one of those? Was it always hidden beneath his coat? "I need you to summon a *yokai* for me so we can go visit Ryujin."

"I'm not sure this is a good idea," Raiden warned. "Mamoru told us not to let her out of the building until she has more experience."

"It's a *fantastic* idea," Shota said, his eyes gleaming with excitement. "Come on, Rai. Who in their right mind passes up the opportunity to go visit a dragon king?"

"Whoa. Back up a second." I raised a hand. "What do you mean, a *dragon king*?"

Shota blinked. "You've never heard of Ryujin?"

I frowned, a vague memory from one of my mother's fairy tales coming back to me. "Isn't he like a sea god or something?"

"Yes," Raiden said tightly. "A very powerful one, who probably isn't too keen on having visitors dropping in on him without notice."

Shota rolled his eyes. "And just how are we supposed to send him notice? A message in a bottle?" He snickered at his own joke, and I couldn't help grinning. He was such a goofball. "Stop being such a stick in the mud, Raiden. You know how much I've always wanted to visit the sea god. And besides, he might know something about this mess with Mount Koya and Kai."

"Well why didn't you say that in the first place?" I asked. "Of course I'm interested in anything that'll help rescue my mother."

"I knew I could count on you!" Shota beamed at me. "See? She's much more sensible than you," he said, shooting a look at Raiden.

"I guess Ryujin probably *does* know something about it," Raiden conceded reluctantly, "but that doesn't mean he's just going to help us. *Kami* aren't always benevolent, and Ryujin is a very powerful one. He might put us through a test or demand a favor in exchange for his help."

"What else is new?" I propped a hand on my hips. "It seems like ever since I stumbled into this mess I've been making deals and forced into uncomfortable situations. If this Ryujin guy can help us, it's worth a shot." I turned back to Shota. "What is it you want me to do?"

Grinning, Shota unhooked something from his keychain and held it up. "This is a *yokai* charm," he said, dangling a tiny turtle carved out of glowing iridescent blue stone in front of my nose. "It has the power to summon *Umigame,* the Great Sea Turtle." He said the name with reverence, as if we were talking about a legendary creature. "None of us have ever been able to use it, but since you're a powerful *yokai* shaman, you'll be able to summon him with no problem."

I took the turtle charm from Shota. It flared brightly in my hand, reacting to my power, and I cursed as pain stabbed my brain through my eyeballs.

"Calm down," I snapped at it. "I just want to look at you."

To my surprise, it did.

"Look at that!" Shota elbowed Raiden in the ribs. "She's a natural."

"She is." Raiden looked as if he wasn't sure whether he should be impressed or annoyed. "Mamoru is going to be *really* upset if we get her killed."

The excitement buzzing through my veins was instantly dampened by a healthy dose of fear. "Is this journey going to be really dangerous?"

"Dealing with *kami* is always dangerous," Shota said, shooting an annoyed look at Raiden. "As is dealing with *yurei* or *yokai.* It's par for the course of being a shaman. Honestly, Aika, don't let Raiden get you all riled up about it. I've studied up about Ryujin, and he's not a malevolent deity. In fact, Japan's first emperor was rumored to be his great-grandson, so in a way he's an ancestor of our imperial line. He likes humans, for the most part."

"It sounds like he should," I mused, trying to remember the tale my mother had told me about him. Unfortunately, like much of my toddler years, the memory was fuzzy. "If there's the slightest chance he can help me find my mother, we have to go. Besides, going to an undersea kingdom has always been on my bucket list."

"Exactly!" Shota patted me on the shoulder. "All we have to do is get to the coast, and then you can summon him. It'll be easy-peasy."

Raiden scoffed at that. "If we're going to go, we need to do it now, before Mamoru comes looking for us." He gave me a pointed look, as if to say, *You agreed to this.* "Meet us at the elevator in ten minutes."

I grabbed my clothes, then rushed down the hall for a quick shower. I wish I'd had clean clothes to change into, but there was nothing for it. I was just thankful I'd thought to wash my clothes and hang them on the *kimono* rack. Luckily, they were mostly dry, and a quick blast with the hair dryer got them the rest of the way there.

I put them on, ran a brush through my long hair, then left it loose so it could air dry. I checked my reflection one more time, then, after a moment of consideration, swiped the tube of lipstick across my mouth.

Hey, I was visiting a dragon king, wasn't I? Might as well make the effort.

Knowing this was as good as I was gonna get, I hurried out of the room to meet the others. Raiden and Shota were already fully dressed and waiting. They both looked me up and down, and I felt the tips of my ears heating up under their intense male regard. Had they noticed my lipstick? God, I didn't want them thinking I'd been trying to dress up for either of them. I was trying to impress the dragon god, not them.

And yet, I found myself standing a bit taller, my lips curving into a little smile of their own. There was something about being the center of male attention that gave me a confidence boost, and though I wasn't totally certain how I felt about either Shota or Raiden, it was clear they were both interested in me.

Then why did Shota push me away?

"So, where are we going?" I asked as we got into the elevator.

"To the rooftop shrine," Shota said as the elevator doors closed. He pressed the "R" button, and we began going up.

"Rooftop shrine?"

"It's exactly what it sounds like," Raiden said. "You'll see when we get there."

The doors opened, revealing a sprawling Zen garden with a huge shrine in the center. Finely crushed gravel had been raked into straight lines that ran across the length of the roof, interspersed with circles that surrounded carefully placed rocks and boulders.

Swathes of grass were strategically grown in paths so that one could navigate through the garden without disturbing it. Several

Japanese maple and dogwood trees were planted all around, their leaves providing splashes of color. Walls made of honey-colored oak surrounded us on all sides, blocking out the noise and bustle of the city while still allowing the early morning light to gild everything.

"Wow," I said as Raiden and Shota stepped onto the grassy path that led to the shrine. "This is amazing."

Raiden smirked. "Wait until you see the inside of the shrine. The Takaokas never do anything by halves."

I followed them up to the shrine, pausing just before the massive *tori* gate to bow. The gate was at least twelve feet tall, and the shrine twice its height, a gorgeous wooden structure painted white and vermillion, with a bark-covered roof with edges that curled like parchment paper.

A few feet from the gate was a covered fountain carved into the shape of a sea dragon, and we gathered around it to wash our hands and mouths to purify ourselves. Picking up the bamboo ladle, I poured water over my left hand, then my right hand, then back into my left hand, which I lifted to my mouth. The cool water flowed over my tongue as I swished it around to cleanse my mouth, then spat it back into my left hand before dumping it into the fountain's run-off tray.

I rinsed my left hand one more time, then stepped away from the fountain so I could shake my hands off and dry them. Raiden nodded in approval, and I bit back a sigh of relief. I was afraid I'd done the steps out of order, as I hadn't visited a shrine in ages. Not since I was a little girl.

"So," I said as we began to ascend the stone steps leading to the shrine entrance. "Is there a reason we're visiting the shrine instead of driving to the beach?"

"Because driving in morning rush hour is for schmucks," Shota declared. His eyes lit up as he lifted his head toward the twin lion-dogs guarding the shrine. "Why bother when you can shrine-travel?"

"Shrine-travel?" I echoed, looking at him as if he'd lost his mind. "What on earth are you talking about?"

"All *Shinto* shrines and Buddhist temples are connected to the *Reikai* in some way or another," he explained, his eyes lighting up. "Shamans can ride the spiritual currents of the *Reikai* that pass between temples and shrines to get from one place to another."

I couldn't believe what I was hearing. "So you're saying the shrines are like portals?"

"Pretty much. Cool, ain't it?" Shota grinned as we stepped under the eaves of the shrine. The doors were open, and there were torches flickering inside, illuminating the *haiden*, or worship hall, with its rows of benches that faced the *honden* that housed the shrine's *kami*.

I thought we were going to go inside, but Shota and Raiden headed straight for the *suzu*—a gigantic brass bell that hung from the eaves of the shrine and had a long, thick rope attached to it that trailed to the ground.

"We use the bell to get the *kami's* attention and access the

Reikai," Raiden explained at my questioning look. "Since we're traveling as one, we have to hold hands." He offered me his right hand.

Nodding, I gripped Raiden's hand, hoping he didn't notice my palm was growing damp with nerves. "Is it possible to get stuck between shrines?" I asked. "Like, end up in the *Reikai* by accident?"

Raiden frowned. "I've never heard of that happening. Now hush," he said, lowering his voice. "Shota needs to concentrate."

We fell silent as Shota bowed twice in front of the shrine, then grabbed the rope and gave it a mighty tug. The bell gonged once, then twice as Shota tugged it again, a deep, melodious sound that vibrated in my chest and swept away the anxiety lingering there.

I half-expected Shota to let the bell go so he could clap—which was traditional when making a wish using the shrine bell—but instead he grabbed Raiden's hand. I gasped as a flash of blinding light engulfed us and lifted my free hand to shield my eyes. Suddenly we were flying through the air at what seemed like the speed of light, and the bright light was shifting and twisting all around us in a dizzying kaleidoscope of colors. I felt like I was trapped in a tie-dye spin, and my stomach pitched with nausea.

A second later, blackness slammed down around us, and we came to an abrupt stop. Reeling, I clutched Raiden's arm for balance, and maybe also to reassure myself that he was still here.

"It's okay," Raiden said, pulling me closer to him. His voice was close enough to my ear that his warm breath brushed across my cheek, and magically, the knots in my stomach vanished. "Your vision will clear in a second."

He was right. Gradually, the blackness faded away, replaced by a gorgeous view of the beach. *Ocean Beach,* I realized as I caught sight of the Sutro Baths ruins down below. We were standing on one of the grassy swells of land leading down to the Baths—a popular tourist hotspot in San Francisco. A salty ocean breeze whipped around us, tugging at my still-damp hair, and I instinctively leaned into Raiden's warmth as the chill nipped at my cheeks.

"Hey," Shota said from behind Raiden. My cheeks flamed, and I hastily stepped out of Raiden's arms to see him watching us, his expression carefully blank. "Let's get down to the shore so we can call up this sea turtle."

He turned on his heel before I could answer, heading for the path that zigzagged down to the beach. My heart clenched, and suddenly I felt conflicted, as if I was being disloyal to Shota by clinging to Raiden. But how did that make any sense? Shota had pushed me away earlier. For whatever reason, he'd put up a boundary.

Pushing the thought away, I glanced around to see if there were any other people around. That was when I saw the tiny stone shrine tucked into the rocks behind us.

"So that's how we got here," I murmured, crouching down to study it. "Can I shrine-travel using these things too? I don't see any bell to ring."

"No," Raiden said. "We can't use the mini shrines to travel *to* places, unless they're specially built for that purpose. We can only use them as a destination point." I looked up at him and noticed there was a hint of pink in his cheeks that immediately made me feel better about my own flaming face. "We should get down to the coast before the tourists arrive." He offered me his hand.

I hesitated for a split second before taking it. That *zing* of electricity shot up my arm again, and from the way Raiden's grip tightened around my hand as he pulled me up, I knew he felt it too. For a moment, I thought he'd pull me closer again, but he let my hand go the moment I was on my feet, turning away before I could see the look in his eyes.

"Come on. Let's go."

Biting back a sigh, I followed him down the dirt path. We caught up quickly enough to Shota, who was now scampering down the path like a happy puppy who'd been let off his leash. He glanced back at us once to make sure we were following before continuing his descent.

"Shota has been dreaming of meeting Ryujin ever since we were teenagers," Raiden said by way of explanation. "He found that charm when he was fifteen and has carried it with him everywhere since. He probably knows more about undersea *kami* and *yokai* than anyone else in the world. I hope he doesn't start fanboying all over Ryujin when we meet him."

Raiden's lips twitched into a reluctant grin. "I wouldn't be the least bit surprised if he asks Ryujin for an autograph. Too bad you can't really sign with paper and ink underwater." A curious expression crossed his face. "Unless maybe they have a way of writing on things underwater?"

"Stone tablets?" I suggested as we finally reached the surf. "Sounds like a hefty autograph to carry to the surface."

"I can hear you guys, you know," Shota grumbled, leading us past the Baths and toward a group of caves off to the right while Raiden and I snickered. "Let's go over here, where no one can see us. While it would be pretty cool if we ended up on the national news for summoning a giant sea turtle, I don't really want to piss off Mamoru."

"Umm, yeah." I was keen on keeping as low a profile as possible. We followed Shota onto a narrow path that clung to the side of the cliff and edged our way around it for a good half mile. Finally, when we were far enough from the beach that we were no longer near shallow water, Shota brought us to a stop at a small landing wide enough for the three of us to stand together and gestured toward the waves.

"All right, Aika, it's show time," Shota said, his voice alight with excitement. He dug out the *Umigame* charm from his pocket and handed it to me. His fingers briefly closed around mine in a reassuring squeeze, giving me another case of the warm fuzzies. "Do your thing."

I took a deep breath as I opened my palm to look at the charm. It blazed in my hand, but instead of telling it to pipe down, I gathered my power around me and latched onto the *yoki* spilling out of the charm.

"Rise, Umigame," I called in Japanese, my voice echoing with power. *"I summon you from the ocean depths."*

A bright green ball of energy burst from the charm and hurtled straight for the ocean. It hit the water with tornado-like force, throwing water in every direction as the sea began to spin. Foam sprayed up from the whirlpool as the ocean bubbled and frothed below us, and the three of us backed away from the ledge, fear rising in my chest to choke me.

"Take cover!" Raiden barked as an enormous wave began to crest. He dragged Shota and me up against the cliff, which thankfully curved inward, providing a tiny bit of shelter. We watched in horror as the wave climbed to five, ten, fifteen feet of frothy madness.

This is really *going to suck.*

Sucking in a breath, I squeezed my eyes shut and clung to Raiden and Shota as the wave crashed into us. The icy water smashed us into the cliff wall, but since we were already pressed against the rocky face, it didn't hurt as much as I'd anticipated.

"Dammit!" Shota gasped, spluttering as the water sluiced back down the cliffside. "My pants are ruined!"

Raiden snort-coughed, hacking up sea water. Or at least I thought that was what he was doing—I couldn't see him as I was bent forward, coughing out a lungful of water myself. "You should have thought about that when you asked to go riding in on a sea tur..." His voice trailed off.

"Holy shit," Shota breathed. "You really did it, Aika."

Slowly, I lifted my head to the ocean. My mouth dropped open in awe, and the miserable wetness and the lightheaded feeling of barely escaping death faded away. Floating in the ocean, right in front of us, was a *massive* sea turtle. He had to be about thirty feet long and nearly as wide, with a gorgeous iridescent shell and dappled blue and black skin that covered his head and limbs. His body was turned sideways, and he regarded me out of his enormous left eye.

"You summoned me?" he asked in Japanese, his voice echoing in the air even though he didn't open his mouth.

"Umm." I swallowed, my throat *very* dry all of a sudden. "Yes," I said, stepping forward. *"My friends and I would like safe passage to Ryujin's kingdom. Can you take us there?"*

"Hmm." The *Umigame's* eye narrowed. The top of my scalp began prickling, and I stiffened as the sensation swept me from head to toe. Was it doing some kind of weird scan on me? Shota and Raiden shivered next to me, and I wondered if they were feeling the same thing. *"Yes, the three of you are strong enough to ride."* The *Umigame* drifted closer to us until the side of its shell scraped up against the cliff wall. *"Jump onto my back."*

I swallowed, peering over the edge of the cliff—it was a twenty foot drop at least. How were we going to get down there without breaking something?

"Don't worry," Shota said, correctly interpreting the look on my face. He unzipped a pocket on the pack he'd slung over his back and withdrew an *ofuda.* *"Hiyaku!"* he cried, tossing the strip of paper into the air. *Soar.*

The *ofuda* lit up, then exploded with a huge *pop*, like a kernel of corn in the microwave. My eyes widened as a huge white feather floated down in its place, coming to hover just beyond the ledge.

"*Ofudas* aren't only good for warding off *yurei* and *yokai*," Shota said as he hopped onto the feather without a care in the world. It shivered slightly beneath his weight, but it held. "Hop on!" He held a hand out to me, as if he were merely asking me to cross the street instead of board a giant feather.

Swallowing hard, I took his hand. He squeezed my hand, giving me an encouraging smile that banished some of my nerves. Carefully, I pressed my foot against the feather to see if it would hold. I fully expected the fluffy strands to part, but they held, resisting the pressure. Satisfied, I stepped onto it, then moved aside so Raiden could join us.

"*Koka suru*," Shota ordered the feather. *Descend.* The feather slowly drifted down, depositing us onto the giant sea turtle's back. The moment it touched the *Umigame's* wet shell, it disintegrated, turning into a soggy piece of paper. "One-time use only," he explained as he settled, cross-legged, onto the turtle's back.

"You guys have to teach me how to use those sometime. They seem really useful," I said as Raiden and I sat down on the hard, damp shell. Those *ofuda* charms were looking more and more appealing by the second. "How many different kinds of *ofuda* are there?"

"A lot," Raiden said, "but we can at least teach you the warding ones that you can use to keep *yokai* and *yurei* at bay." His features tightened with concern. "We should have taught you before we left."

"It's okay," I said, feeling a sudden wave of sympathy for Raiden. He'd probably never had to babysit someone like me before. "I'm sure I'll be fine with you and Shota here."

"Of course you will," Shota said breezily, patting the turtle shell. "Now would you mind doing the honors and getting us under way?"

I turned around to face the back of the *Umigame's* head, even though I knew he couldn't see me looking at him. *"Are we going to be able to breathe while we're riding on your back?"* I asked, goosebumps prickling over my flesh as it occurred to me that I didn't understand the logistics. We didn't even have anything to hold onto. *"How do we stay on?"*

The *Umigame* chuckled. *"There is no need to fear,"* he said. *"I will not let you die while we travel. Are you ready to go?"*

I swallowed. "Ready as I'll ever be."

"Good."

And with that, the *Umigame* dove beneath the waves.

I held my breath as water rushed all around us, expecting to be blasted off the turtle's back by the currents. But I stayed right where I was, comfortably seated on the turtle's back, my butt parked between the two grooves I'd settled in. Looking back, I noticed that Raiden and Shota were still there as well. Shota gave me a thumbs up, and Raiden actually grinned. Their hair was waving in the water behind them, a ghostly green sheen on their faces, but other than that they looked totally normal.

"You don't have to hold your breath," Raiden said, bubbles coming out of his mouth. My mouth dropped open in shock—his voice was slightly warbly, but perfectly understandable. "The *Umigame's yoki* is protecting us." He gestured around us, and I gasped as I realized a shimmering sphere had surrounded us like a giant glowing bubble.

"So this is why we can talk and breathe?" I asked, gesturing to it.

"Yes." Shota's eyes lit up as he looked around the ocean—he was like a kid who'd stumbled into a hidden gateway to Candy Land. "You guys, this is the coolest thing ever!"

"I hate to admit it, but he's right," Raiden said, his normally stoic expression nowhere to be found. His face was slack with amazement as he looked around. I had to agree—the view down here was incredible. Schools of fish were swimming all around us, shimmering waves of fins and scales in a variety of shapes and sizes. Long tendrils of kelp waved at us from the ocean floor, and brightly colored fish darted in and out of the underwater forest, looking for food while hiding from predators.

Off in the distance, I spotted what looked like a pair of sea otters chasing each other through the water, and there were some manta rays sailing through the currents as well. Many of the fish steered clear of us, unwilling to become the *Umigame's* lunch, but an elephant seal drew close, curious. I held my breath as it sidled up against the shimmering barrier, wondering if it would try to come up to us. But it couldn't pass, and after a minute, it swam away.

"Looks like the sharks won't be able to get to us, then," Raiden said, sounding satisfied. "I wonder what happens when we get off the *Umigame's* back, though?"

"My yoki will protect you for several more hours after you disembark," the sea turtle said. *"Beyond that, you will have to ask Ryujin, or one of his children, to offer you protection from the sea."*

"Sweet," Shota and Raiden said simultaneously. They exchanged identical grins, and I couldn't help laughing. Personality-wise they seemed completely different, but in this moment their shared blood shone through clearly.

Boys will be boys, I thought, turning my attention back to the view. *I might as well enjoy it while I have the chance,* I thought as we sped through the water, plunging into the ocean depths. Because I had a feeling we were headed straight into trouble.

10

It took us several hours to reach Ryujin's palace, and I spent most of that time flat on my back on the turtle shell, catching up on some much needed sleep. Yes, I know the idea of sleeping underwater while surrounded by amazing undersea sights sounds a bit crazy. Believe me, I spent the better part of the first hour gawking at all the fish and animals. It wasn't every day that you got to fly past a humpback whale and her calf, or watch a great white shark chase a sea lion.

But those exciting moments were interspersed with long stretches of nothing but kelp forests and schools of fish, and there was only so much of that a girl could take. I needed my beauty sleep if I was going to go toe to toe with a dragon god. And seeing as how Raiden had passed out as well, it stood to reason there was no harm in taking a deep sea nap.

"Hey, guys," Shota said next to my ear, interrupting a very nice dream in which I was receiving my diploma from medical school. "Wake up. We're approaching the palace now."

I groaned, stirring a little. As I did, I immediately became aware that two warm bodies were pressed up on either side of me. Tensing, I opened my eyes and sat up slowly. Sure enough, both men had cozied up to me while I was sleeping. Shota was sitting up on my left, his eyes gleaming as he stared straight ahead at whatever had caught his attention. Raiden was on my right, sleeping like the dead. Both of their bodies were pressed up against mine, and my cheeks blazed as I realized I'd probably snuggled up with them unconsciously for warmth. The *Umigame's* shield protected us against the worst of the cold, but there was still a distinct chill down here.

"Look ahead," Shota said, shifting his gaze and grinning down at me. "You won't believe your eyes."

Groaning, I pushed myself up to see what the big fuss was about. And gasped. Off in the distance, perched atop what looked like an undersea volcano, was an immense palace constructed of pink coral and sea glass. It glittered as though it was encrusted with jewels, and as we grew closer, I realized it *was* encrusted... with something. Fish scales, maybe? We were still too far off to tell. A towering gate of stalactite-shaped coral surrounded the palace, and stationed around it were...

"Are those jellyfish?" Raiden asked, looking over my shoulder at the palace. I'd been so caught up by the splendor of the palace, I hadn't noticed him sit up. "Holy shit, this place looks like something straight out of *The Little Mermaid*."

"Do not let Ryujin hear you say that," the *Umigame* warned, a hint of amusement in its deep voice. *"He finds the insinuation quite*

offensive, as he built his palace long before Hans Christian Andersen was ever born."

I blinked. "You know who Hans Christian Andersen is?"

"I may be old, but I am not senile," the turtle said, sounding a bit miffed. *"The ocean currents bring more news than you might think."*

"Of course," Shota said, his voice soothing. "And you guys end up with all the books and treasure that are lost at sea, too. You probably know a lot about what goes on above the surface."

"Yes, and the sea birds bring us news too. We are very well informed."

Well that'll teach me to make assumptions, I thought to myself as the *Umigame* pulled up a few feet away from the front gates. The jellyfish guards shifted, their tentacles wrapping tightly around their spears, and I tried not to notice the crackling energy that clung to said tentacles. I had no doubt that if those guards decided to turn us into shark bait, our odds of survival were *not* good.

"Thank you very much," I said to the turtle, swimming off his back. I knew, logically, that the water pressure should be crushing me at this depth, and yet, I swam through the water as easily as if I were in a kiddie pool. Even though it made me nervous, I approached the sea turtle's great head, then leaned my body against it in a sort of half-hug. "I know you are powerful enough that you didn't have to help us."

The sea turtle chuckled again. *"It has been many a century since a human last rode atop my shell."* He nudged me with his head, and I floated back a few feet, not sure if he was nuzzling me or trying to push me away. *"Good luck with your audience with Ryujin. I will await your call again."*

Raiden and Shota swam to my side, and we watched the sea turtle swim away. I marveled at how fast he sliced through the currents, reducing his huge form to a mere spec in the distance in a matter of seconds.

"That was really something," Raiden murmured.

"Yeah. And we're only just getting started." Shota rubbed his hands together.

As one, we turned to face the jellyfish guards. They stood silent, waiting, and I swallowed, trying to figure out where to look at them. They didn't seem to have eyes, as far as I could tell, or even mouths. Could they talk?

"Speak, human," the one on the right said, and I started. Like the *Umigame*, its voice was disembodied, and yet somehow I knew that it had spoken rather than its partner. "What is your business here at the Dragon Palace?"

"We are here to see Ryujin," I said. "We have important business to discuss with him."

"And what business is that?"

The three of us exchanged looks. "It would be best if we discussed that with him directly," Raiden said.

The two guards shifted. "Ryujin does not grant an audience to just anyone," the second guard said. "Is he expecting you?"

"Well, no," Raiden admitted. "But we've come a long way just to see him. Don't you think he'd at least be a little interested to hear why we've gone through all this trouble?"

"Nobu," a melodic voice drifted through the waves, and the guards turned. My mouth dropped open at the sight of a *ningyo* —a Japanese mermaid—swimming out toward us from one of the coral towers. Her lower half wasn't exactly what I envisioned in a mermaid—instead of one long tail, she had three, covered in persimmon-colored scales and tipped with long, translucent fins. Her upper half was completely bare, with flawless alabaster skin and high, perky breasts that were partially covered by the thick mass of black hair that flowed from the top of her head in waves around her. And though her face was beautiful, she had shimmering orange horns curling from the top of her head, and some kind of strange burnt orange tattoo slashed across both of her high cheekbones.

"Who are these humans?" she asked, curiosity gleaming in her iridescent eyes as she looked us over. Her ruby lips curved into a smile, exposing sharp fangs, and a shiver crawled down my spine. "They look tasty."

Raiden stepped forward, his stance wary. "I am Takaoka Raiden," he said, and the three of us bowed. "These are my friends, Shota and Aika. We came here to speak to Ryujin. Can you take us to him?"

The *ningyo* fluttered her eyelashes at Raiden. "That depends. What can you offer me in return?" She licked her lips seductively, and I felt a sudden flash of jealousy at the way she was looking at Raiden. But slapping the *ningyo* in her pretty, albeit fanged, face wasn't going to get us anywhere.

"Please," I said, stepping in front of Raiden before he could respond. "An evil shaman named Kai has taken my mother prisoner. We are trying to get her back, and we think Ryujin might be able to help, if only we could talk to him. Isn't there any way we can gain an audience with him?"

The flirty smile vanished from the *ningyo's* face, replaced by a sympathetic look that made me hate her a lot less. "Well why didn't you say so?" She tossed a skein of hair over her left shoulder, exposing one of her nipples. Shota made a choking sound behind me, and Raiden coughed. "Of course I'll take you to see him. Kai's escape is the most exciting thing we've heard about in centuries, and my father is bored to tears. He'll be happy to talk to you."

She waved at the guards to open the gates, then turned around and floated through them as if she hadn't just flashed all of us. I glanced sidelong at Raiden as we followed. His cheeks had reddened, though he wore his default stoic expression, and I wasn't sure if I should be amused or annoyed.

And what do you have to be annoyed about, anyway? I chided myself. *He's a man. I'm sure his cheeks would turn just as red if you lifted up your shirt and flashed him right now.*

My face flooded with embarrassment at the idea, and that was when Raiden turned to look at me. "What are you blushing about?" he asked, arching a brow.

I lifted my chin. "I could ask you the same question."

Raiden rolled his eyes. "Come on. At least I didn't suck in a lungful of water like someone else we know." He jerked a thumb toward Shota.

"What?" Shota asked defensively. "Fish are kind of my specialty, in case you haven't noticed. It's not every day you get to see a mermaid in the flesh." He eyed the *ningyo's* retreating back. "That's one fish I won't be taking out my sushi knife for," he muttered, and I choked back a laugh.

"My name is Amabie, by the way," the *ningyo* said as the palace doors swung open, revealing a hallway made of crystal that glowed with phosphorescent blue algae. Red, purple, and gold coral ran through the crystal floor, making it seem like we were literally walking across a reef as we entered. "My apologies for not introducing myself earlier—it's been too long since we've had human visitors." She flashed a fanged grin over her shoulder at Shota, whose eyes went wide.

"Amabie?" Shota echoed faintly. "As in Amabie of the Harvest?"

"The very same." She laughed at the astonished look on his face, and the sound was magical, like a faerie running her fingers over the strings of an enchanted harp. My mind suddenly filled with memories of sunny days at the park and hot summer evenings lying in the sand and watching the sunset. "I was only joking when I said you all looked tasty earlier—I don't eat humans. Although I'd be willing to taste that one," she added, licking her lips as she looked at Raiden.

"I'd appreciate it if you could keep your fins to yourself," I said in an acid tone, putting myself in front of Raiden. Amabie's blatant interest in him was getting my back up, though I wasn't sure why. After all, it wasn't as if I owned him, right? And besides, what kind of person did that make me, getting possessive over Raiden when I was still struggling with the feelings I had for Shota?

The last thing you should be thinking about are romantic relationships, Aika.

Amabie raised her eyebrows at me. "As you wish," she said, throwing a flirty glance toward Shota. "That one is cuter, anyway." She winked, drawing closer to him. "You look like you could handle a girl like me."

Shota laughed. "Trust me, you don't want to get anywhere near me," he said. "I'm a sushi chef by trade."

"I *love* sashimi," she purred, running a hand down his arm. I gritted my teeth as jealousy flared in me. "You should cook for me sometime."

There was a beat of silence, and for a second, I thought Shota was going to flirt back. But instead, he looped his arm through mine and pulled me close.

"Sorry," he said easily, ignoring Raiden's glare. "There's only one woman I cook for these days, and I don't think she's up for sharing."

Amabie huffed, then turned around, her tails flicking a spray of bubbles in our faces. "Your loss," she said haughtily.

I glanced down at Shota's and my intertwined arms as we followed Amabie through the palace. Raiden didn't look pleased to see the two of us holding hands, and once again, I felt like a disloyal bitch. I wished I could talk to them about what was going on between us, because it was obvious that there were some strong feelings brewing, and yet none of us wanted to acknowledge what was happening.

But we had more important things to think about, and now was not the time for this conversation. Unable to handle the growing tension between the three of us, I pulled away from Shota and focused on our surroundings.

Opalescent sea shells decorated the walls, and above, more golden coral snaked across the ceiling like a series of chandeliers. Instead of having lights attached, iridescent fish flitted amongst them, casting glittering light every color of the rainbow across the coral-laden crystal floor. Even that was different here, though, because instead of stretching out like spider webs through the crystal as it had in the floor outside, it writhed beneath our feet like pink sea anemones.

"So what's the big deal about Amabie?" I asked Raiden in a low voice, leaning in close enough so only he could hear.

"Legend has it that she appeared on the coast of a small, struggling town during the Edo period and predicted six years of good harvest," Raiden said as we were led down a hall that forked off to the left. This one was different from the last, and I felt like we'd stepped into a latticework of blue coral that stretched up all around us like a living gazebo. "She told the townsfolk that if disease spread, to show a picture of her to the afflicted, and they would be cured."

"And did they have a six-year harvest?"

Raiden nodded. "They were one of the wealthiest towns in the country for those next six years. So wealthy, in fact, that they drew the attention of the emperor himself. No one died of sickness during those years, at least until the original painting of Amabie, painted by the town potter, was burned by a vindictive competitor who was jealous of the potter's success. The town succumbed to sickness not long after that, and over half the people were wiped out before they abandoned it to start over somewhere else. It's a ghost town now," Raiden said sadly.

"That's terrible," I murmured, filled with sadness for the townsfolk and their fate. How awful must it be to have such wealth and prosperity, only to have it taken from you because of one man's jealousy?

"The human who did that is burning in hell now," Amabie said, her melodious voice turning dark with anger. She stopped in front of a pair of huge double doors and turned to look back at us, a fierce grin on her face. "As do all who cross a *ningyo*. Our curses are very powerful."

The three of us exchanged nervous looks as Amabie threw the doors open. "Father," she sang cheerfully, sailing into the room as if she hadn't half-threatened us a second ago. "We have visitors!"

"Not now," Ryujin snapped, waving a clawed hand. "I'm on the phone."

The three of us stopped short at the sight of him—he was gigantic, at least thirty feet long, and his upper body towered over us a good fifteen feet in the air. His sinuous form was covered in scales of every color blue I could think of, and even a few I'd never seen. They shimmered in the light filtering in through the translucent glass skylight above. His yellow, reptilian eyes crackled with annoyance as he held an enormous conch shell to his ear.

"Uhh...is he talking into that thing?" I whispered to Raiden.

"It looks like it, doesn't it?" he whispered back, his eyes glued to Ryujin. His face had gone white, and his expression was numb, as if shock had turned him to stone. I couldn't blame him—I'd seen some strange things in the last twenty-four hours, but a gigantic undersea dragon definitely took the cake.

"Tell International Oil they can take that ridiculous counter-offer and shove it up their asses," Ryujin snarled, exposing yellow fangs that were the size of Raiden's arm, and three times as thick. "Two-hundred million is my final offer."

Amabie flicked her tails in annoyance. "He'll be off the phone soon," she told us, as if it were normal for a thirty-foot-tall dragon to have phone conversations using a conch shell. "My father's a day trader, so he's always got his ear glued to that stupid conch shell."

"A day trader?" Raiden asked, sounding as incredulous as I felt. "Your father is in the stock market?"

Amabie flashed another one of her fanged smiles. "He special-izes in hostile takeovers. Specifically, he goes after corporations that pollute the oceans."

"Look, I don't give a damn about how much they've improved

their safeguards or what they're being valued at," the dragon snarled, leaning backward as he slashed angrily at the air like he was attacking the person on the other end of the phone. "The last time they put a boat in the bay, they spilled oil all over it." His voice turned soft and deadly, which was even worse than when he'd been yelling. "And don't think I don't know about how that reactor is still leaking into the bay. I don't give a damn what the scientists say about it; I can prove it." His voice got even quieter. "And I have this friend in the media..."

A self-satisfied smile spread across his face, exposing far too many teeth. "Why yes, I do think my offer is quite generous, given the circumstances. I'll have the contracts sent over. And tell them to stop dumping those barrels of chemicals in the bay. My people are getting tired of filming them."

Ryujin put the conch shell down on an enormous rock shelf sticking out of the wall and blew a disgusted sigh out of his nostrils. "What is it you want, daughter?" he asked, turning his great head toward us. "You know better than to walk in..." He trailed off, his eyes widening with surprise as he finally noticed us. "And who are these?" he demanded, lowering his neck so that his head hovered right in front of us. It was a lot bigger up close than it had been fifteen feet up, and I resisted the temptation to step away even though my knees were knocking together.

"They're shamans, visiting from the surface," Amabie said, swishing one of her tails toward us in introduction. We immediately sank into low bows. "They say they've come seeking your counsel."

"It has been a long time since a shaman has dared visit my

domain," Ryujin rumbled. A rush of bubbles rippled over us as he spoke, and I flinched. "Rise, humans," he commanded imperiously. My spine immediately jerked upright, as if of its own accord, and from the way the guys started next to me, I knew they'd done the same. A shiver crawled down my spine at the power in Ryujin's voice—could he control us with his words?

His yellow gaze swept over us again, assessing, then lingered on me. "A *yokai* shaman," he said, his voice lightening with wonder. "It has been even longer since I have last seen one of your kind. Where did you come from?"

"Umm. San Francisco." I shifted nervously as I spoke. Ryujin was eyeing me as if I were an exciting new treasure he'd found, and I wasn't sure I liked it. "How do you know I'm a *yokai* shaman?"

Ryujin snorted, spraying us with bubbles again. "Your aura, of course. You should know your *ki* would be different from theirs." His eyes narrowed as he looked at Raiden and Shota, who were standing so still they didn't even look like they were breathing. "Why doesn't she know this?" he demanded of them.

Raiden finally seemed to unfreeze, and he stepped forward, angling his body so that he was between me and the giant sea dragon. "She's only just found out she's a shaman, Ryujin-sama," he said, his tone respectful but firm. It seemed that, unlike the rest of us, he'd found his balls again—there was no trace of fear in him. "Her mother wasn't one, and her father has been dead since she was a child, so she knows very little."

"And yet you brought her down here?" Ryujin sounded

surprised. "Why would you risk putting such a rare shaman in a dangerous situation like this?"

Raiden stiffened, and I pushed in front of him before he said something foolish. "Ryujin-sama," I said, bowing low again. "We knew the journey was dangerous, but there was nothing Raiden could have done to stop me from coming. My mother has gone missing, and I fear that Kai has taken her. We need your help to get her back."

"Kai?" The dragon drew himself upright. "I'd heard he recently escaped, but why would he..." He stopped, his eyes gleaming with understanding. "Of course. He is trying to draw you out. That is why he took your mother."

"For what reason?" Shota asked, speaking for the first time since we'd entered the room. He seemed to have regained himself and was buzzing with excitement all over again. "Why does Kai want Aika-san so much, Ryujin-sama?"

Ryujin gave us all an annoyed look, shaking his huge head. "I suppose the three of you are still too young to have been told the full story of Kai," he said. He waved a huge claw, and three giant cushions appeared on the floor. "Sit, and I will tell you the story of Kai. Or rather," he said, his voice deepening like ominous thunder, "I will tell you the story of Kai, Haruki, Kaga, and Fumiko, and how their choices led to the downfall of shamankind."

aruki. The name rippled across my skin, causing the hairs on my arms to stand at attention. I felt a tug in the center of my chest and found myself looking at Raiden. His entire body had gone still, and I knew the name had inspired a similar reaction in him. Did he know who Ryujin was talking about?

"What do you mean, the downfall of shamankind?" I asked Ryujin. "The shamans are still here, aren't they?" I swept a hand to indicate the three of us. "We're proof of that."

Ryujin shook his head. "You are the scattered remains of what was once a great empire," he said, his deep voice tinged with sadness. "Shamans were the spiritual leaders of Japan, often even more important than the clan chieftains they ruled along-side. A few became political leaders as well, such as Himiko, the Queen of Yamatai." His yellow eyes flickered. "It was Kai who ended her line."

"Really?" Raiden leaned forward, looking very interested. "I thought it was Haruki who killed her."

"Few know the true tale of what transpired between Haruki, Fumiko, Kaga, and Kai," Ryujin rumbled. "Now are you going to keep asking questions, or are you going to let me tell the story?"

Raiden's cheeks reddened. "My apologies, Ryujin-sama," he said, bowing. "Please proceed."

Ryujin settled down, satisfied. "Nearly two thousand years ago, Japan, which was known as Wa at the time, was ruled by Clan Yamatai. Wa enjoyed several decades of peace and prosperity under the rule of Himiko, Yamatai's clan leader and Wa's esteemed empress. Her beauty was legendary, her power absolute, and she was Amaterasu's favored child. Or at least, that is what the stories say."

Ryujin's wide mouth curved into a fanged smile that made me shiver. "What the stories do not tell you is that there were three more clans: Earth, Fire, and Lightning. They did not like the Yamatai, and each believed that they were the rightful rulers of Wa. They were the only ones that had not fully submitted to Yamatai's authority."

"Let me guess," I said when Ryujin paused to take a breath, or maybe just for dramatic effect. "The three clans were spirit shamans too?" Mamoru had already mentioned that Himiko was a *yokai* shaman, so that seemed pretty obvious.

"Yes," Ryujin said, sounding pleased at my deduction. "Originally, there were seven shaman clans. They ruled different territories, and there was constant fighting between them as some sought to rule all of Wa. But one clan, the water clan, broke away from the mold, from the sacred teachings these shamans had clung to for hundreds of years. Instead of calling upon *yurei* to do their bidding, they began to use *yokai*. This set them apart from the other clans, and gave them the advantage they needed to conquer Wa and claim it as their empire."

Raiden and Shota exchanged looks of surprise. "I always thought it was five clans," Shota said. "This is so fascinating, Ryujin-sama!"

"I am pleased you are enjoying the history lesson," Ryujin said, a little dryly. "Most of the other clans ended up picking sides, and were swallowed up by either the Yamatai Clan or one of the three elemental clans, depending on whether or not they were willing to learn the ways of the *yokai* shaman, or if they were purists, like the other clans were. The Saitos believed that the Yamatai were abominations, and that their use of *yokai* spirits would bring the wrath of the gods. That was nonsense, of course, as we would have stripped the Yamatai of their power long before things ever came to a head," he added with a scoff. "But the Saitos were set in their ways, and they feuded with the Yamatai for a long time."

"So what changed?" I asked. "Who extended the first olive branch?"

"Queen Himiko did," Ryujin said. "She offered her daughter, Fumiko, to whichever of the clan chieftains could prove their worth. Whichever man won her would rule over Wa at Fumiko's side, and the other two would become advisors and join their clans with the others."

"I'm sensing there's a 'but' coming up," Shota said as my stomach tensed.

"A very big 'but.'" Ryujin nodded. "Haruki, Kai, and Kaga competed fiercely for Fumiko's hand. It is said that she cared for them all dearly, but in the end, chose Haruki. The two had known each other since they were children, and she considered Haruki to be the best choice to rule at her side."

Raiden, Shota, and I exchanged uneasy glances. "Is this the part where you tell us that Kai didn't take well to this?"

"He did not," Ryujin rumbled, his tone turning dark. "In the middle of the night, someone slit Kaga's throat in his bed. The next morning, Haruki and Kai both accused each other of the deed, and challenged each other to a duel. Fumiko begged them to stop, but neither would back down. The two fought on an empty plain, with many witnesses present. Kai fought valiantly, but he was no match for Haruki. The lightning shaman was older, and far more experienced."

Ryujin paused again, and I was surprised to find there was a lump in my throat. Tears stung at my eyes, and my heart was an aching pit. I didn't know why, but I felt very strongly about these ghosts from the past, ghosts I had never met. Glancing at Raiden, I noticed that his entire body had gone rigid, his eyes glued to Ryujin. It was clear to me that the story was important to him somehow.

"As you may or may not know, we *kami* are fickle creatures. Sometimes we stand back and watch, and other times we like to stick our noses into the business of the children we have created.

It just so happens that Amatsu Mikaboshi, the god of primordial chaos, had been watching this conflict for some weeks and carefully whispering in Kai's ear while he was sleeping. He chose this moment, when Kai was about to be defeated, to whisper in his ear again and make him an offer. He told Kai that he would lend him his power, if, in exchange, Kai allowed him to become his avatar." Ryujin's voice turned into a growl. "It was the greatest mistake Kai had ever made."

A dark chill ran down my spine. "Did Kai win the duel?"

"Oh yes," Ryujin hissed. "With Amatsu's power at his fingertips, he was far more powerful than Haruki. He easily overcame the Saito Clan Chieftain and was about to deliver the killing blow. But before he could, Fumiko ran onto the field, begging him to stop. She threw herself on top of Haruki, and Kai accidentally killed them both."

"How awful," Shota murmured, and I had to agree. I couldn't even imagine what Kai must have felt at the moment Fumiko had thrown herself in front of Haruki. To know that you were responsible for the death of the person you loved most...

"Kai was crushed by Fumiko's death. He gathered her body up and tried to call her spirit back, but before he could, Haruki's spirit grabbed her and took her away with him to the afterlife. Enraged, Kai swore vengeance upon both the Yamatai and the lightning clan. Then he gave himself over to Amatsu's dark power. Amatsu took control of the earth clan, mercilessly slaughtering anyone who dared oppose him, and prepared to mount an attack against the Yamatai."

"That must be why there are so few shamans today," Shota murmured. "They all got purged."

"Not all. Fortunately for your kind, several dissenters from the earth clan escaped, and they ran to Himiko's court to tell her what had transpired. Himiko gathered her forces and went to confront Kai. She saw immediately that he had been corrupted by Amatsu's power and tried to exorcise the dark god from him. But Amatsu was too powerful, and he would not be denied. The two clans ended up in a horrific battle, and Himiko called upon Amaterasu for help. Together, the shaman queen and the sun goddess managed to bind Kai and Amatsu into a heavily warded box. But before they did, the chaos god put a terrible curse on Himiko, and all of her line."

A horrible feeling churned in my gut, and I found that I was leaning forward at the edge of my pillow. "What was the curse?"

"Amatsu knew that so long as the line of *yokai* shamans continued, he would never truly be able to take power. He put a curse on Himiko to ensure that she would never again be able to bear children, which effectively ended her line, as Fumiko was her only heir. It was a powerful curse that not even Amaterasu herself could undo, and it led to the eventual downfall of the Yamatai Clan." Ryujin sighed heavily. "It was a great loss for all of Wa."

"So Aika isn't descended from Himiko, then?" Raiden asked sharply. "She isn't from the Yamatai line?"

"Oh, undoubtedly her clan descends from Yamatai, but it would have been one of the other shaman clans that were absorbed and taught the ways of the *yokai* shaman," Ryujin said. "But no, Aika does not have Himiko's blood running through her veins. Amatsu's curse made that impossible."

"I see," Raiden said. His hands were clenched into fists, and when he locked gazes with me, my breath caught at the pain in his eyes. What was going on?

"This has been really interesting, Ryujin-sama," Shota said, "but I'm afraid it doesn't really explain why Kai wants Aika. If she's not a descendent of Himiko, then she shares no relation with Fumiko, his long-dead lover."

"That is what you would think," Ryujin said, a twinkle in his eye, "but fate often surprises us. I cannot tell you more," he said when Shota opened his mouth again. "You will have to find that out yourself when you confront Kai."

"But that's not fair!" I protested hotly, forgetting that I was talking to a massive dragon god. "You obviously know the answer—why don't you tell us!"

"Because it is not the right time, child," the dragon answered. He lowered his head to look me in the eye directly, and I swallowed as his dragon breath bubbles rushed over me again. Thankfully, he did not seem angry. "Right now, the three of you need to get to Kai's tomb. The wards around it have been weakened over the centuries, but they are still strong enough. That is why he has been using *yokai* to do his bidding. If you can get to him and bind him again before he frees himself, you can get your mother back and stop a great evil from being unleashed upon the world."

"That's not going to be easy," Shota said, sounding troubled. "If the tomb has been opened, Kai and Amatsu will be using their combined powers to keep everyone from getting in through the front entrance and sealing them away again. That's probably why they've called every high-level shaman in the area over there—to try and break through so that Kai can be sealed away again."

"There is another way to get into Kai's tomb," Ryujin said. "It is a secret entrance, accessible via an underground cavern. Usually it is impassible due to the high tide...but I can help with that, for a price."

"What's the price?" I asked, latching onto the ray of hope Ryujin's words offered. If we could get past the barrier and into Kai's domain, we could find my mother and get her back.

"Aika," Raiden interrupted, his voice strained. "Do you mind if I talk to you for a minute? In private?"

I blinked, turning toward him. A muscle was ticking in his jaw, and he looked like a coiled spring, ready to explode at any moment.

"Uhh, I guess. If that's all right with you, Ryujin-sama?" I asked the great dragon.

Ryujin inclined his enormous head, a glimmer of understanding in his eyes. I frowned—did he know what was bothering Raiden? What was going on here?

"There is a small room right outside the audience chamber you can use. But don't keep me waiting," he warned as we stood up. "I have a business to run, and time is money."

Raiden and I bowed, mumbling our thanks, then backed out of the audience chamber. The moment the doors closed, Raiden grabbed my arm and yanked me into a room just off the side of the hallway—an oversized storage closet, I realized.

"Aika," he said, grabbing me by the shoulders. His face looked drawn, his skin pale. "We need to turn back now, before it's too late."

"What are you talking about?" I asked. Goosebumps broke out across my skin at the urgency in his voice. "We've got a way into Kai's tomb, a way that none of the other shamans know about! We have to take advantage of this opportunity."

"You need to stay as far away from Kai as possible," Raiden said firmly. "It's obvious this is a trap, and that he needs you for something important. Maybe you're the final piece he needs to break out of his prison."

"I've already thought of that," I said tightly, "but I can't leave my mother to rot in his stupid cave. We need to get her out of there."

"And how do you propose we do that?" Raiden crossed his arms over his chest. "You do realize that Kai is possessed by the god of chaos, right? He's not just going to sit back and let you waltz out of there with your mother."

"I realize that, but we do have the attention of a powerful sea god right now," I pointed out. "One who just said he's willing to help us. That's got to be a good thing, right?"

"Yeah, he said he'd help us in exchange for a price," Raiden growled. "He's not giving us a free pass, Aika."

"And I'm not asking for one!" I shouted, smacking his hands away from me. "But unless he asks me to sacrifice babies for him, it's a price I'm willing to pay! This is my mother we're talking about, Raiden!" My eyes began to burn again with unshed tears, but I didn't bother blinking them back this time. After all, it wasn't like he'd be able to see them underwater.

I'd thought the mention of my mother would make Raiden back off, but instead his eyes grew even darker. "Has it ever occurred to you," he said, his voice low and angry, "that you might be Fumiko's reincarnation? And that's why Kai wants you so badly?"

What?

"That's impossible," I sputtered, even as I felt that tug in my chest again. "I can't be Fumiko's reincarnation!"

"And why the hell not?" Raiden demanded. He took several steps toward me, backing me against the wall. My treacherous body reacted as he caged me there with his strong arms, pumping heat through my veins, and I had to make a conscious effort to even my breathing. "None of us have seen a *yokai* shaman for thousands of years, and then you happen to appear out of the blue, with no idea what family you've come from. At the same time, Kai awakens from his prison, which has been undisturbed this entire time. And you're trying to tell me this is a *coincidence*?"

I swallowed hard at the blazing anger in his eyes and looked away. His words were like a knife to my heart, twisting deep, because I couldn't deny there was a certain amount of logic to them. I didn't believe in coincidences, not really. And yet...

"Ryujin said that Himiko's line died out when Kai was sealed away," I said when I'd managed to find my voice. I met Raiden's angry gaze squarely. "That means I'm not a descendent of Fumiko."

"So? That doesn't mean you're not a reincarnation."

"And it doesn't mean I *am*, either!" I shoved at Raiden's chest, tired of this argument. As usual, he didn't move, which only made me angrier. "You have absolutely no proof that I'm Fumiko's reincarnation. We don't know why Kai wants me at all, beyond the fact that I'm a *yokai* shaman, and to be honest, I don't really care. I'm going after my mom whether you like it or not, and if Ryujin is willing to offer me help, I'm going to take it. With or without you."

Fuming, I ducked underneath Raiden's left arm and pushed past him. "Aika—" he began as I stalked out of the room.

"Save it." Head high, I flung open the audience chamber doors and strode to the dais. Raiden was right on my heels, and Shota was glancing at us curiously. Ignoring them, I stopped behind my seat cushion and bowed deeply.

"I apologize for the delay, Ryujin-sama," I said. "My friends and I are very interested in your generous offer. Please, tell us what you will do to help us, and we will do whatever we need to in return."

"Are you certain?" Ryujin said, looking down at me curiously. "You have not even heard what it is that I want from you yet."

My face flamed as I realized my mistake.

"My apologies, Ryujin-sama, for my companion's hasty words," Raiden said quickly, stepping in front of me and saving me from further embarrassment. I blinked, surprised that he was stepping in even though I'd just pissed him off. "I'm afraid her excitement has carried her away. We would like to hear out your terms before we agree to them."

"A wise decision," Ryujin said. I let out a tiny sigh of relief at the amused tone of his voice—at least he wasn't mad, or trying to take advantage of my slip-up. I knew from the old stories that other gods weren't quite as forgiving.

The dragon king opened his mouth to speak again, but before he could, the doors flew open.

"Father!" a female voice cried, and we turned to see a smaller sea dragon with pearly white scales swim into the room. She had golden eyes like Ryujin, and looked extremely agitated.

"What is it, Tama?" Ryujin asked, his expression shifting to alarm. "Is it your mother?"

The sea dragon nodded. "She is growing weaker, Father. I am not sure she will be with us much longer."

Ryujin's expression darkened. He turned his turmoil-filled gaze back to us and extended one of his huge arms. His claws unfurled to reveal two giant gemstones, one that looked like pure moonlight, and another that blazed like a dying sun.

"These are the jewels of the rising and ebbing tides," Ryujin told us. "You can use these to lower the tide that blocks the cavern entrance and seek passage through it to Kai's tomb. I will lend you these, if you go to Sarushima and procure a monkey liver for me."

"Monkey Island!" Shota exclaimed. "You're going to send us there? I've always thought it was just a legend!"

"You will not be going," the dragon king said sternly. Shota deflated visibly, and for a moment I felt bad for him. "I require one of you to remain behind as a guest and keep my daughter company."

Amabie, who had been watching quietly from her father's side, drifted over to Shota. "I wouldn't mind showing him around the castle," she said, looping his arm into hers. I forced myself to ignore her as she snuggled against Shota—I was *not* going to let my jealousy distract me from the real problem at hand.

A pained look crossed Shota's face. "I'm not sure the two of you should go by yourselves," he said, taking a step toward me. "I've heard stories about those monkeys, and—"

"There is no choice in the matter," Ryujin said firmly. "One of you must remain behind, and I must have that liver. My wife is dying," he said quietly, his great head drooping a little. "She has been ill for some time now, but in the past few weeks it has gotten worse. Only the monkey liver can cure what ails her, and none of my subjects have been able to procure one for me."

"Then we will get you one," I said, feeling sympathetic for the dragon king. Raiden shot me a look, but I ignored him. I knew all too well what it was like to stand aside and watch as someone slowly wasted away from an incurable disease. If there was a way to save his wife, and get what we needed in the process, then I was glad to help.

Something in Ryujin's gaze shifted, and he studied me for a long moment, silent. "You have a noble heart," he said gravely. "Both of you do. I believe you will keep your word." His expression changed, turning businesslike. "Any monkey liver will do, in theory, but I desire the strongest one, for the best chance of my wife's survival. Should you bring back the liver of the monkey king himself, I will give you a special weapon you can use to defeat Kai."

"A special weapon, you say?" Raiden said, sounding *very* interested. "What kind of weapon?"

"I will reveal that to you once you come back with the liver," Ryujin said imperiously. "Now do we have a deal, or not?"

12

"Thanks for coming with me," I said as Raiden and I swam out of the palace without Shota. Since we'd agreed to Ryujin's terms, we'd been forced to leave Shota in Amabie's care, a fact that rankled me a lot. "I know you think this is a dumb idea."

"I would never make you face something like this on your own," Raiden said as we floated past the gates. He sounded a little miffed. "You're an untrained shaman about to go up against an entire island of monkey *yokai*. What kind of guy do you think I am, that I'd make you do that by yourself?"

I flinched at the hurt look in his eyes. "I just figured you were angry at me, since I'm not doing what you want."

Raiden sighed. "I'm angry because I think you're playing right into Kai's hands," he said, scooping a hand through his hair. It floated around his face in the water, a black cloud of fine strands, and I was struck by the urge to smooth it back from his face just to see what it would feel like underwater. "But it is our duty as shamans to stop him, and if Ryujin really does have a weapon we can use to bring him down, we need to do whatever we have to in order to get our hands on it."

He turned his body to face mine, and my heart stuttered when he lifted a hand to my cheek. "I don't want anything bad to happen to you," he said softly, rubbing his thumb against my skin. "You're already carrying such a big burden with your mother as it is, and I know it's unfair that all this is coming down on your shoulders. But this thing with Kai...it's bigger than any of us. We can't let him win, Aika. Do you understand?"

"Of course I do." The stakes were pretty obvious now that I'd heard the story from Ryujin. But Raiden was staring so intently at me, it made me wonder if there was something hidden between the lines of his warning. "Why wouldn't I understand?"

"It's just...things are more complicated than you think." He hesitated, as if he wanted to say more, but he just shook his head. "You should call the *Umigame* now."

"Sure." My stomach sank with disappointment as his hand fell away, but I did my best not to show it. I lifted my wrist and touched the turtle charm I'd added to my bracelet, summoning the *Umigame* back to us. He appeared in less than five minutes, speeding around the side of a huge coral reef in the distance.

"You're pretty fast for a turtle," I teased as we floated onto his shell.

"Turtles are only slow on land," he huffed back. *"Where do you want to go?"*

"Monkey Island. Do you know where it is?"

"I know where everything is."

"Is it close by?" I asked, patting the turtle lightly on the shell.

"Closer than the last journey. Relax now. We will be there soon."

Nodding, I settled down on the *Umigame's* back. After a moment of hesitation, Raiden joined me.

As the turtle sped off into the ocean's great wide beyond, Raiden and I lay down on our backs. We stared up at the distant ocean surface, like we were sunning ourselves on a beach instead of riding on a giant turtle shell. Even with the water swirling around us, I could feel Raiden's body heat caressing my skin. He was close enough to touch, our hands barely an inch apart, and as he turned his face toward mine, my heart skipped a beat. There was such intense longing and regret in his eyes...a longing mirrored in my own heart, if I was honest with myself. I wanted to reach out and touch him, to run my hands down his chest and explore the tanned skin and muscles hidden beneath his shirt, just out of reach.

The look in Raiden's eyes deepened as if he could sense my intention. He shifted a little closer, reaching for my hand...

"Umm." Heart hammering, I quickly propped my head up beneath my hand, turning my body sideways to create distance. How could I feel this way, when just a little while ago I was turning green with envy over Shota?

"What do you know about Sarushima?" I asked, desperate to put my attention on something, *anything*, else. "Do the monkeys have superpowers, or are they just normal monkeys?"

Raiden stared at me for two very long, tension-filled seconds, his hand still outstretched. That tug in my chest intensified, but I resisted, refusing to give in to the urge to wrap myself up in him. I needed to sort out my feelings for these two before I made any moves. I refused to be the asshole who strung two different guys around because I couldn't make up my mind about which one I wanted.

"I don't know a lot about Monkey Island," Raiden finally said, dropping his hand. "I think they're normal-sized monkeys, but they can talk like humans, and they've built some kind of society on the island. Beyond that, I'm not sure."

"Right. That's why there's a king, I guess." I chewed on my lower lip as I thought about that. "Do you think my *furi* might come in handy? Since it's kind of like a monkey?"

Raiden shrugged. "Not sure. It's worth summoning him, though, especially if it turns out that the monkeys can't talk. We'll need a translator." His lips twitched a little. "You end up saying the damnedest things sometimes when you become a shaman."

I laughed. "Yeah, I never thought I'd find myself needing to communicate with a tribe of monkeys."

"Trust me, this isn't even going to come close to the weirdest thing you'll ever encounter," Raiden said. "My parents and grandparents have told me all kinds of crazy stories about their encounters with *yurei* and *yokai* in Japan."

"Oh really?" Yesterday, I would have blown this off as nonsense, but my eyes were open now. After all, knowledge was power, and I needed to know everything I could if I wanted to defeat Kai and save my mother. "Like what?"

"Well, there was this one time my mom went to a hotel in Japan to help out with a group of *makuragaeshi* that kept flipping pillows." Raiden smirked.

"What do you mean flipping pillows?" I asked, pursing my lips as I tried to remember something about the creatures. Unfortunately, they'd never featured in the stories my mother had told me.

"*Makuragaeshi* are these childlike spirits that sort of look like samurais." He waved off the comment. "They like to haunt rooms and play pranks on the guests. So they'll take a sleeping person's pillow and put it under their feet or step into ash and track footprints on the ceiling. That sort of thing."

"So your mom went to Japan to deal with a bunch of supernatural pranksters?" I asked, raising an eyebrow.

"Supernatural pranksters that looked like children dressed up for Halloween, yes." Raiden shook his head. "It was kind of ridiculous when you think about it, because they're harmless, but the client paid a lot of money because they were losing money..."

"Oh, do you guys do a lot of jobs like that?" I asked, gesturing at him. "You know, remove harmless spirits for money?"

"Not as many as you think, but we rely on enough of them that it bugs me." He shrugged. "It pays the bills, though, and besides, no one wants to deal with horrible monsters all the time. Jobs like that do help shamans learn the ropes." He smiled at me. "Normally, that'd be the type of job I'd take someone like you on for training."

"Oh, are there lots of easier spirits and such?" I asked, surprised the jobs were so common.

"Tons of them," Raiden said, nodding, before he launched into a story about another hotel that had trouble with a *mokumokuren*. He spent the rest of the journey telling me more stories from his family's history. As he talked, he grew more animated, his eyes sparkling with laughter as he painted me the most outlandish pictures using only his words and hands.

Watching him talk about his family business made me wish we'd met under better circumstances. In a world where my mom hadn't been diagnosed with cancer, and my father had survived, I would have been brought up with the safety and security of a real family. A shaman family, going by what the *furi* had told me, where I would have been taught to use my powers from a young age. My father probably had his own set of crazy family stories, stories that would have been both entertaining and educating. He had likely been the only man alive who knew the truth about what had happened to the *yokai* shamans after Yamatai had crumbled away into nothingness.

"Do you think there might still be *yokai* shamans around?" I asked suddenly, interrupting Raiden. "If my father was one, he had to have come from a family of them. Could I have relatives out there somewhere?"

"I hope so," Raiden said, but the hint of doubt in his voice wasn't reassuring. "I just figured that if you did, wouldn't your mother have known about them? It's very uncommon to marry someone and have no idea about their familial connections."

I bit my lip. "Mom says that my grandparents are back in Japan, and that she had a falling out with them. They didn't want her to marry my father, so the two of them eloped, and ended up moving to America while she was pregnant with me. I don't have any idea who they are—Mom didn't even have pictures of them in the house. Do you think that her parents knew my father was a shaman? What if that's the reason they didn't want her to marry him?" My stomach plummeted at the thought. Did that mean my mother's parents would reject me too, if I ever met them face to face?

"It's all too possible," Raiden said sadly. "Shamans used to be revered, but ever since that Inoue Enryo guy came onto the scene, our reputations have gone down the drain."

"Enryo?" The name rang a bell, but I couldn't put my finger on it. "Who's that?"

Raiden let out a disgusted sigh. "He was a doctor of philosophy who made it his personal mission to debunk *yokai* and *yurei* myths," he said. "He basically managed to convince all of Japan that most of the superstitions they've believed in for thousands of years are lies, and to throw away their traditions and turn to science instead." His eyes flashed with anger. "It isn't that I don't believe in science, or that some of Dr. Inoue's work wasn't unfounded. A lot of the myths and superstitions Japan has clung to *are* false. But the old gods have faded away as we move further and further into the age of technology. We're losing touch with our ancestors, with our spirituality."

A pang of sadness hit my heart, and I found myself reaching for the hand I'd spurned earlier. "That has to be really hard," I said softly, "being continuously rejected by society."

I felt guilty now for dismissing Raiden so thoroughly when he'd first told me I was a shaman, despite the evidence staring me in the face. As a pre-med student, I was one of the science-worshipers, even though I was also a spiritual person. While I still believed that modern medicine was one of the greatest achievements of mankind, I was a *reiki* practitioner, too. It was all too obvious that there was still a lot we didn't know.

And ignoring the very real existence of spirits and monsters was only going to push us further away from answers, not closer.

"I'm used to it." Raiden shrugged as if it were no big deal. But his hand tightened around mine, and that familiar pain glimmered in his eyes again. "That's why my family started our investigation company. So we could continue to make use of our abilities, and worship the old gods, without being ridiculed or turned destitute. That could be what happened to your father's family, Aika. They might have been poor, and your mother's family didn't want her to marry him because of their lack of social status or wealth."

I flinched. "That sounds so cold," I said. But it also wasn't uncommon amongst Japanese families. "I need to ask my mother about all this," I added, urgency filling my words. "She's the only one who can give me answers about my heritage."

Raiden's expression hardened, and he nodded. "We'll have to get her out of there then."

The turtle shell tilted backward, and I sat up, realizing we were headed toward the surface. I squeezed Raiden's hand tighter as nervous energy pumped through my veins. It was one thing to say you were going to an island of monkeys—another thing entirely to actually set foot on one. And on top of it, we were going to have to kill the monkey king and take his liver. A shudder rippled through me at the thought of reaching into a dead primate's abdomen and pulling out his organs.

You're studying to become a doctor, Aika, I reminded myself. *Now's as good a time as any to get used to sticking your hands into someone else's guts. Even if you're doing it without sterilized gloves.*

The *Umigame* gave one last push with his enormous fins, and we broke the surface with a huge splash. Sea water slapped me in the face, and I sputtered, trying to maintain my balance on the turtle shell. The sun hung high in the air above us, blazing with the ferocity of a summer afternoon even though it had been early fall back in San Francisco.

"Guess we're close to the equator," I said as a warm breeze drifted around us. I picked at my sodden shirt, realizing the hot air was going to bake the sea salt into my skin and clothing. "You wouldn't happen to have an *ofuda* that dries clothes, would you?"

Raiden grimaced, pulling out a sodden wad of paper from his pocket. "These are all ruined," he groaned. "I should have thought to ask Shota for his waterproof pack. Maybe your *kyuubi* can dry us off?" He glanced dubiously at my charm bracelet.

I snorted. "Maybe, but she'd probably singe all the hairs off your body just for fun." Wiping my hair out of my eyes, I turned and got my first look at Sarushima. The beach seemed to stretch out across the coast, with dense green vegetation just beyond it. Even from here I could see that the place would be ideal for fishing and having a beach day. Better still were the huge persimmon trees dotting the landscape complete with bright orange fruit that glittered like gemstones in the bright sunlight.

"Well, no time like the present," Raiden said, getting to his feet. "Thanks for the ride, *Umigame*," he called. He executed a perfect swan dive into the water, barely making a splash.

Show-off.

"I have another matter that requires my attention," the *Umigame* said, *"so I cannot stay. But I will come when you call."*

"Thank you." I patted the turtle on the shell, then carefully slid down the side of it. Raiden popped up just as I reached the water, and a jolt of surprise hit me as he caught me in his strong arms.

"Thanks," I said as he cradled me against his chest. I looked up at him and was surprised to see he was smiling down at me. "You didn't have to do that, you know."

"No, but I wanted to." He brushed my sopping wet hair out of my eyes, his smile fading a little. My pulse jumped as he dipped his head a little closer to mine, our breath mingling in the salty sea air. "I know you don't like it, but I can't help that I want to protect you, Aika. It's just who I am."

My heart melted at the sincerity in his tone, and I wanted so badly to tilt my head back and let him kiss me. But the *Umigame* chose that moment to dive back beneath the ocean, and we were immediately caught up in a gigantic wave.

"Hold your breath, Aika!" Raiden shouted. He ducked beneath the wave, still holding me with one arm, and tried to swim his way out of it. My heart jackhammered in my chest as he pumped his legs, but even though we made it through the initial wave, another, smaller one caught us and flung us straight toward the shore. We crashed into the surf, and Raiden somehow twisted us around so he landed first, putting his body between me and the sand.

"Raiden!" I cried as his head smashed into a rock. His eyes rolled back in his head, and he moaned in pain.

"Shit!" I scrambled to my feet, nearly getting knocked over by another wave, and slid my hands beneath Raiden's armpits. "Come on," I groaned, pulling him away from the surf as fast as I could.

I managed to drag him beneath the shade of a tree before I collapsed in the sand next to him, my arms aching. I just wasn't built to carry a guy nearly twice my weight across any kind of distance. But there was no time to sit back and relax—I needed to make sure Raiden was okay.

"Raiden," I murmured urgently, grabbing him by the shoulders. I'd propped him up against the tree trunk, but he was already sliding sideways. "Raiden, I need you to open your eyes."

He was completely unresponsive. *Shit.* Bracing him against the trunk with one hand, I used my other to find his pulse. It was still there, but weaker than it should be considering he was strong, young, and healthy. Panic began to set in when I realized he wasn't going to wake up, and I fought against the urge to hyperventilate.

Calm, I ordered myself. *Stay calm.* I was going to be dealing with this kind of stuff on a regular basis when I graduated. But that was a long way off—I was still only in my second year of pre-med. I didn't have any experience triaging injured people.

"Okay," I murmured, straddling Raiden so I could use my legs to keep him upright. I pressed one hand against his chest to keep him against the tree trunk and slid the other behind his head to check for injury. I found a large knot on the back of his head and swallowed hard when my hand came away bloody.

"Dammit!" I figured he had a concussion, but I'd really hoped he'd avoided cutting his head. How bad was the injury? Did I dare move him again to check on it? It wasn't as if I had anything to stitch it up with, or even a bandage to put around his head.

I knew from my studies that it was best to keep concussion victims upright and not move them too much. Brain bleeding was a serious thing and could result in death if the damage was severe enough.

"Oh God," I breathed, tears stinging my eyes. Raiden wasn't going to die, was he? He couldn't die. I didn't think I could bear it if he lost his life trying to protect me. Why wasn't there anything I could do to help him? I could do a *reiki* healing, but that wouldn't help much, not for an injury this severe. He needed medical attention, and I was powerless to provide it.

A sudden ache burned in my chest, and I pressed my hand against the pain. Right where I'd been stabbed yesterday. A jolt of excitement hit me as I remembered the *furi*, and how it had healed me. Was it possible it could help Raiden too?

Trembling, I lifted my wrist and touched the monkey charm dangling from my bracelet. *"Maji,"* I said, willing the *furi* to appear with all my might.

The tiny charm flared, and the *furi* appeared next to me in a swirl of blue light. It blinked its bright red eyes as it took in the scene, its black and yellow spotted tail swishing curiously.

"Am I interrupting something?"

My cheeks flamed as I realized I was still sitting on top of Raiden.

"It's not what it looks like," I snapped, pressing my hands against his chest as he began to slump forward again. "He's hurt. I need you to heal him."

The *furi's* eyes widened in alarm. "I cannot do that," he protested. "You must get him to a healer."

"There is no healer around here!" I cried, my frustration boiling over. "You healed me when I was stabbed with that knife. Why can't you do the same thing for Raiden?"

"I did not heal you," the *furi* said patiently. "I simply absorbed the blow in your stead." He pressed a hand to the dark fur on his chest. "I heal much faster than you, and the knife did not go into your heart, so I was able to survive the blow. Had the knife gone into your heart, or your head, I would have still absorbed the blow, but I would have died. It is not the same thing as healing."

My stomach sank. "So you don't have any healing powers?" I asked, my voice sharp with desperation. "Nothing at all that can help me?"

"No, but he does." The *furi* glanced down at Raiden. "Check his pockets."

Frowning, I did as the *furi* asked. His right pocket held only his wallet and some loose change, but in his left were a few of the *yokai* charms I'd seen in the lacquered box. "What is he doing with these?"

"I do not know, but—"

Several loud, animalistic shrieks ripped through the still air, sending a bolt of fear through me. The *furi* shrieked back, jumping in front of me just as a group of monkeys burst from the tree line. They began lobbing stones and hard, green persimmons at us, and I ducked as the *furi* blocked and caught the projectiles, flinging several of them back at our attackers.

"Run!" the *furi* cried. "Get out of here!"

I jumped to my feet, then slung Raiden's arm over my shoulder and tried to drag him to his feet. But he was still out cold, and I could barely move him an inch. "Come *on!*" I wailed, tears streaming down my cheeks. "Wake up, you big idiot! I can't leave you here to die!"

A strange scuttling sound came from behind me, and the monkeys' screeching instantly turned from angry to pained. Whirling around, my mouth dropped open in astonishment as I saw a horde of crabs rushing up the beachside, swiping at the monkeys with their clacking pincers. They were gigantic, each one the size of a Saint Bernard, with purple-orange shells and a strange pattern on their backs that looked like the face of an angry guy.

"Are those...samurai crabs?"

"Raiden!" My heart jumped at the sound of his voice, and I looked over to see he was staring blearily at the monkey-crab battle. "Come on, stay with me now," I said urgently as his eyelids began to droop again. "You have to get up!" I hated to move him, but it was clear we weren't safe here.

Two of the crabs scuttled forward, nearly scaring me out of my skin. "Get back!" I cried, holding Raiden tightly against me. But to my surprise, the crabs didn't cut us into tiny pieces. Instead, they arranged themselves in what looked like a two-crab conga line, stopping right in front of us.

"Put him on our backs," the first crab said, his voice echoing in the air. "We will carry him to safety."

I hesitated for a split second. Where was "safety?" How did I know I could trust these crabs? But it was clear that the monkeys were our enemy, and the crabs *were* fighting the monkeys, so accepting their help was probably a safe bet. The enemy of my enemy and all that.

"Furi!" I screamed, trying to get my own monkey *yokai's* attention. He was right in the middle of the fray, bashing two monkeys' heads together repeatedly. "Help me!"

The *furi* tossed the two monkeys effortlessly aside, then leapt over the battling animals so he could get to me. Without asking questions, he grabbed Raiden's legs while I slid my hands beneath his armpits. Together, the two of us lifted him onto the backs of the samurai crabs.

"Hurry!" the lead crab cried, scuttling forward. But three of the monkeys saw us, and they attacked us in earnest. The *furi* screamed, launching himself at the monkeys, but this only drew the attention of the other monkeys, and more broke away to get to us.

Furious, I grabbed the fox charm on my bracelet. *"Kyuubi!"* I cried, willing the nine-tailed fox to appear with all my might. She did, but instead of materializing in front of me, fully formed, she appeared as a swirling ball of fire with a fox head. A *hitodama*. Without thinking, I snatched her up and slammed her into my chest, just like Raiden had done.

Power flooded me, so fast and furious it stole my breath. I swayed on my feet for a moment as I was overcome by the heady rush of *ki*. It scorched my veins, turning my breath to fire, and when I looked down, my entire body was covered in flames.

"No time," the *kyuubi* growled in my head, and I realized that the fiery presence scorching my insides was *her*. "Attack!"

The fire in my veins leapt at her command, and it took everything in me to rein it in. "Watch out!" I yelled, the only warning I gave to the crabs before I unleashed the fox fire burning beneath my skin.

A burst of blue fire exploded from my outstretched hands and slammed into the two closest monkeys. Horrific screams tore from their lips as their flaming bodies were flung backward across the sand.

The rotten-egg stench of burning hair filled the beach, and for a moment the only sounds were the screams of the two dying monkeys. As their cries faded away and their bodies turned to ashen smudges on the beach, the rest of the monkeys pointed and screeched at us, hastily backing toward the forest.

The crabs saw their chance and scuttled quickly in the opposite direction. Unfortunately, the flames had taken hold of me, feeding on my rage, and before I knew what was happening, I was sprinting after the retreating monkeys. Each step I took turned the sand beneath my feet to molten glass, but I didn't care. I wouldn't stop until I burned them all to ashes.

"AIKA, STOP!"

Raiden's voice, weakened but full of desperation, stopped me in my tracks. I glanced back to see him struggling to lift his head from the impromptu crab stretcher he was lying on. "Don't...lose control...still...have to get the liver..." he croaked, and then his eyes rolled back in his head.

"No!" Fear gripped me by the throat, and I ran toward Raiden, the murderous monkeys completely forgotten. As I approached, the fire wreathing my body died away, leaving me feeling a lot more like myself.

"Raiden, please wake up!" I smacked his cheek lightly, trying to get him to open his eyes. But it was no good—he was out again.

"Weak human," the *kyuubi* said, her voice full of derision. "Not strong enough for you."

"Shut up," I snarled at her. To my surprise, she fell silent, her blazing fire reducing to a simmer inside me. The anger coursing through me faded almost completely, and I realized it was connected to the *kyuubi's* fire.

Acting on instinct, I pressed my hand against my chest, then curled my fingers into a fist and *pulled*. The fox's *hitodama* popped free of my chest with a loud sizzle, and I flung her away.

As soon as the *hitodama* hit the sand, it exploded into the *kyuubi's* full, over-sized form. "Cover us," I ordered her. She stared at me for a long moment, her glowing eyes full of annoyance. Then, without a word, she dutifully took up position between us and the forest. Several of the monkeys were still watching from the safety of the trees, but they scrambled away when the *kyuubi* barked, exposing her wicked-looking fangs.

"You're learning," the *furi* observed from behind me. I turned to see him watching me, something like approval glinting in his eyes. The crabs were already scurrying away, heading up the beach. "Come, let's not lose our hosts."

The *furi* and I hurried after the crabs, who had organized themselves in three single file rows. Pushing myself between them, I found the two carrying Raiden. He was pale as death, and my lungs constricted with anxiety. I didn't know if his lack of color was from the bleeding or the pain, but it was a really bad sign.

"Where are we going?" I asked the crabs. "Is there a healer there?"

"No healer," the lead crab said. "Safe haven."

I swallowed back the tears clogging my throat and focused on keeping pace with them. *One problem at a time, Aika,* I told myself. *Get out of danger. Then figure out what to do about Raiden.*

The crabs led us for a mile down the beach, then up a treacherous path that wound up a rocky cliffside. My heart was in my throat the entire time as I worried that Raiden was going to fall off, but strangely, he didn't budge from the crabs' backs. Maybe they secreted some kind of sticky substance that kept him stuck there? Or perhaps they had the same kind of magic the *Umigame* did that kept us from flying off his back while we were hurtling through the water at ridiculous speeds.

As we climbed further up the cliff, I noticed the stones lining the edge of the path gradually turned into walls made of huge chunks of stacked stone, not dissimilar to how Japanese castle battlements were constructed. As the path grew narrower, the crabs reduced themselves to a long, single file line.

We switchbacked several more times along the path before we finally got to our destination—a cave entrance in the face of a rock wall flanked by a huge *sanmon* gate. Two enormous statues of *Fujin* and *Raijin*, the gods of thunder and lightning, had been installed inside the gate, and as we passed through it, I could have sworn their stony eyes were watching me, crackling with hidden power.

Under different circumstances, I would have paused outside the gate to get a better look at the statues. Instead, I hurried on into the dark, cool cavern, following the crabs into a tunnel system. To my surprise, peat torches burned from wall sconces set into the rocky walls, filling the cool air with a scent that could only be described as smoky dirt. The initial cavern entrance split off into several tunnel systems, and many of the crabs dispersed throughout these. But ten or so of them stayed with Raiden, and they led us into a small cave with a single mat lying on the ground and a clay jug filled with water.

"This place is too small for the likes of me," the *kyuubi* said, looking around. She'd shrunk herself to the size of a Great Dane, though she still retained her usual shape. "But it is a good place to hide from the monkeys."

"I'm glad you approve," I said dryly as the *furi* and I slowly lowered Raiden to the mat. His skin was clammy, his forehead covered with beads of sweat, and he let out a moan of pain as his head touched down on the mat. My heart twisted at the sight of his suffering, and I remembered the charms I'd taken from his pocket.

"Okay, so what do I do with these?" I asked, pulling them from my own pocket. There were three—a rat, a weasel, and a bird. "I don't see how any of these are going to help Raiden."

The *furi* sat back on his haunches. "Summon the *kamaitachi*," he said. "He will be able to heal your friend."

I frowned, glancing back down at my palm. "Which one is that?"

"The weasel," the *furi* said as if that were obvious. "You are not familiar with the *kamaitachi's* legend?"

"Not really," I admitted. "Don't think my mom told me that one." I plucked the tiny weasel charm from my hand and shoved the other two charms back in my pocket. *"Maji, kamaitachi,"* I ordered it.

The familiar swirling blue glow appeared by my elbow, solidifying into a ferret-sized creature. It had dark brown fur and glowing yellow eyes, and instead of forelegs, it sported sickle-like blades that jutted out of its elbow joints. On any other kind of animal, I would have found those incredibly intimidating. But the *kamaitachi's* whole body was shivering with delight, its eyes glowing and its nose twitching like crazy. It was so freaking adorable I knew I would have tried to pet him if Raiden wasn't dying.

"I haven't been summoned in ages," he chittered in a high, squeaky voice that instantly reminded me of Alvin and the Chipmunks. The weasel-like *yokai* turned around in a circle, completely unafraid of the other *yokai* in the room as it took everything in. But he froze the moment he laid eyes on Raiden, lying prone on the mat. "Did you summon me here to heal him?"

"Y-yes," I managed to choke out. "Do you think you can?"

"Of course. It'll take just a minute."

Quick as a flash, the *kamaitachi* darted over to Raiden. He raised one of his sickle arms, and before I could so much as blink, slashed Raiden's cheek.

"What the hell are you doing?" I screeched, horror-spiked adrenaline rushing through me. I made a grab for the evil little weasel, but the *furi* pushed me back against the wall.

"It's all right, Aika! Let the *kamaitachi* do its job."

"What are you talking about?" I cried as the *kamaitachi* leaned over Raiden's bleeding face. My stomach turned as it began lapping up the blood trickling down Raiden's cheek. "Are you crazy? That thing is freaking eating him!"

"No, it is not," one of the crabs said, startling me. I'd totally forgotten they were here, and now that I was paying attention, I noticed three of them were in the room with us. The rest were standing out in the hallway, which the *kyuubi* was guarding. "This is how the *kamaitachi* heals. Sit and watch."

"He heals by injuring people?" I asked incredulously, unable to believe what I was hearing. But then I reminded myself that nothing about this situation was normal. I'd just spent six hours underwater without breathing. Who was to say that a weasel couldn't heal someone by cutting them open?

Sucking in a shaky breath, I turned to watch the *kamaitachi*. It was still licking Raiden's cheek, but to my amazement, the wound had completely disappeared. With each stroke of the weasel's tongue, a little bit more color oozed back into Raiden's face, until his pain-pinched features finally relaxed. The *furi* released his hold on me, and I dropped to my knees beside Raiden again, picking up his hand. The pulse in his wrist was steady and strong, and after a moment, he opened his eyes.

"Aika?" he asked, staring up at me dreamily. The softness in his gaze made my heart soften, but the reaction was eclipsed by relief. "Where are we?"

"We're on Sarushima," I said, a little breathlessly. "You got knocked out when we crashed into the surf. How are you feeling?"

"Good," Raiden said, sounding surprised. He sat up easily. "Fantastic, actually." He turned, then jolted as he came face to face with the *kamaitachi*. "Whoa!"

"Whoa!" the *kamaitachi* squeaked back. His nose twitched, and he leaned back. "You smell like you need a bath."

The *furi* laughed at that, and the crabs clinked their pincers together in a way that sounded amused instead of angry. Even the *kyuubi* chuckled.

"Well, excuse me," Raiden said, his mouth curving a little. "I haven't had time to take a bath since I crawled out of the ocean.

Are you the one who saved me?" The *kamaitachi* nodded, and Raiden ran his big hand down the creature's spine, petting him. "Thanks. I owe you one."

"I found him in your pocket," I said, feeling strangely left out. "Were you planning on summoning him yourself?"

Raiden shook his head. "I'm a *yurei* shaman—I can't summon *yokai*, remember? But I figured we might be able to use a few of these, so I grabbed them as a precaution." He gave me a crooked smile that made my heart do backflips in my chest. "Guess the hunch paid off."

"Yeah." A sudden flood of emotion hit me, and I threw my arms around him. "I'm so glad you did," I whispered in his ear as tears threatened to choke me for what seemed like the millionth time in the last twenty-four hours. "I really thought you were going to die."

Raiden's arms tightened around me. "Never," he said fiercely, burying his face in my hair. My heart sang with joy as his lips pressed against my ear. "I've learned from my mistakes, Aika. I'll never leave you again."

Something about the way he said that set an alarm bell off in my head, and I leaned back. "What do you mean, again?" I searched his face, but his gaze went blank, as if someone had grabbed a pair of blinds and yanked them down.

"Excuse me," one of the crabs said, interrupting the moment. Blushing, Raiden and I broke apart. We'd completely forgotten about our captive audience. "I hate to intrude, but my people would like to know what it is you are doing on Sarushima. Have you come for the persimmons?"

Raiden and I exchanged looks of confusion. "Persimmons?" he asked the crabs. "I didn't know there were persimmons on this island."

"Ah." The crab shifted a little. "Then you are here for the monkey livers." Was it just my imagination, or did they sound relieved?

"Yeah. Ryujin sent us to get one for him." Remembering my manners, I bowed to the crabs. "Thank you so much for saving us from the monkeys. I don't know what I would have done without you."

"Think nothing of it," the crab said. "If we hadn't come along, I'm sure your *yokai* would have protected you." The crab's eyes swiveled to look at the *kyuubi*. "You have some very strong friends."

I cracked a smile. "Even so, we are very grateful." I hesitated, then added, "Is there something that you want from us in exchange for your help?" I didn't think we had time for yet another quest, but it seemed rude not to offer something. Despite what the crab had said about me and my powerful *yokai* friends, it was highly likely Raiden still might have died, or at least been severely injured. Their interference had bought me enough time to summon the *kyuubi* and merge with her so I could beat the monkeys back.

"As a matter of fact, we were hoping you might be willing to help us drive the monkeys off the island," the crab said. "In exchange, we will help you procure the liver you seek."

"Drive the monkeys off the island?" Raiden echoed. "But isn't it their island?"

"No!" The crabs clacked their pincers angrily. "Those filthy monkeys invaded our land and stole what was ours. Before they came to this island, it was called Heikeshima. We planted a beautiful persimmon grove in the heart of the island and feasted off its bountiful fruits. But the monkeys were jealous and wanted the persimmons for themselves, so they climbed up into the trees and threw heavy rocks and sticks to keep us away. Now they have built a castle at the edge of the grove, and they defend it fiercely."

"That's awful," I said, feeling a wave of sympathy for them. "And you haven't been able to get rid of the monkeys? Is it just that there are more of them than there are of you?"

"No," the crab said. "It is not the numbers. The problem is that the monkeys hide up in the persimmon trees, out of our reach, so we cannot kill them. Crab legs are no good for climbing trees," it said sadly, clicking its pincers once again. "We could cut the trees down, but then we would not have our persimmons anymore. And we have worked very hard to grow those trees— we do not want to destroy them just to get rid of the monkeys."

"I get it," Raiden said slowly. "So you want us to help you get rid of the monkeys, so you can take back the persimmon grove. And in exchange, you'll help us get the monkey king's liver?"

"Yes."

"Very well," he said, folding his arms. "We will help you, but first you must help us get the liver."

"Raiden!" I scolded. "They've already saved our lives. I don't think we're in a position to make demands like that."

"It does not matter," the crab said, surprising us both. "Both tasks can be done at the same time, since they both require breaching the monkey stronghold."

"So what, do we just get in, and I kill the monkey king and take his liver?" I asked. I still felt squeamish at the idea of disemboweling a monkey, but I would do it if that's what it took to save my mother.

"Oh no," the crab said. "The liver you seek is not located inside the monkey's body."

"It's not?" Raiden and I asked at the same time, sounding equally bewildered.

"How is that possible?" I asked. "Don't the monkeys need their livers to be inside their bodies to survive?"

"Yes, but these are not the same kind of liver. What you seek is a special kind of liver that the monkeys hang in the persimmon trees to dry." The crab sounded especially disgusted by this, as if he couldn't stand the idea of his precious persimmons being contaminated by monkey livers. Admittedly, the idea sounded pretty gross to me too. "The monkey king's liver grows in a special tree that he keeps in his room, so you will need to get him to invite you in there in order to take it."

"Eww." I wrinkled my nose at that. "Are you telling me I have to seduce the monkey king?"

"Sounds like it," Raiden said. He sounded just as repulsed as I felt. "How would she even do that? It's not like the monkey king is gonna get the hots for a human girl. He's into monkeys, isn't he?"

"Perhaps," the *kyuubi* said, stepping into the room. She bared her fangs in a gamine grin that sent a shiver down my spine. "But with my abilities at your disposal, I don't believe that will be a problem at all."

13

A s it turned out, the *kyuubi* wasn't just good for setting things on fire or tearing into things with her claws and fangs. She was also good at creating illusions, and she used her magic to turn Raiden, me, and several of the crabs into monkeys dressed as *kabuki* dancers.

Wow, I thought, looking Raiden up and down. He was dressed in a red and gold checkered *kimono*, and I had to choke back my laughter at the sight of his hairy monkey face all painted up with red, black, and white *kabuki* makeup. There was absolutely nothing of Raiden's features in that monkey's face. Even his long black hair was gone, though the *kyuubi* had taken the fur on top of his head and styled it into a topknot.

"I don't know what you're laughing about," Raiden said, then jumped at the sound of his own voice. His words had come out sounding more like a screechy monkey's than his own baritone. "You look like Chewbacca's long-lost wife. If she decided to take up a career as a *geisha*."

"I do not know who this 'Chewbacca' is, but I hope you are not complaining about my disguise," the *kyuubi* said archly. She flicked her tails, sending dust motes flying about the room. "I followed the crab's directions exactly."

"No, of course not," I assured her, trying not to flinch at the sound of my own strange voice. For the first time, I started to realize just how powerful a *yokai* the *kyuubi* was—this level of illusion magic couldn't be easy. "We look great." I looked toward the crabs, who looked very similar to Raiden. "This is what we should look like, right?" I asked anxiously. I really didn't want to have to go through all this again. We'd already lost way too much time.

"Yes," one of the crabs said, talking in the same screechy voice. "We are ready to go. But before we leave, I have a gift to give you."

The crab stepped forward, pulling something from his robes. "This is an *osuzumebachi* charm," he said, holding out a charm that was shaped like a tiny bee. I shivered—the *osuzumebachi* were giant Japanese hornets so big that they were sometimes called "sparrow bees." "You can use this charm to summon a nest of them, and use them to attack the monkey king at the right time. The monkey king is allergic, and if he is stung by even one bee, it will kill him."

"And what about if I'm stung by one of these?" I asked, taking the charm gingerly. I felt like I was literally picking up a hornet's nest, and the last thing I wanted to do was drop it. "Aren't the *osuzumebachi* poisonous?"

"Yes, but these are bound to the charm, so you will be able to control them," the crab said. He paused, then added, "If you are able to control the *kyuubi*, you should have no trouble with the *osuzumebachi*."

I glanced at Raiden. "But these aren't even *yokai*, are they?"

Raiden shuddered. "They might as well be," he said as I fastened the charm to my bracelet. "For all you know, the *osuzumebachi* in there are a *yokai* version that are even larger than the regular ones."

"That doesn't make me feel better. At all."

Finished with the illusions, I summoned the *kyuubi* into my body, and we headed out. She simmered in my chest as we approached the monkey statue that marked the edge of the monkey king's territory; she was clearly unhappy with having to ride along inside me but aware that she could do nothing about it.

The statue was a massive thing, standing nearly fifteen feet tall and made of polished wood, making me think it had been carved from a singular tree trunk. Rubies glittered in place of its eyes, and they sparkled with malevolence, following us as we moved past.

A shiver wracked me as I wrapped my arms around myself and tried to ignore the feeling we were being watched. I knew it shouldn't matter since we were being hidden by the *kyuubi's* illusions, but it was possible they had weird monkey magic that would get us spotted. I really hoped they didn't, but after what I'd been through so far, I couldn't discount anything.

There's no point in worrying about it, I told myself firmly. But as we walked, I began to notice there were monkeys all around us, frolicking in the trees. My heart began to hammer in my chest, and I hoped like hell they weren't about to start throwing stones at us. Even with Raiden and the *kyuubi*, I didn't think we could take an entire army of these guys.

Hmph, the *kyuubi* scoffed at the idea that we were outgunned. But she didn't refute my fears, and that said it all, didn't it?

Thankfully, the monkeys seemed too lazy to pay us much mind. Most of them were lying on the ground drinking beer and sake. One was even lying in a pile of persimmon seeds, his bloated belly full as he snoozed in the sun. The crabs bristled next to me at the sight of him, but they didn't give us away. I could tell they wanted to reach out and throttle that monkey for eating their precious fruit, but they seemed to know that wouldn't help us.

No, the only way out of this mess was finding the monkey king.

As we moved across the sandy path, a huge stone fortress came into view. The blocks were immense, easily a couple feet tall and just as wide. It must have taken an army of monkeys to push them into place. They were piled on top of one another haphazardly, but they were so thick and tall that they cast a shadow over us even though we were almost a hundred feet away.

"Wow..." I breathed, shielding my eyes as I stared out at the sight of the fortress's walls. It was a good thing we planned on sneaking inside, because there was no way we were breaching that wall.

"Yeah..." Raiden muttered, glancing at me. "That's pretty

intense. How the hell did they get all those blocks there?" He pointed toward the wall. "It's over twenty blocks tall and at least twice as wide. Those things have to be measured in tons."

"They captured many of our people and forced us to drag the stones into place," the crab beside me said. "Then, when my brothers would fall from overwork, they'd eat us and mix our shells into the mortar."

"You mean that fortress is held together by your family?" I gasped. Shock and horror filled me at the thought, and suddenly I had newfound sympathy for the crabs.

"Yes." The crab nodded. "Now you can see why we want the monkeys to leave. They are not honorable neighbors, and instead visit cruelty and pain upon us."

"Well, I'm glad we came along then," Raiden said gruffly. His jaw had clenched, and he glared fiercely up at the fortress. "This is exactly the type of thing we shamans should be fixing."

"Don't get ahead of yourselves. We must still gain access to the king," another crab said as we approached the gate in the center of the wall. Unlike the wall surrounding it, this gate was made from lacquered wood and banded together with dark iron. Two monkeys leaned lazily against the frame on either side of it, their eyes lidded with boredom.

As we approached, the left one looked up and eyed us carefully. "What do we have here?" he asked, reaching up to rub his jaw between his thumb and forefinger.

"We are the famed *kabuki* dancers Komorebi, and we have come to perform for your king," the first crab said, dropping into a low bow. We followed suit, bowing low to the guards as the other monkey pushed himself to his feet and took a plodding step closer.

"Is that so?" he asked, glancing at the other guard as he reached down and touched my shoulder with one slender finger. "I don't recall hearing about any dancers coming."

"Well, you know how it is," the first monkey said, shrugging. "Us guards never get told nothing." He shook his head. "We'd better let them through or the king will put us back on kitchen duty." He made a face. "I do hate cleaning the drains."

"But what if it's a trick?" He poked me again before grabbing my hair and tugging on it. Not hard enough for it to hurt, but enough for me to feel it.

"Ow," I cried, leaping to my feet and pushing him away. "What do you think you're doing?"

"Making sure you're real," the monkey said, rolling his eyes. "There was a *kyuubi* around earlier. So we have to be real sure you're not imposters."

"Well, are you satisfied?" I asked, crossing my arms over my chest and glaring at the monkey.

"Aika..." Raiden said, his tone low and full of warning. He and the others straightened out of their bows, following my lead. But the monkey only shrugged.

"Fine," he said, "but I hope for your sakes you're the real deal. If you dance badly, the king will crack open your skulls and eat your brains."

Great, I thought as the monkey strode back toward the gate and rapped on it with one fist. *No pressure.*

Golden light rippled across the surface for a moment before the gate creaked open on hinges in desperate need of oil. I stood there watching it inch open to reveal an ornate floor covered by polished black tile. It led off into the distance toward an immense house with golden monkeys stylized across its walls. The thatched roof glimmered in the sun like spun gold, and as the two guards stood aside and gestured for us to enter, I knew I was staring at the monkey king's palace.

Normally, I would have been filled with wonder at the sight. I was pretty sure no human had been here for centuries, if ever. But the sight of hundreds of monkeys gathered inside the gated area stopped me short.

They weren't just normal monkeys. They were the size of freaking elephants.

"Go on," the right guard said as a cold sweat broke out over me. He shoved me lightly through the entryway. I opened my mouth to protest, but the moment my foot touched the black tile, a buzz of electricity shot through me.

"Send in the next act!" an angry voice boomed in my head. It was like a trumpet blasting directly into my eardrums, and I instinctively clapped my hands over my ears. "I am bored, and hungry!"

"That does *not* sound good," Raiden muttered as he and the crabs were shoved in after me. His expression was stoic as usual, but the thread of worry in his voice knotted my stomach. I turned back to the courtyard just in time to see the palace doors open. Out stepped another monkey clad in a deep red *kimono* covered in flowers. He glanced around for a moment, features drawn and panicked, but as his eyes settled on us, relief washed over his features.

"You've arrived just in time!" he cried, rushing toward us in bounds that carried him across the distance in a few moments. He reached out, grabbing my hand and pulling me forward. "We have no time to waste. The king is very upset today because a *kyuubi* burned two of his subjects to death. He is scouring the island for the evil *yokai* as we speak."

"How awful," one of the crabs said as the *kyuubi* chuckled inside my head. I could tell she wanted to come out and have some fun with these monkeys, and I had to rein her in. "Have they found any clues yet as to the *kyuubi's* whereabouts?"

"No, and that's only made him angrier." The monkey swallowed hard and glanced at us. "You'd better get in before he starts throwing a tantrum. I hope you guys are good... for your own sakes."

14

W ith those ominous words echoing in our ears, we were shoved inside the throne room. For about half a second, I was amazed at the splendor of it all. Monkeys carved from jade decorated the walls, and paintings framed with gold hung between them. The walls themselves were made of thick black stone that glinted in the light of the fireflies buzzing overhead.

In the center was a massive coral throne decorated with gemstones every color of the rainbow. Unfortunately, that's where the splendor ended, because sitting upon that throne was a monkey who was even more enormous than the ones outside. And when I say enormous, not the hulking, muscled, King Kong kind of ginormous. No, this guy was more like Jabba the Hutt, with rolls of belly fat cascading over his knees as he lounged on his cushion-piled throne. All around him, female monkeys dressed in lingerie prostrated themselves. One of them, dressed in a bright pink teddy, was actually lying on his giant belly, feeding him bits of peeled persimmon.

The entire scene made my stomach roil, and it took everything in me to keep the look of revulsion off my face.

"You must be the dancers," the monkey king cried, his jowls quivering as he spoke. His eyes darted between us, then settled on me. I watched him lick his lips as he looked me up and down, and I had to fight the urge to recoil.

"Yes, we are the famed *kabuki* dancers Komorebi!" the lead crab said, stepping forward and gesturing at us with one hand. His brilliant emerald robes flourished around him with the motion, snapping in unseen wind as he shifted and swayed to unseen music. He spun to reveal his swords, but instead of drawing them, he brought one leg up in a delicate arc, holding it there for a moment before shifting in midair to his other foot.

As the lead crab started to settle back into a crouch, the monkey king sat up and roared. The whole room seemed to shake as he shoved the scantily clad monkey off his bulbous belly, sending her tumbling to the ground.

"Your *kabuki* dance bores me!" he snapped, slashing through the air with one claw. Two monkeys appeared from either side of the center stage area. One of them grabbed the crab in mid-movement and jerked him roughly to the side. My mouth fell open in shock as the monkey king looked us over before pointing one stubby finger at Raiden.

"You entertain me!" He shook his head, making his fat cheeks flap around his face. "And no more of the dancing stuff."

"Very well," Raiden said. I could feel the waves of anger radiating off him, but he stepped forward calmly. As he did, I watched him sweep one of his stone tablets into the air and mouth something. Then he spun, so his back was to the monkey king, and raised his arms overhead. Light exploded from the tablet he'd palmed and bathed us in glowing blue. Raiden quickly palmed the spirit as it burst forth and slammed it into his chest. The female monkeys gasped as more tendrils of light wreathed him in blue, and he spun around on one leg while kicking his other out.

"Prepare to be amazed," Raiden said with a smirk. He held out a hand, palm up, toward the king, then snapped his fingers. A flurry of confetti shot out of his sleeve and flickered through the air. The king and his concubines looked up at the display, and while they were distracted, Raiden stepped forward and whipped a golden bandana from his pocket.

"My apologies," he said, offering it to the king. "You seem to have gotten some there." He pointed at the monkey king's cheek, offering him the bandana.

"Oh, well, thank you," the king said, glancing at the bandana before reaching to take it. But when he jerked it toward his face, it didn't come away from Raiden's grip. Instead, a blue scarf appeared on the end of it. The king pulled again, this time producing a green scarf.

"What sorcery is this?" the king asked, taken aback and dropping the golden handkerchief in his hand. "Do you seek to make a fool of me?"

184 | JASMINE WALT & J.A. CIPRIANO

"I would never—"

Raiden was interrupted by the king lashing out, smacking him broadside across the face and batting him across the room like he was a rag doll. He hit the wall with a thwack and slid down it.

"No!" I screamed as horror sliced through me. I took a step toward Raiden, but the king glanced at me and licked his lips.

"You. Entertain me." His eyes narrowed. "Do not fail me. This is your troupe's last chance. Failure will not be pleasant."

I swallowed, unsure of what to do. I wasn't a magician, or a dancer, and I'd thought both the crab and Raiden's acts had been pretty good. How the hell was I supposed to top that? By waiting tables for him?

Excuse me? the *kyuubi's* voice echoed irritably in my head. *Have you forgotten me already?*

Oh. Right. *Sorry,* I said to her, a little sheepishly. In my moment of panic, I'd completely forgotten about the powerful *yokai* inside me. *Are you up for some monkey barbecue?*

I could practically feel the *kyuubi* wrinkle her nose in disgust. *Monkeys taste revolting,* she said. *I have something a bit more... sophisticated in mind.*

Something in my head shifted, and suddenly the *kyuubi's* entire plan was laid out in front of me. When I realized what she had in mind, a shiver of revulsion went through me...but the plan was pretty genius, and I didn't have anything better in mind.

Put your big girl panties on, Aika, I told myself. *Your mom's life is on the line.*

"Well?" the king asked, slapping his giant belly with one hand. "Are you going to do something, or do I just order the cook to prepare the stewpot?"

"Don't threaten me with a good time," I said airily, pushing away my self-doubts. I sidled forward until I was close enough to touch him, then reached out and ran my fingers across his large belly, trailing them up toward his third chin. Another wave of revulsion hit me, and it took everything I had not to recoil. "Or I just might get too excited to perform." I giggled and batted my eyelashes at him. "And you wouldn't want that, would you?"

Before he could respond, I sauntered away, showing off everything the *kyuubi's* illusion had given me, even though my skin was crawling. I knew it wasn't my body the king was ogling, but it still made me feel dirty.

There was nothing for it, though. I needed to get the king's liver, and if seducing him was the only way, then I would make myself the sexiest monkey that fat bastard had ever laid eyes on.

After I'd reached the center of the room, I threw my hands up above my head and called on the *kyuubi's* power. It answered easier than I'd expected, flowing into me like liquid magma and filling my veins with fire.

Taking care to use my *kyuubi's* power over illusion to ensure my act didn't remind them of the fight on the beach and give us away, I raised my hands heavenward and smiled coyly at the monkey king.

"Are you ready?" I asked, batting my eyes at him as I wove together living flame with my fingers like a spider spinning her web.

With each movement, ballerinas made of sapphire flame leapt from my fingertips, and while I'd been worried the king would catch on to what I was doing, he seemed so enthralled by my conjured dancers I knew we had nothing to worry about.

My ballerinas danced above my head as I spun back around and brought my hands around. This time the entire room warped, changing under the force of the *kyuubi's* power as the illusion I'd called upon took hold.

A moment later, everything in the room but the king and me seemed to vanish, and we were standing atop Mount Fuji. Stars glittered in the sky overhead as the ballerinas danced themselves into flaming oblivion. As they dissipated into the ether and the king turned his eyes back to me, his mouth fell open. He twisted around as much as his fat body allowed him, trying to figure out how he'd been transported.

"Are you prepared to enter a world of illusion?" I purred, my lips quirking into a sly smile. I raised one finger to my lips while bending at the waist and shimmying backward slightly. "Where pleasure and decadence are only the appetizers?"

Not waiting for a response, I stepped forward and took his hand, pulling him to his feet. Except he didn't actually move—he only thought he did, thanks to the illusion the *kyuubi* and I were expertly weaving.

"What's going on?" he asked as I sidled next to him, moving my body against him as I shimmied to my own internal beat. As I did, the *kyuubi* smirked in my brain, and her power leapt over me. Fire leapt from the ground around us as our bodies began to writhe, perfectly in tune with each other. The king moved around me, his hands gripping my waist and running up my body, and I wasted no time flaunting myself while being careful to keep him from touching any of my more intimate parts.

Under normal circumstances, I wouldn't be caught dead seductively dancing with a two-ton Jabba the Gorilla. But I threw myself into the illusion so I wouldn't think too much about it, and instead pretended I was dancing with a hot guy. Someone I didn't mind bending over and shaking my ass for.

Suddenly, the image of the king flickered, and Raiden was the one dancing with me. My mouth dropped open at the sight of him dressed in nothing but a pair of black jeans and boots, his washboard abs fully on display. What the hell? Where had he come from? Wasn't he still lying on the ground in the throne room?

Careful, the *kyuubi* said, her voice rife with amusement. *Illusions can take on a life of their own if you don't control them.* The image flickered away, revealing the monkey king again, and I quickly masked the shock on my face before he noticed. In my efforts to try and pretend he was Raiden, I'd actually *turned him* into Raiden. My face flamed, and I threw myself back into the dance.

Thankfully, the monkey king hadn't noticed anything amiss. Probably because he was too busy ogling my furry ass. I swiveled my hips a few more times, then, as the dance wound down, I raised my hands and summoned more fire. It leapt through the air like firecrackers, hitting the star-strewn horizon above and crackling into flares of color and sound that, in turn, danced and gyrated, replicating our own dance in the night sky.

"Are you not entertained?" I asked, leaning in close to the king as another firework exploded overhead, dazzling us in brilliant amber light. I exhaled on his neck as I continued, "I only aim to please, my king."

The king opened his mouth to say something, and I stepped back. With a snap of my fingers, I undid the illusion. It shattered into crystalline fragments that rippled in multi-hued patterns before dissipating into the ether, leaving me standing in a low curtsy before the king while he sat on his throne, looking stunned.

"Amazing," he muttered, still staring at me as the room went dead silent. I hazarded a glance around, and as I did, I saw everyone watching us with mouths agape. Raiden stood on unsteady feet, his eyes wide. A surge of concern for him momentarily wiped out my sense of accomplishment, until I caught a glimmer of what looked like pride in his eyes. Was he impressed with what I'd done? How much had the others been able to see? I sincerely hoped he hadn't seen the entire illusion.

Before I could continue down that train of thought, the king was on his feet and coming toward me. He reached out, taking my left hand in his and bringing it to his lips. "Please, I must have more. Come back with me to my chambers and give me another show."

I could practically feel Raiden tense like a bowstring behind me, and my own spine went taut in response to the wicked gleam in the king's eyes. But I ignored the sensation. This was what I'd wanted, right? The chance to get him alone and steal his liver.

"Yes, I'd love to." I smiled coyly at the monkey king, batting my long lashes at him. "You'll find my show is *much* better in private."

15

"Now then, how about you show your king just how playful you can be?" the monkey king growled teasingly as we entered his personal chambers.

The room was lavish to the extreme, filled with decadent pillows. The walls were all mirrored, as was the ceiling, and the carpet was thick and black. In the center stood a massive bed covered in plush red pillows and satin sheets. It looked like the bedroom of a Lothario, not an impressively obese monkey.

"Come on, don't be shy now that we're all alone." The monkey king waddled over to the bed and plopped down on it. The whole thing strained under his bulk as he shifted on top of the satin sheets, causing his robe to fall open and leave him nearly uncovered. A flash of heat flitted across my cheeks as I turned my gaze back toward his face, but he must have seen me looking, because he smiled, revealing his yellowed fangs.

"Oh, don't worry, I'm sure we'll find a way for you to properly accommodate me." His grin widened, and I swallowed hard. This was going to go south real fast if I lost control of the situation.

"I think you're quite right," I said, taking a tentative step into the room. My bare feet sank into the plush carpet, and I was surprised to feel it caress my flesh like it was alive. Another shudder scrambled down my spine as I looked around the room.

"What's wrong?" he asked, concern etched into his voice as he watched me look around in confusion. "Do you need something? I can assure you, I'm happy to satisfy all your needs." The purr that entered his voice left no doubt in my mind as to what "needs" he was referring to.

"I just..." I looked down at my feet and twisted my fingers anxiously. "I had heard about your magic liver and was hoping to see it. But it doesn't seem to be around here, so maybe it was just a rumor." I pouted, looking up at him through lowered lashes.

"A rumor?" the monkey king boomed, lifting himself up on his massive arms so he could lean forward. This time his robe fell off his shoulders to reveal the biggest pair of man boobs I'd ever seen in my life. Or was that monkey boobs?

He shoved himself off the bed with a massive heave and landed on the carpet with a heavy thud that shook the floor. My palms grew sweaty as he plodded toward me, and I surreptitiously wiped them on my thighs before allowing him to take my hand in his. His own flesh was hot and sweaty, and everything inside me screamed that I should run. But I let him drag me toward a massive window on the left wall, hoping that his plan was to show me the liver and not toss me out the window for daring to ask to see it.

Huffing, the monkey king grabbed the silver curtains and yanked them aside. I gasped as a beautiful grove of persimmon trees was revealed. The trees were a deep, vibrant green, and the orange fruit sparkled like the fish I'd seen flitting through the sea.

"Wow," I murmured as we stepped through the open window and onto the balcony. The air outside was surprisingly cool against my flesh, and as I stood there next to him, the king pointed to the closest tree. Its trunk was as thick as a rhino and its bows hung low enough over the balcony that I could have reached up and plucked a persimmon if I was so inclined.

"There," the king said, pointing to the branch with his free hand. As I followed his finger, I saw what looked like a sliver of brown encrusted with gemstones that glowed with preternatural power. The thing was so large, I had a hard time believing it would even fit into a monkey, even one as big as the king.

"Your liver is truly splendid," I said, smiling at him and batting my eyes. "I wonder... no... I couldn't ask that... surely..."

"What is it?" he asked, raising an eyebrow.

"Could I, well... could I touch it?" I asked, my cheeks heating as the king watched me carefully. "It's just so big, and I've never seen one that nice..."

"I don't know," the king said, taking a step back and looking me up and down. "Do you really want to?"

"Yes! I'll be gentle, I promise," I said, excruciatingly aware of how this conversation would sound to anyone listening from beyond a wall. God, I was so glad that Raiden wasn't within earshot, or I would die of embarrassment.

"Well, I suppose it'll be fine as long as you're gentle," the monkey king said. I blinked, and the next thing I knew, he'd reached out and plucked the liver from the branch. He held it out to me, and as I took it from him, I was surprised by how firm it was in my hands. Heat radiated from it, and as I lifted it up to get a better look at it, I knew this was exactly what I needed.

"Your liver is amazing," I whispered, taking a step back and reaching into my pocket. My fingers closed around the *osuzume-bachi* charm, and as they did, I jerked it free from my pocket and focused my power. "*Maji!*"

As I spoke the word, a cloud of two-inch hornets exploded from the palm of my hand. I was immediately overcome by the presence of what felt like a billion tiny voices in my head all asking for directions.

"What are you doing?" the king cried, taking a step backward and throwing up his hands to protect himself. That turned out to be a big mistake, because the hornets interpreted the motion as an attack, and they swarmed him instantly. The king screamed as they dive-bombed him, their huge stingers striking repeatedly, and he fell back against the balcony railing, flailing wildly.

"Why are you doing this?" the king wailed, and for a moment I felt bad.

Huge welts began to swell all across his body as he railed uselessly at the swarm.

Your pity is wasted on this useless lump of flesh, the *kyuubi* sneered in my head. *He is greed personified, and must pay for his sins.*

The *kyuubi's* words strengthened my resolve. "I'm doing this for the crabs," I said, taking a step forward. "You've stolen their land, killed their brethren, and in general you've conducted yourself with dishonor." I touched my chest with my thumb. "We came to your island peaceably and you attacked us with stones. Now you will feel the pain of that inhospitality a thousand-fold."

And with that, I spun on my heel, shoving the liver into a hidden pouch inside my clothing. The monkey king bellowed from behind me as I raced out of the room, and a cold sweat broke out across my forehead. But I refused to look back. Heart pounding, I flung the bedroom doors open, and ran straight into the two guards positioned outside. Their faces creased in confusion, and one took a step forward, as if to stop me.

"Get out of my way!" I snarled, pulling my fist back. Fire wreathed my fingers, and I plowed my flaming knuckles straight into the monkey guard's face. Pain exploded through my hand, and I cried out—I'd never actually hit someone in the face before. But from the way he flopped backward onto his butt, screeching and clawing at his burning face, I knew he had to be hurting a lot more than I was.

"How dare you!" the other monkey screamed, baring his fangs.

His hand went to the *katana* at his waist, but before he could draw it, I blasted him with more of the *kyuubi's* flames from both hands. The monkey managed to dodge the first blast, but the second one hit him in the chest, and he went down screeching just like his companion.

The blast the monkey had dodged hit the wall, and flames began to race across it. Cursing, I spun on my heel and raced back into the main room, wanting to get out of there before the place went up in flames. I had a feeling I'd be burning it to the ground on my way out.

"Aika!" Raiden cried as I burst into the hallway. He grinned at the sight of the flames wreathing my fingertips, and without missing a beat, he drew the swords at his belt. The *katanas* glinted in his hands, flashing through the air to disarm the closest guards, and Katsu's aura blazed all about him.

"Can you do something about that door?" Raiden shouted, pointing toward the sealed door with one of his *katanas*. He used the other to lob off a monkey's head, and I grimaced as it went flying across the room, spraying the floor with blood.

"Got it!" I summoned more of the *kyuubi's* flames and blasted the door with both hands. The sapphire flames hit it with an explosion of light and sound, blowing it outward across the courtyard and startling the guards outside. Raiden and I began to run toward it, but I stopped short as the *osuzumebachi* buzzed in my head.

"What is it?" Raiden grabbed my arm. "We have to go!"

"The hornets knocked the king from the balcony," I said quickly, my heart hammering. "He's coming around the side of the palace!"

"Shit," Raiden swore. More guards converged on us, and he slashed at them with his swords. I lobbed more fireballs to drive them back, but after a little while, I began to feel faint. Borrowing the *kyuubi's* flames was starting to tax me in a way I'd never expected. My vision darkened around the edges and I began to sweat.

"If you drop the illusion, it will be easier," my *kyuubi* said, her voice strained as it rippled across my mind.

"Okay," I said, allowing it to shatter. Our forms reverted to normal, and as they did, the king came running toward us, the hornets still chasing him. He was swollen to kingdom come, but that didn't bother me nearly as much as the look of rage on his face. His eyes bulged as he saw me.

"You!" he snarled. "You tricked me!"

Panicked, I lobbed one more fireball at him. The effort practically made stars shoot past my eyes, and worse, the monkey king dodged. My blast sailed by him and slammed into the lacquered gate beyond. The wood blew outward in a spray of debris that scattered bits of wood across the entryway.

"I missed," I mumbled, stumbling back into Raiden, who was busy fending off the monkeys. His chest was heaving and he was drenched in sweat. It was obvious he couldn't keep this up much longer either, even with the help of an ancient samurai master.

"No, you don't!" one of the crabs cried as it burst through the doorway and snapped at a monkey guard who'd been sneaking up on us. It put one claw to its mouth and let out a large whistle.

The bushes beyond the gate came alive with crabs, and they flooded into the courtyard, running roughshod over the monkey army.

"Help them," I gasped, touching the *osuzumebachi* charm. As I spoke, some of the hornets broke off, attacking the guards and keeping them at bay. Pushing past the tiredness trying to settle into my limbs, I grabbed Raiden by the collar and pulled him out into the courtyard. Monkeys and crabs were fighting all around us, but I ignored them.

"We need to get to the gate!" Raiden yelled.

"I know!" I snapped, pushing him in front of us. "Break through with your fists of fury. I'll keep them from stabbing our backs."

He shot me a look I couldn't decipher, then charged, slashing and parrying the monkeys in our path. Their swords clanged while I directed the hornets. Thankfully, the king was too busy being attacked by an avalanche of crabs to pay us much mind, and even though it was only seconds, I was grateful when we broke through the last defenses and escaped the courtyard.

More crabs and monkeys were battling out here, but that was okay. We were almost clear.

"We need to get to the beach and summon the *Umigame*, so make sure you save some strength," Raiden shouted, slashing at another monkey and splitting his armor open. The monkey's blood splashed across us, hot and sticky, but I was too busy running for my life to be grossed out by it. I could feel my power fading fast, and part of me hoped I wouldn't need much to summon the giant turtle. If I did, we were screwed.

"This way!" Raiden cried, pushing me to the left. I followed along, trying to avoid the monkeys, and only throwing fireballs sparingly to conserve magic.

"Might I suggest becoming invisible?" the *kyuubi* asked, and I could have sworn I heard worry in her voice.

"You can do that?" I asked aloud.

"Do what?" Raiden asked, but I ignored him, focusing on the *kyuubi*.

"In a manner of speaking." The light around us bent like we were in those *Predator* movies. Raiden ran his sword through the closest monkey guard, and as it toppled forward, I expected the rest to come running. But they completely ignored us, as if we weren't even there.

"Wow." Raiden looked stunned. "This is fantastic, Aika." He smiled at me, and everything but his perfect white teeth faded away.

"Aika!" Raiden caught me as I fell forward, his strong arms wrapping around me. I was so weak...so very weak...

"Conserve your strength," he said, and I felt him sweep me up against his chest. "I'll get us to shore."

I managed to nod as he tucked me against his body, barely able to keep my eyes open. The sound of trees rustling around us, and pounding footsteps, told me that we were running through the jungle. I wanted to open my eyes, to keep a lookout for any enemies, but my lids were too heavy, and they wouldn't budge.

The next thing I knew, the tang of salty air hit my nostrils. Sea spray splashed against my exposed legs as Raiden waded into the water, and I felt him press something hard into my hand. "Call him," he gasped, and I realized it was the *Umigame* charm. "Just call him."

"Okay," I whispered, letting go of the *kyuubi's* power and the *osuzumebachi*. As I did, a wave of strength rushed into me, and I grabbed hold of it, funneling it into the turtle charm.

"Please come..." I whispered, and with that, everything faded away.

16

Thankfully, the turtle did come to take us back to Ryujin's palace, though I was completely out of it by the time he arrived. I slept during most of the ride back, but even so, I was exhausted by the time we made it back. Dealing with Raiden's near-death experience, performing in a *kabuki* play, seducing a monkey king, and escaping his enraged subjects really took it out of a girl. The last thing I wanted to do was go and fight a centuries-old shaman possessed by an evil god.

"Come on, Aika," Raiden said gently, coaxing me off the *Umigame's* back. "We've gotten this far. Don't give up on me now."

"Yeah, yeah," I muttered. But I let Raiden put his arm around me and guide me to the gate. The jellyfish guards seemed surprised we'd returned so soon, and they opened the gates for us immediately.

As we were about halfway to the entrance, the palace doors

burst open. "Raiden! Aika!" Amabie shouted, swimming toward us. Tama, the sea dragon from earlier, was on her heels, and Shota was riding on her back. Relief swept through me at the sight of him, unharmed. "Did you procure the liver?"

"Sure did," Raiden said, hefting the pouch I'd put the liver in. "The monkey king's liver, just as promised."

Tama's eyes brightened. "Really?" she said as Amabie took the pouch. "That's excellent news! This will cure Mother for certain."

"We'll see," Amabie said shortly. She turned, her three tails flipping restlessly behind her. "Let's bring her the liver. Father is already waiting in her chambers." She sped off to the castle faster than we could follow.

"Come on," Shota said, waving us onto Tama's back. "This is way faster."

We climbed onto the dragon's back, and she shot off after Amabie. "I can't believe you got back so fast," Shota said. "Ryujin thought you'd be gone for at least two days."

"Well, we had a crab army to help us," I said.

Shota's eyes widened as we passed through the front entrance. "A crab army? You've got to tell me all about it!"

"Later," Raiden said as we sailed up the huge double staircase that curved around the entryway. We flew through a maze of halls, the dragon swimming so fast I didn't even attempt to keep track of where we were going. She stopped outside a huge white door trimmed with pink sea shells, and Amabie tugged it open.

"Mother," she called as we hopped off Tama's back. "The shamans have returned!"

"Do they have the liver?" a weak female voice answered. We followed Tama into a humongous parlor room with dragon-sized furniture, then into a similarly gigantic bedroom just beyond. Lying on a bed the size of a small island was a female dragon that had clearly once been beautiful. She was lithe and sinuous, with deep green scales, but many of them were blackened with rot, and the water around her was clouded with something icky. Raiden threw out an arm before I could get closer, pushing us both back against the bed.

"We shouldn't get any closer," he muttered. "The gods only know what might happen if we catch the same sickness."

Ryujin was sitting next to his wife, clutching her clawed hand with his own. His eyes brightened with relief when Amabie pulled out the liver and handed it to him.

"They brought it," he said, holding it up for inspection. "The monkey king's liver, no less. Eat it and be well, my love."

Amabie and Tama helped prop the dragon queen up onto the pillows so she could eat. Her deep silver gaze was lackluster, but she opened her maw anyway and ate the liver. The moment she swallowed it, a change came over her. Her scales began to ripple, the rot melting away. Light poured out from the skin beneath, bathing her in a soft glow.

"It's working!" Ryujin cried. Amabie and Tama both squealed, hugging each other in excitement as their mother's entire body radiated with power. She raised her head to look at us, and a thrill went through me at the sight of her eyes—they were blazing brightly, alert and full of life.

"I am healed," she said, a note of amazement in her gravelly voice. "For the first time in months, I feel as though I can get out of bed!" She stretched her long neck out toward us. "Do I have you to thank for my recovery?"

"Indeed we do," Ryujin said, his entire face shining with happiness. He inclined his head toward us—the equivalent of a dragon bow. "You have done extremely well, shamans. We shall have a feast in your honor tonight, and to celebrate my wife's recovery!"

"Yes, a feast!" Amabie and Tama cried. The two of them enveloped their mother in hugs. "We shall dance and sing again, like we used to do every evening before you fell sick!"

As I watched Ryujin's family celebrate the return of their queen's health, the persistent, dull ache in my heart, which I'd barely been aware of, lifted a bit. *I've done this,* I thought dazedly. Maybe I'd used shamanism instead of medicine, but I'd cured someone of a fatal disease. And all it had taken was a monkey liver.

If I was capable of this much, what else could I do? Was there a different path that could lead me to a cure for my mother, one that didn't involve chemotherapy? The idea was certainly a good motivation for continuing to learn more about shamanism.

"Ryujin-sama," Raiden said, breaking my train of thought. "We are overjoyed to see that your wife is recovered, and of course we should celebrate. But Aika and I really must be going. May we have the jewels and weapon we were promised?"

"Of course," Ryujin said, waving a hand at us. "But we can handle all that tomorrow. You two will be staying as honored guests tonight and will attend the ball this evening."

"We will?" I blurted without thinking. Ryujin narrowed his eyes, and I hastily added, "Of course we would love to, but the urgency—"

"I understand the urgency," Ryujin said. "Perhaps better than even you do. But you have tired out the *Umigame* from all your travels today, and he needs to rest. As do you," he said pointedly. "A warrior is no good in battle if his mind is clouded from lack of sleep."

"Agreed," the dragon queen said. "You shall all stay the night, and I will sing in your honor!"

Seeing no way out of this, the three of us bowed. "We are honored to be your guests for the evening," Shota said. "But we have nothing to wear."

"Oh, that won't be a problem," Amabie said. She and Tama disengaged themselves from their mother and swam toward us, their mouths curving into crafty smiles. "Tama and I will dress you," she said, hooking her arm through mine.

"Uhh..." Raiden looked a little panicked. "I'm not sure that's necessary," he said as Tama curled her body around him and Shota.

"Don't be silly," Shota said, grinning. He clapped Raiden on the shoulder. "I've been hanging out with these two all day—they're great fun. We're going to have a blast tonight. I guarantee it."

"It has been a very long day for you both," Ryujin said. I glanced up at him, surprised at the compassion in his voice. "Amabie, why don't you show our guests to their rooms so they can get some rest before the ball tonight?"

"Why are we having a ball again?" Raiden asked in a pained voice. It was obvious that he wanted to get going, and I had to agree with him. We had more important things to do than attend a ball.

Ryujin laughed, a booming sound that echoed in the chamber. "To honor your great victory, of course," he said, his eyes gleaming. "You didn't think you would be able to return with the monkey king's liver, a feat no one here has been able to manage, and leave without fanfare, did you? We are going to have the grandest of celebrations!"

"Our balls are renowned throughout the sea," Amabie said, swimming toward me. She hooked an arm through mine, her eyes shining. "Come on, Aika. Let's get you to your room. We have just enough time that I might be able to turn you into a princess yet."

17

I n the end, there was no way to leave, even if the dragon king hadn't invited us to his ball. As he'd said, the *Umigame* had made one too many trips today and was exhausted. We wouldn't be able to ride him again until tomorrow, so we might as well stick around and enjoy the festivities.

"It's still creeping me out that this even works," I said as Amabie's maid arranged a fish scale clip in my hair. She'd dragged me back to her suite, and I was sitting in her boudoir while her maids fixed me up. At first I'd been reluctant—after all, Amabie's flirty behavior with Shota wasn't winning her any favors with me. But she was the princess, and I couldn't refuse such a generous gesture without coming off as a total jerk.

Amabie gave me a strange look. "What do you mean?" she asked as a second maid laced her up into yet another ball gown. This one was a brilliant orange that matched her scales—the eighth one she'd tried on tonight. And there were several more candidates I had a feeling she would try on before she made a decision.

I gestured to myself. "All of this. I'm wearing a dress, jewelry, and makeup, and I look almost exactly the same as if I were standing on land." Yes, the skirt was waving a tiny bit in the water, and my hair wasn't staying completely still. But it was still a lot better than I'd anticipated.

"Well, you certainly couldn't get away with this outside the palace, but so long as you are in my father's domain, there is no reason why you can't enjoy nearly all the creature comforts you experience on land." Amabie sniffed as the maid bent to check my makeup. "In many ways, we sea-dwellers have it better than you."

I didn't know about *that*, but I decided it wasn't worth arguing over. Instead, I studied my reflection in the vanity mirror across from me.

Somehow, Amabie and her maid had turned me into a princess, just as she'd promised. They'd found a backless dress in her closet with—big surprise—a mermaid-style skirt that hugged my body and made me look like I actually had real curves.

It was made of a satiny fabric that looked like mother of pearl shot through with some kind of shimmery robin's egg blue thread, and the skirt was embroidered with fish scales of the same shade. The maid had swiped pastel pink across my lips and given me a smoky eye look with shimmering teal eye shadow that, at first, I'd worried would be too much with my pale skin. But strangely, it wasn't. It just tied everything together and made my dark eyes look sexy instead of boring.

"All I need are heels, and I'd be red-carpet worthy," I joked when the maid stepped back to study me.

"You look wonderful," the maid said, her fish lips widening into what was probably a smile. "Princess?" she asked, looking toward Amabie for approval.

Amabie paused what she was doing and came around to look at me. A slow smile curved her lips as she looked me up and down. "Raiden won't be able to keep his hands off you."

My cheeks flamed. "I'm not doing this for Raiden," I said, smoothing my dress self-consciously. Oh god, what was he going to think when he saw me? Was I too overdressed? I couldn't remember the last time I'd dressed up for anything, and even though Amabie had made me look like a princess, deep down I knew I wasn't one. I was just a struggling student.

And my mother was dying of cancer.

What was I doing?

"I can't do this." I bolted out of the chair, heart hammering in my chest. This was all *way* too much. Panicking, I yanked the pearl clip out of my hair and tossed it on the vanity.

"Hey!" Amabie's eyes flashed with outrage. "What do you think you're doing?" she demanded as I tried to unzip the dress. "I spent a lot of time getting you into that!"

Tears burned my eyes as I struggled, and failed, to unzip the dress. The angle was too awkward to reach. "I'm sorry, but I can't go to your party," I said, refusing to meet Amabie's angry gaze. "Give the dragon queen my best."

"Aika!" Amabie called as I burst out the door. I shut the door behind me, then hurried down the hall before she could come after me—

And ran straight into a rock-hard chest.

"Aika?" A familiar set of strong arms wrapped around me, and to my utter mortification, I looked up into Shota's concerned face. "What's going on? Are you okay?"

"L-let me go," I stammered, pushing ineffectually at his chest. "I don't want you to see me like this."

"What are you talking about?" Shota asked, holding me out at arm's length. "You look..." He trailed off, his expression going slack with shock. His eyes grew darker as they slowly moved up and down my body, and my mind skidded to a halt as I recognized the look in his gaze. It was the same hungry look my last boyfriend would give me when he saw me in an outfit he thought was hot. The one that told me he'd be demanding sex by the end of the night, and that I'd have to find yet another excuse to bail.

Except with Shota, I had a feeling I wouldn't want to bail if things ever got that far between us.

"Incredible," he murmured softly. He slid his left hand up my bare arm, and I shivered a little as his rough palm glided over my skin. My body went completely still as he cupped my cheek with his hand and used his other arm to pull me closer to him. He was wearing an old-fashioned suit, I realized dimly, made from some kind of velvety, dark teal fabric. It had long coat tails and big brass buttons, and it should have made him look ridiculous. But the damned thing fit him like a glove and somehow only made him look even more handsome.

"This isn't about how I look," I spluttered, trying not to let myself get distracted by the look in Shota's eyes. The warmth from his hands kindled a fire in my own body, one that was doing its damnedest to drive everything else out of my head aside from the need to touch him. Why was he touching me like this, after all the effort he'd made to put distance between us? "It's just..."

"There you are!" Amabie exclaimed. I cringed at the sound of her voice, my shoulders hunching. I didn't want to face the mermaid princess, not after I'd stormed out on her. "I was worried something had happened to you, but it looks like you're doing just fine." She crossed her arms over her breasts, pouting. "Why do you like her so much better than me, Shota? Is it because I have too many tails?"

"Aika and I are friends." Shota's arm tightened around my waist, and I instinctively knew he was frowning at her. "What did you say to her in there?"

"She didn't say anything wrong," I said wearily, pushing out of his embrace. "I just got overwhelmed, that's all. I feel guilty about getting all dressed up and going to a party while my mother is locked up in a dungeon somewhere."

Amabie's expression softened. "If I could sneak you out of the castle and get you back to the surface, I would," she said, taking my hand. "After what you did for my mother, it is a small price to pay. But the *Umigame* is your fastest way back, so there is little point in doing anything until he is ready to go. And besides, we really *would* like you to come. It has been an age since we have last celebrated anything."

She squeezed my hand, a little harder than necessary, and in that one gesture, I understood. This moment was important to Amabie, was important to everyone in the palace, and if one of the guests of honor decided not to show up, it would ruin the whole thing. The feast was in celebration of the dragon queen's return to good health, and my absence would steal the spotlight away from that. Trying to run away was a selfish thing to do.

"I understand," I said, bowing my head. "I'll be there."

"Excellent." Amabie beamed, and for once, her fangs didn't seem quite so scary. But the expression quickly disappeared as her hands flew to her face. "Oh no!" she shrieked, her eyes widening almost comically with horror. "I spent too much time focusing on you. I still have to finish getting ready!" She whirled around, and I jumped back to avoid getting smacked by her fins as she hightailed it back to her room. Naturally, because I have the best luck, my back slammed into Shota's chest.

"Umm." I turned around before I gave in to the urge to lean into him. "I guess I should finish getting ready too."

"Huh?" Shota cocked his head, giving me a puzzled look. "I thought you were already ready."

"Well I was, until…" I lifted a hand to my cheek, then remembered that my makeup was waterproof. None of the tears I'd shed had stained my cheeks or ruined my smoky eyes, because I was underwater. Really, the only thing that I'd messed up was my hair. It was hanging loosely around my shoulders now, instead of twisted up into the knot Amabie had secured earlier with a clip.

"Aika," Shota said, taking me by the shoulders. He tilted my chin up, forcing me to meet his gaze. "I promise, you're going to be the most beautiful woman at that ball tonight. You've got nothing to worry about."

"And how do you know that?" My voice was steady despite my tripping pulse. This man did things to my heart rate that should probably be illegal.

"Because," he said, "I can't take my eyes off you."

The simple sincerity in those words knocked the breath out of me. No guy had ever said anything like that to me, and in that moment, I wanted to let my guard down. What would it be like to have a man in my life I could rely on? The concept was completely foreign to me. It had always been me and mom—I'd been so little when my father had passed away, I didn't remember him at all. I'd had a few boyfriends, but nothing serious, and once my mother had been diagnosed, my love life went completely out the window.

My mother had done her best to take care of me, but she couldn't always be there for everything. I'd learned to become self-reliant, to stop looking to other people to solve my problems for me. I'd come to understand that if I wanted to accomplish anything, I had to do it myself.

Friends were nice to have if you wanted a good time, or if you needed the occasional ear. But they couldn't fight your demons for you. They couldn't solve your problems. Those were things you had to do on your own.

And yet, it seemed that Shota and Raiden were helping me do both.

"Aha!" Raiden called, startling us both. Shota instantly jumped away from me, looking guilty as hell as Raiden came around the corner. "I was wondering where you were." He looked me up and down, his dark eyes gleaming. "You look beautiful."

"T-thanks," I stuttered, warmth rippling through me. There was no denying the admiration in his eyes, and yet the moment was dampened by the way Shota was standing off to the side, staring resolutely ahead. Why was Shota acting like he'd just been caught with his hand in the cookie jar? I tried to meet his gaze, but he refused to look at me.

Was I insane? Had we not been having a moment just a few seconds ago? Why had I suddenly ceased to exist?

"Is everything okay?" Raiden asked cautiously, glancing between us. Suspicion glinted in his eyes. "Were you guys in the middle of something?"

"Not at all." Shota smiled at both of us, but it didn't quite reach his eyes. And he still wouldn't look at me directly. "You two look fantastic," he said, gesturing to Raiden's outfit, which was similar to his but in deep red. "I'm going to go ahead of you. See you guys in the ballroom."

"Okay..." Raiden trailed off as Shota walked away. He turned to me, a quizzical expression on his face. "Are you sure nothing happened?"

"Nothing at all," I said, tucking my hand into Raiden's arm. I was tired of letting Shota twist my feelings into knots. For once, I'd let myself enjoy Raiden's company without feeling guilty. "Shota had just come by to tell me you were looking for me."

"That I was, and boy, am I glad I've found you." Raiden smiled down at me, and my skin tingled with anticipation as he gestured to the stairway ahead. I had a feeling there was a double meaning to his words. "Shall we?"

I smiled back, deciding that for once, I was not going to overanalyze. "We shall."

18

For someone who supposedly hadn't celebrated anything in decades, Ryujin sure knew how to throw a party. The moment Raiden and I descended the curved staircase leading down to the foyer, we were instantly enveloped in a sea—pardon the pun—of guests who had all managed to flock to the palace on such short notice. I'd thought they would all be varieties of undersea *yokai*, but to my surprise there were lots of regular marine animals as well. Manatees, sea lions, otters, sharks, penguins—even a few orcas were in attendance.

I wondered how wise it was to put so many predators and prey in the same space. An orca was eyeing one of the otters with an unhealthy amount of interest. But it turned out I had nothing to worry about—heads instantly began to turn toward us, and whispers spread through the crowd like wildfire.

"Guess they're not used to seeing humans down here," I murmured to Raiden as we merged with the crowd. Servants were taking coats from the guests and directing the flow of traffic toward the ballroom.

"Ryujin did say it had been ages since a shaman last visited," Raiden pointed out.

One of the servants spotted us and quickly snatched us out of the throng. We were ushered to the entrance and handed off to a *ningyo* dressed in a brilliant silver gown. She introduced herself as the hostess, then took our hands and led us to a balcony at the top of the staircase. We stepped just inside the double doors and found ourselves overlooking the ballroom.

"Honored guests," she sang, drawing the attention of the guests down below. They all turned to look at us, including Ryujin and his wife, who were seated on thrones. To my surprise, the two of them had shrunk themselves down into smaller forms, likely so they could mingle and dance with the guests. "Please welcome Takaoka Raiden and Fujiwara Aika, the shamans who helped save our queen's life."

The crowd broke out into raucous applause and cheers that completely stunned me. I wasn't used to receiving so much praise and attention. Raiden, on the other hand, had no problem with it—he waved at the crowd below and nudged me to do the same. Shyly, I gave them all a small wave, and the cheering grew even louder.

Against my better judgment, I sought out Shota in the crowd. He was standing in the middle of the room, looking up at us, and for just a moment, I caught an expression of such intense longing on his face that it stunned me. But it disappeared the moment I locked gazes with him, so quickly that I wondered if I'd imagined it.

As I stared down at him, trying to decide what the hell to think, Raiden tucked me against him once more. I tore my gaze from Shota's as we descended the staircase together.

"You're doing great," Raiden assured me, even as my stomach began to flip-flop. He squeezed my arm, as if he sensed my distress. "I'll be right here with you the whole time."

I glanced at him, envious of his calm demeanor. "You act like you've done this before."

"The Takaoka family attends social functions like this all the time," Raiden said simply. "It's par for the course when you own a multi-million dollar corporation."

We reached the ballroom floor, and for a moment, I was terrified that everybody would rush toward us. But to my surprise, the guests parted, clearing a path to Ryujin. The dragon king and his wife looked expectantly toward us, and suddenly I felt like the biggest idiot.

Duh. Of course you can't just melt into the crowd and become a wall-flower. You have to pay your respects first.

Raiden and I reached the dais, then sank to our knees and bowed our heads to the floor.

"Good evening, Ryujin-sama," Raiden said, and I was thankful he was speaking for both of us. "We are very pleased to be here as your guests of honor tonight."

"You may rise," Ryujin said.

As Raiden and I got to our feet, I was painfully aware that the entire ballroom had fallen silent. Even the musicians had stopped playing. I wasn't exactly agoraphobic, but I did hate being the center of attention. My skin prickled with anxiety, and it took everything in me to meet the dragon king's gaze calmly and pretend there wasn't an entire room of people watching me.

"As you all know now," Ryujin said, pitching his voice so the whole room could hear, "these two shamans risked their lives to bring our queen the coveted monkey king's liver so she might partake of its healing properties and become well again. That she sits here with me tonight is entirely due to these two brave humans, and I would see them rewarded for their efforts."

Ryujin lifted a hand, and a servant who had been standing in the shadows came forward. He bowed to Raiden and me, then offered me a huge leather pouch. My nerves buzzed with excitement as I took it from him and carefully opened it. With bated breath, I reached in and pulled out the jewel of ebbing tide. It blazed in my hand like white fire, and my skin hummed in response to the contact. It was like a low-level electrical charge was coursing through my body.

"As promised, the jewels of rising and ebbing tides," Ryujin said as I pulled out the other stone. "They must be returned by the next fortnight. You may either return them in person or give them to the *Umigame* to ferry back to me when you are finished with them."

Raiden and I both swore that we would see the jewels returned.

We bowed again, then straightened up, expecting Ryujin to give us the weapon he'd promised. Instead, he told the crowd to enjoy the ball, and the guests all erupted into applause again.

My stomach sank in disappointment at the dragon king's obvious dismissal, and part of me wanted to protest. But Raiden caught my eye, and I knew he was thinking the same thing I was —that it would be suicide to make a scene in front of so many people. Wordlessly, he offered me his arm, and we turned away, prepared to melt into the crowd and endure the endless hours of conversation awaiting us. I immediately zeroed in on Amabie and Shota standing just a few feet away. Amabie was hanging on Shota again, but he looked so damn uncomfortable that I didn't feel jealousy at all. Taking pity on him, I headed toward him.

"Aika! Raiden!" Shota darted forward, escaping Amabie's clutches. "The two of you did amazing up there." He smiled broadly at us, as though the awkwardness from earlier had never happened.

"Thanks." I smiled, even though I didn't really feel like I'd been awesome. My stomach was a pit of worry, and I felt like it was going to swallow me whole. Raiden had been right. How were we supposed to go up against Kai without any kind of advantage? We'd been counting on that weapon.

"Don't look so disappointed, you two," Amabie said. She lowered her voice. "My father told me to have you meet him in his suite after the ball so he can give you the weapon. He does not want to do this in front of all these people. Any one of the *yokai* here could be in league with Kai."

A shiver crawled down my spine at the serious tone in her voice. It made perfect sense, and I immediately felt bad for doubting the dragon king. "I suspected it was something like that," Raiden said. He sounded calm, but his shoulders had tensed subtly, and I knew he was on his guard now. Why hadn't I thought about this?

Amabie nodded. "I will take you to him when the time comes." Straightening, she tossed her hair over her shoulder and put on a sparkling smile. "I'm so glad you're enjoying the party," she said in a louder voice that was obviously for the benefit of everyone else. Craning her neck, she waved at another *ningyo* across the room, one who bore a striking resemblance to her. "Ooh, look, my cousin Arie arrived! Let me introduce you, Shota."

"I—whoa!" Shota said as Amabie yanked him away. He cast Raiden a long-suffering look as she dragged him across the ballroom floor. I realized then that Shota was hanging out with Amabie for the same reason I'd let her maids dress me up earlier—the princess was too important to offend. Some of the heavy weight on my chest lifted, and even though I still didn't love watching Amabie drape herself all over Shota, I at least didn't feel like I wanted to murder her anymore.

"So," Raiden said, pulling my attention back to him. I blinked when I noticed he was offering his hand to me. "May I have this dance?"

My heart skipped a beat at the warm look in his eyes. "I'm not really familiar with ballroom dancing," I said shyly, glancing toward the couples whirling across the dance floor.

"Lucky for you, my mother thought it would be fun to sign me up for lessons when I was fourteen," Raiden said, smirking a little. "I don't think this is exactly what she had in mind when she said I would need to use the skill someday, but there's no time like the present, right?"

I couldn't help it—I laughed. "Your mother made you take ballroom dancing as a teenager?" I asked, finally taking his hand. "I'm having a hard time envisioning you waltzing around a room in a tuxedo."

Raiden grinned. "You're about to see it right now."

My stomach leapt as Raiden guided me to the dance floor, and I realized that everybody was going to be looking at us again.

Get over it, I told myself sternly as Raiden and I took up our positions. He put his left hand on my waist, and my skin tingled beneath my dress as he slowly slid his hand up my side until it was curled just beneath my shoulder blade. Gently, he took my left hand and placed it on his upper bicep, then clasped our free hands together.

"Just follow my lead," he murmured. He stepped forward, his knee brushing against my thigh, forcing me to step back. Then to the side, lifting me a little so I was on my tiptoes. Flustered by the unfamiliar dance, and the feel of his hands on my bare skin, it took me a moment to realize we were doing a kind of box step. But Raiden was good at leading, and his strong arms and sure steps quickly disguised my missteps. Soon enough, I lost myself to the rhythm, and we floated across the room as if we'd been doing this for ages.

"You're a quicker study than I thought you'd be," Raiden said as we waltzed past a pair of skeleton-like *yokai* dressed in white robes.

I smiled. "I think it helps that we're underwater. If we were on land, I'm pretty sure I would have face-planted by now."

"I would never let that happen." He pulled me closer, close enough that my breasts brushed up against his chest for a split second. An electric thrill went through my body at the brief contact. "We haven't known each other very long, Aika...but you're important to me. I don't want anything bad to happen to you."

A warning bell went off in my head, and I began to pull back. "If you think you're going to talk me out of going after my mother—"

"No." Raiden tightened his grip on my shoulder blade, preventing me from backing away. "I know there's no chance of talking you out of that...and to be honest, I wouldn't like you as much as I do if you were the kind of woman who just sat back while someone she loved was in trouble."

"Oh." That took the wind right out of my sails. A warm, fuzzy feeling began to grow in my chest, and it took real effort for me to hold back the sudden smile that wanted to bloom on my face. "Then why are you saying this to me?"

"I just want you to know that I have your back," he said, his voice pitched low beneath the music. "That you can trust me."

"I trust you," I said, a little confused now. "Why wouldn't I?"

Raiden raised an eyebrow. "Because you think I'm planning to find a way to leave you behind and go fight Kai by myself. Or am I wrong?"

"I—" My words died in my throat as I realized the truth of his words. He was right—I *had* instinctively assumed the worst. But was that really unwarranted?

"I can't help it, Raiden," I said, hating the defensive note in my voice. "You've got a controlling streak, and you've already made it clear that you don't want me to go."

"That's true." He lifted his hand from my shoulder blade and brushed a stray strand of hair from my cheek. "I can't help the way I feel, Aika, but I know we have to do this together," he said as tingles skipped across my skin in the place he'd touched me. "Amatsu is the god of chaos, and he's very good at pitting people against each other. The best defense we have against him is to remain a united front. That's not going to happen if you and I are both standoffish with each other."

"I already said that I trust you," I said, a little mulishly. "I can't say I'm going to blindly follow along with everything you say, but I promise I won't try to deceive you or work around you. We're in this together."

"Good," Raiden whispered, pressing his forehead against mine. "That's all I wanted to hear."

The kernel of resentment that had taken hold of me melted away beneath the warm look in his eyes. Sighing, I relaxed, letting Raiden carry me away on the steps of the dance. He pulled me a little closer to him as he guided me across the room, and in that moment, there was no denying the magnetic attraction between us. Resisting Raiden's embrace was like the ocean trying to resist the moon's pull. I didn't know that anything would come of this, especially since we'd only just met...but was it really so wrong that I wanted to give in to what I felt?

We finished the set, then went to one of the refreshment tables to grab a drink. Shota joined us, and a trio of kappa immediately came over and tried to start a conversation with us. As the five of them launched into a conversation about catch wrestling, my thoughts drifted to the worry that had been niggling in the back of my mind. A worry that I'd forgotten about while I'd been enjoying Raiden's embrace.

Why had Raiden been so relieved when I'd told him I trusted him, and that I wasn't going to work around him? Was he worried that something might happen when we got to Mount Koya, something that would turn me against him? I couldn't imagine what that could possibly be. I didn't know Raiden that well, but I was pretty sure he was committed to taking Kai and Amatsu down. If that wasn't enough to bring us together, what was?

There must be something he isn't telling you. Some piece of the puzzle he sees, that you don't.

"Aika." Amabie touched my shoulder, and I turned to see her standing behind me with a grave expression on her beautiful face. "It's time."

I blinked. "Ryujin's already gone?" I hadn't noticed him leave. But a quick glance confirmed he was no longer sitting at the throne, though his queen was up there, entertaining a group of their subjects. He must have slipped out while we were dancing, I realized.

"Yes. Let's not keep him waiting."

I got Shota and Raiden's attention, and the three of us quietly slipped out of the ballroom with Amabie. Our escape didn't go completely unnoticed, but Amabie took us through a servant's entrance, rather than the grand staircase, so most of the guests didn't see. She led us up a set of stairs, down two hallways, then up a second set of stairs before we finally emerged into one of the main hallways on the second floor.

As promised, Ryujin was waiting for us in his living room suite. He'd reverted back to his normal dragon size and was reclining on a gigantic chaise lounge as we entered.

"Ah, good," he said, lifting his upper body as Shota closed the door behind us. "Come. I have your weapons, as promised."

We stopped a few feet away from the chaise, waiting expectantly. Ryujin waved his hand, and a wave of sparkling dust swirled from his clawed fingertips, coalescing into a four-foot box of obsidian.

"Open it," he commanded.

Slowly, Raiden knelt in front of the box. The muscles in his back flexed as he carefully lifted the lid, revealing a *katana*. It was an ornate weapon with a gold cross guard and the image of a dragon painted on the black sheath in gold leaf. Moving closer, I saw that the cross guard had been forged into a pair of sea dragons that chased each other around the hilt of the sword.

"Holy crap," Shota whispered as Raiden drew the blade. I gasped—instead of normal folded steel, it seemed to be forged out of some kind of iridescent blue metal, something that looked a lot like...

"It's a dragon blade," Raiden said, confirming my thoughts. "Made out of dragon scales, one of the strongest substances in the world."

"The blade's name is Raiken," Ryujin said. "A fitting weapon for someone of your namesake. It has the power to call down lightning."

"Damn," Shota said, sounding extremely impressed. "That's pretty badass."

"It is," Raiden said, sheathing the blade. "I...I'm not sure I'm worthy of such a kingly gift." The uncertainty in his voice knocked me off balance, and I stared at him. I'd never heard him sound so unsure.

Ryujin arched a brow. "Are you refusing my gift?" he asked.

Raiden straightened. "Of course not, Ryujin-sama." He stood up and strapped the sword to his belt. "I will treasure this always."

"Good." Ryujin narrowed his eyes. "Denial does not suit you, Takaoka Raiden. And it will not serve you well in your fight against Kai. I suggest you stop pretending not to know who you are."

Raiden hesitated. "I understand," he said, bowing. Shota and I exchanged looks, and it was clear from the look on Shota's face that he didn't have any better idea of what Ryujin was talking about than I did. We waited a few beats for either of them to elaborate, but Raiden and the dragon king simply stared at each other, some kind of silent understanding passing between them.

"Ryujin-sama," I finally said, breaking the silence. "While I definitely see that the sword you gave Raiden is a powerful weapon, I can't help but worry whether or not it will be truly effective against Kai. Surely Amatsu won't be taken down so easily, even with a lightning bolt." He was an ancient god, after all. I'd be very surprised if taking him out was that simple.

The dragon king laughed. "You are quite right." He waved his hand again, and two more boxes appeared. "Which is why I have two more weapons here." He floated one of the boxes over to Shota, and one to me.

"Holy shit!" Shota exclaimed, his voice filled with pure glee. I turned to see him lift a sickle weapon with a long chain attached to the end. The blade was wickedly sharp and appeared to have flames etched into the sides. "A *kusarigama*!"

"Damn." Raiden moved closer so he could look at the weapon over Shota's shoulder. He gave a low whistle. "That's a thing of beauty."

"Its name is Kasaiha," Ryujin said. "The blade will summon flames when you wield it against an enemy, so be mindful when you use it."

"That is badass." Shota's eyes gleamed. "Baiken is going to love this!"

"Baiken?" I asked.

"My battle *yurei*," Shota explained. "Raiden isn't the only one walking around with a cool samurai at his disposal." He stuck out his tongue at Raiden.

Raiden snorted. "Yeah, but mine's an actual *daimyo*. Yours is just a swordsman."

I shook my head as the two of them started to bicker. Even though I'd seen Shota's keychain before, I'd forgotten that he also had the power to summon spirits. He hadn't used his shaman powers at all beyond paper magic, which made it easy for me to forget he had them. But then again, there hadn't really been an opportunity for him to do so.

"Enough!" Ryujin roared, silencing Raiden and Shota. "Aika, aren't you going to open yours?"

"Oh. Right." My nerves tingled with excitement as I opened the box, but the feeling vanished, replaced by extreme disappointment. Instead of a weapon, there was a long velvet pouch nestled within.

"What is this?" I asked as I picked it up. It was stiff, with rectangular edges, as if there was a really big envelope inside, or a piece of thick paper.

"Inside that pouch is an *ofuda* that can be used to seal Amatsu and Kai back in the prison Amaterasu fashioned for them," Ryujin said. "It is a very powerful ward, but it is not water resistant, so do not take it out until you are above the surface again. You will have to apply the *ofuda* yourself, Aika. Do you think you have the strength to do it?"

Oh. I swallowed. "I don't have any experience with *ofudas*," I admitted.

"It's fine," Shota said quickly, surprising me. "I'll teach her."

"See to it that you do," Ryujin said, his voice growing stormy. "I have enjoyed many centuries of peace since Amatsu was locked away, and I have no desire for that peace to be disrupted again. Humankind does plenty of damage to the oceans without that bastard's interference." His eyes blazed with anger. "You must not fail."

"We won't," Raiden said, surprisingly calm in the face of the dragon king's barely leashed wrath. The gravity of Ryujin's words crashed down on my shoulders like an anvil, and I found myself painfully aware that my mother's life wasn't the only thing at stake if we didn't get Kai back into that box. It wasn't just one death we were trying to prevent.

It was millions.

19

"This is definitely *not* how I imagined my first trip to Tokyo going," I spluttered as Raiden, Shota, and I grasped the edges of the dock. A splinter dug into my finger, and I winced, then tried to find another spot to grab on. Dammit, why was nothing *ever* easy? Couldn't we catch a break just once?

Raiden only grunted, already halfway out of the water. *He makes it look so effortless,* I grumbled to myself as I watched him pull himself out of the ocean and onto one of the many docks outside the back of the Fish Market. Thankfully, Raiden was willing to share some of his strength—he got down on his knees, then grasped my hand and pulled me out of the water.

"Thanks," I panted as he set me on my feet. Shota was right behind me—he hauled himself up, then shook out his hair like a wet dog, splattering me with more water. A chill wind blew straight through my wet clothes, and I shivered. "We need to get the hell out of these clothes."

"I'll say." Raiden's eyes dropped to my chest, and they darkened with the same hungry look he'd given me the first time he'd seen me in my ball gown. I glanced down, wondering what he was looking at, and gasped at the sight of my nipples poking out through my shirt.

"Hey!" Mortified, I crossed my arms over my chest. *Both* men were staring at me now, looking as though they wanted to devour me. "My eyes are up here!"

Raiden instantly jerked his gaze back up to my face. "You can't blame me for looking," he said dryly.

"They were...really out there," Shota added unhelpfully. A grin twitched at his lips.

"No kidding." Fuming, I stalked past them, ignoring the dock-workers who were staring curiously at us. Some of them looked like they wanted to approach, but I leveled my best death glare at them, and they quickly backed off.

We'd left Ryujin's palace several hours ago, with the weapons, the *ofuda*, and the jewels in hand. The *Umigame* had brought us to the docks, and we'd instructed him to swim a few miles out this time before going back beneath the water. The last thing I needed was for us to be slammed against a concrete building—my *furi* might be able to protect me, but there was no way Raiden or Shota would survive.

"Hey." Raiden caught up with me. He shoved his hands into his pockets and glanced sidelong at me, a faintly amused look on his face. "Where are you taking us?"

"I'm not taking us anywhere," I said crossly as my shoes squelched on the pavement. We walked through a maze of stalls selling produce, candies, and street food, drawing stares from the shopkeepers and customers. "I just want to get away from all these people."

"We should grab some clothes, then head to a hotel to shower and change," Shota said, looking around. "We need a quiet spot so I can teach Aika the basics of paper magic."

We made it out to the street and ducked into a 7/11 so Raiden could grab some cash out of the ATM. As he slid his ATM card into the machine, I glanced nervously at the sword strapped to his back.

"What exactly are we going to do about these weapons?" I whispered to Shota, noticing that the clerk behind the counter was staring at us. "The second a policeman sees them, we're going to get stopped."

"We'll just grab a bag to hide it in for now," Shota said, sounding unconcerned. "I can use an *ofuda* later on to make it invisible."

I blinked. "You can do that?"

Shota laughed as Raiden pulled a huge stack of yen out of the machine. "Sometimes I forget how little you know about shamanism. I can't wait to teach you."

My annoyance at the world evaporated at the smile on his face, leaving me confused. I couldn't tell whether or not Shota was flirting with me. Every time I thought he was trying to be romantic, he turned away and gave me the cold shoulder, so it was probably best to assume he wasn't. And yet, I wanted to smile back at him, to respond with some kind of wisecrack that would make him laugh again.

Dammit, why was everything so complicated?

With our huge wad of cash in hand, we hit the streets of Tokyo to do some serious shopping. The first place we stopped at was a luggage store, or rather Raiden did, while I waited outside with the weapons. He found a duffel bag big enough to carry the weapons in, and then we hit up a department store and a Family Mart for some clothing, food, and supplies.

I was a little embarrassed to be walking around Tokyo for the first time looking and smelling like a bum, and I half expected the employees at the places we walked into to turn up their noses. But everybody was very friendly and courteous, and if they were repulsed by our limp hair and salty clothing, they didn't say anything about it. Before I knew it, we were back out on the street, our arms loaded down with bags as Raiden hailed a cab. One pulled up almost immediately—a boxy little Toyota that looked like it was fresh out of the 90s, albeit new. To my surprise, the door swung open automatically before I could reach for it.

"Get in," Raiden said, nudging me gently. "I'll put our bags in the trunk."

I did as he said, gingerly sliding along the seats, which were covered with a lacy, doily-like fabric. The driver gave us dirty looks, no doubt because we were ruining his upholstery and stinking up his car with the smell of sea water, but Raiden handed him a twenty-thousand yen bill, which seemed to mollify him some. The two men crowded in on either side of me, their bodies brushing up against me as there was little extra space in the cabin. My nerves buzzed from their close proximity, and I quickly grew very warm, far warmer than the extra body heat could account for.

There is something wrong with me, I told myself firmly as the driver pulled into traffic. Something very wrong. It wasn't like me to crush hard on a guy, but here I was, having intense feelings for *two* people at the *same* time. They both seemed to know it, too—the tension in the space was thick enough to slice and serve on a platter.

Talk about the pink elephant in the room.

On the drive to our hotel, Raiden and Shota pointed out various districts and landmarks. We passed by Tokyo Tower—a huge, red version of the Eiffel Tower that Raiden said boasted a One Piece exhibition and an amazing aquarium. A few blocks north, we drove through the Ginza district, where buildings sporting every brand name known to man, plus a bunch I'd never heard of, towered around us. Dazzled by the concrete jungle, I quickly became lost as Raiden pointed out the various districts and what they had to offer. I'd heard that Tokyo was New York City on steroids, and so far, I considered that an understatement.

Despite the towering skyscrapers and the buzz and hum of technology everywhere, there was still evidence of traditional Japanese culture—signs that pointed to Zen gardens secreted between buildings, tiny shrines perched precariously on pipes running along the backs of apartment buildings, sumo wrestlers dressed in yukatas coming out of the stable after a hard morning training session. It was a strange mixture of old and new, and I wished I could take a few days to explore.

But we weren't here for a vacation. We were here to defeat an evil shaman and rescue my mother. So I buried the excitement in my chest, knowing it was only going to lead to disappointment. Even if we succeeded with our mission—which we would —my mother was likely going to be in no condition to go sightseeing in Tokyo. I'd probably be spending every waking minute at her side in a hospital.

"Do you think your parents are already here?" I asked Raiden.

"Probably. I imagine they're either at the site or at the shaman headquarters here."

I frowned. "Is there a reason we're not going to them?"

"If they find out we're here, they'll lock us both up. They'd never let an untrained shaman like you near the site, and as for me..." Raiden blew out a breath. "Well, you already know. My parents won't risk me."

I nodded. "I'm sure my mom would feel the same way." In fact, she was probably praying I wouldn't come for her—that I'd leave her to die in that awful tomb. But even if I could bring myself to do that, this was bigger than us. If Kai got out of that tomb, Amatsu would be free to wreak havoc on the world. I couldn't allow that to happen.

The cab dropped us off at a swanky hotel in the middle of Shinjuku, where a bellhop immediately took our bags and loaded them onto a cart. I raised my eyebrows when Raiden ordered rooms for each of us. It seemed kind of extravagant considering that we weren't actually spending the night here, but then again, he was rich. Besides, it would be nice to actually have some privacy while I showered and got out of these wet clothes.

After we checked in, we got into the elevator and rode it up to the twentieth floor. "Wow," I said, pressing my nose against the glass window. The city sprawled beneath us, a mecca of color and metal and vibrancy. It looked like something straight out of *Blade Runner*.

"Is that Mount Koya?" I asked, pointing at the tiny blip I spotted on the horizon, far off into the distance.

"Yeah." Shota came to stand behind me, his hands in his pockets. I glanced sideways, and some of my excitement faded at the grim look on his face. "It's too bad we won't be able to go there. It's pretty spectacular."

I nodded. "How are we getting to Kai? Shrine-travel?"

"It's the fastest way," Raiden confirmed. "The shamans will have set up a portable shrine up there. We'll go to Nezu Shrine when we're done here and hop over."

"Okay." I gazed at the mountain, a tiny triangle the size of my index fingernail, for a moment longer, before the elevator doors opened and I had to get off. The three of us went our separate ways—we each had rooms on this floor, but they weren't adjoining.

"Come find me in 2005 when you're ready," Shota called.

I nodded, then slid my plastic key card into the door of my own room. It swung open, revealing a spacious room with a California King-sized bed and a picture window offering another amazing view of the city. Under other circumstances, I would have plopped myself into the chaise lounge parked there and stared for hours. Instead, I dumped my new clothes on the bed, stripped out of my old ones, and hopped into the shower.

"Ahhhh," I groaned as the hot spray hit me. The pulsing jets felt incredible, scouring away layers of salt, sand, and other stuff I didn't want to think about while pounding the tension out of my muscles. There was nothing quite like a hot shower to clear your head after a long day, and this one felt incredible.

I scrubbed myself all over at least three times, then dried off and changed into a pair of clean jeans and a Hello Kitty T-shirt. I didn't want to waste time blow-drying my hair, so I combed it out, then left it loose down my back so it would dry faster. Looking in the mirror at myself, I wished I had the foresight to buy some makeup. There were circles under my eyes from a severe lack of sleep, and my face was pasty white. It was amazing that Shota and Raiden looked at me without cringing.

I sat down on the edge of the bed to put my shoe on, and a wave of tiredness swept over me. Dammit. Longingly, I glanced at the mattress beneath me, which was super comfortable and way too inviting. *Lie down,* an insidious voice whispered in my head. *You can afford a few minutes' rest.*

I bit the inside of my cheek to clear the hazy fog of exhaustion that had descended upon my mind. If I lay down now, it wouldn't be for a few minutes. It would be for a few hours, and I didn't have time for that. Shota was waiting for me...and so was my mother.

I couldn't forget that I was doing all this for her.

Quickly, I finished dressing, then grabbed an energy drink from the mini fridge and downed it before heading for Shota's room. I wasn't really a fan of Monster or Red Bull, but I needed the extra juice if we really were going to face off against Kai today.

Shota's room was only a few doors down from mine. I knocked on the door, and when I got no answer, used the extra key Shota had given me to gain entry. Shota's room was a mirror image of mine, with identical furniture. I could hear the shower running, so I went and made myself comfortable on the chaise by the window and spent a long, peaceful moment enjoying the view. My mind drifted as I stared out at the skyline, and I didn't hear when the water turned off or the door opened.

"Aika?" Shota's shocked voice spun me out of my reverie, and I turned to see him just outside the bathroom with nothing but a towel wrapped around his hips. His lean, muscled body was practically on full display, complete with abs, and my face flamed as I realized my mistake. "I didn't know you were in here!"

"S-sorry!" I shot out of my chair, then tripped over my own feet. Shota lunged forward and grabbed me before I face-planted, but my clumsiness must have been contagious, because somehow we both ended up tangled together on the floor.

"Relax!" Shota's arms banded around me as I flailed around like a fish caught in a net. "You're just making it worse."

I stilled as Shota pulled me against his body. His body heat seeped into me as my curves pressed against his muscular form, and suddenly I was acutely aware that the towel had slipped away. If I just looked down...

No. You are not *looking down.*

"Sorry," I said again, wishing I could just disappear. I was simultaneously embarrassed and aroused, the heat from Shota's body firing me up, turning my core molten. I held very still in his arms, knowing that if I moved my hands just a little, I'd be touching his bare flesh. I could skim them down his back, and maybe over other things too...

"There's nothing for you to apologize about," Shota said, sounding a little breathless. My heart pounded hard as his dark gaze bore into mine, and a thrill went through me when he curled his hand around the curve of my waist. "I gave you a key. I should have known better than to walk out here naked."

Naked. The word, spoken aloud, sent another wave of heat rushing through my veins. My nipples pebbled through my shirt, and Shota's gaze turned molten, almost as if he could sense my desire. My lips parted, and I leaned in a little closer, hoping he would finally take the hint...

Shota cleared his throat, his gaze shuttering. "I should get dressed," he said, pushing himself upright. Cold air rushed between the space where his body had been pressed against mine, sending a chill through me. A healthy dose of shame followed on its heels. "We've got training to do."

Those words, spoken with such clinical dispassion, triggered a wave of anger within me. "Fuck that," I said, grabbing his wrist before he could get up. Shota's eyes widened as I yanked him back against me, his mouth open as if he was about to protest. But instead of letting him, I threw my arms around his neck and kissed him.

As I smashed my lips against Shota's, I felt a *zing* of electricity, as if we'd completed a circuit. There was a heartbeat of resistance, and then Shota groaned, wrapping his arms around me. He pulled me into his lap, then threaded his fingers into my hair, holding me tightly against him as he kissed me hard. I gasped at the feel of his length pressing against my core, and then his tongue was inside me, filling me up with the taste of him. I sucked on his tongue greedily, my hands sliding down his shoulders, over his arms, loving the way his muscles flexed beneath my touch. The exhaustion that had plagued me earlier had vanished, replaced by a deep-seated need to take *more*. I wanted to explore this connection, this current that seemed to flow between us, and see just how far it went—

"Dammit!" Shota cursed, pushing me off his lap. My breath whooshed out of me as I landed hard on the carpet, but that was more from the shock of his rejection than anything else. I flinched at the anger simmering in his tone, etching itself into the lines of his normally carefree face. "Why are you so *tempting*, Aika?"

"Tempting?" I echoed, staring at him. No, it wasn't just anger, I realized as I searched his gaze. There was self-loathing there, too, and I couldn't understand it. "Why are you treating me like

I'm some kind of forbidden fruit? Like I'm a chocolate fudge cake, and you're on the Atkins diet?"

Shota laughed, a bitter sound that tore at me. "I *wish* you were chocolate fudge cake," he said hollowly. He seemed to remember he was still naked, and threw the towel over his lap. I could have told him not to bother—he was still hard, and the fabric only seemed to draw further attention to the bulge I'd only let myself catch a glimpse of earlier. "That would be way easier to resist."

I folded my arms over my chest, ignoring the little thrill his words gave me. There was no denying it—Shota definitely wanted me. "I don't understand why you're trying so hard to 'resist' me," I said, using my fingers to make air quotes as I spoke. "Just a few days ago, you were trying to get me to have dinner with you."

"That was before you met Raiden," Shota said quietly.

I stared. "Raiden? What's he got to do with this?"

Shota raised an eyebrow. "You have feelings for him, Aika. I've seen the way you two look at each other. It's obvious you belong together."

I scoffed. "That's ridiculous," I said. "Raiden and I barely know each other. Just because we may or may not have *feelings* for each other doesn't automatically make him my soulmate." I paused when Shota's gaze shuttered again on the word 'soulmate'. "Wait a damn second. You actually *think* he's my soulmate?"

"What I think is irrelevant," Shota said. His eyes were filled with sadness, making my confused heart ache even more. "The gods clearly have a plan for you, Aika, and I can't let my feelings interfere with it. There's too much at stake."

"And what about *my* feelings?" I cried, thoroughly fed up. "Who cares what the gods think! And what do the gods have to do with this anyway?"

Shota shook his head. "You only have feelings for me because of our history," he said. "They'll go away soon enough. The important thing is that we have to keep our distance from each other."

"This is ridiculous," I sputtered as he got to his feet, wrapping the towel around his waist. "How do you even know that the gods want me to end up with Raiden? You're just making assumptions!"

Shota gave me an odd look. "It's strange," he said as I stood up. "I thought once I explained this that you'd understand, but you're acting like your feelings for Raiden don't matter. Are you really saying that you prefer me over him?"

His words tugged on my heart, and an image of Raiden popped into my head, his face smiling down at me as we whirled across the dance floor together. The thought of severing my connection with him, of pushing him away, was physically painful, and my chest throbbed at the very idea.

"I...I don't know," I said heavily. "But I do know that I want the chance to find out."

Shota sighed, his eyes dimming. "I'm going to go put some

clothes on," he said, turning away. "When I come back, be ready to train."

My heart sank as I watched him retreat to the bathroom. Clearly that had been the wrong thing to say, and yet how could I be anything less than honest? I cared about both Raiden *and* Shota, and I wanted the opportunity to explore those feelings. And yet the two of them seemed to have jointly decided that I belonged with Raiden.

"As if I didn't have a choice," I muttered, sitting back down on the chaise. Anger simmered in my veins. Who were these two men to make decisions like that for me, and without even coming clean on their reasoning behind it? If we weren't under such a time crunch, I would have brought them both in here and forced them to tell me what was *really* going on.

That's exactly why you shouldn't be letting your feelings get involved, I scolded myself. All this love life drama had no place in my world right now, not when my mother's life hung in the balance. I'd told myself that multiple times. Maybe now I should start listening.

When Shota came back out again, I'd regained my composure. Turning, I looked him up and down coolly as he approached. He wore a white button-up shirt and black jeans, those lean, gorgeous muscles all covered up now. Desire flickered inside me briefly before I snuffed it out. I was going to stick to my guns this time. I would *not* let my emotions take over.

"You ready to train?" he asked, pulling a black box from one of the drawers.

"Yep." I joined him at the small breakfast table, trying not to think about all the *other* black boxes he'd brought me, filled with yummy, handmade sushi. My stomach whined a little, and I made a mental note to grab one of the sandwiches we'd bought later. "This is where all our supplies are?"

"That's right." Shota flipped open the lid to reveal stacks of long, rectangular white paper, as well as several bottles of ink and brushes. "There are two things a shaman needs to know when it comes to making *ofuda*. The first part is how to actually craft the *ofuda*, and the second is how to use it."

"That makes sense." I glanced down at the supplies. "So how do we begin?"

Shota picked up one of the stacks of papers from the box. Unlike the others, these had *kanji* drawn on them in black ink. They were folded up, so I couldn't make out precisely what they said. "I prepared these earlier," he said, holding them out to me. "It's all the same spell, so you can see progressively how you get better."

"Okay." I took one of the *ofudas* from him. It was a small piece of paper about the size of a playing card, folded up so I couldn't read it in its entirety. I was a little disappointed that we were skipping the part where I actually got to make these, but on the other hand, I knew we didn't have a lot of time. "What now?"

"Shut your eyes, and try to feel the spell. Even if you don't know what it is, you should feel the magic inside like one of those Jack-in-the-Boxes. All you have to do is wind it up and let it out," he said, reaching out and putting his hand over the top of mine.

"Okay," I said, swallowing. The warmth from his hand seeped into my skin, settling my nerves a little. Unfortunately, it was also very distracting, and I had to make an effort to focus on the *ofuda*. As I did, I felt a spark of power within it. It reminded me of a present held together by a single ribbon, and as I had that thought, I found the mental ends of the ribbon fluttering in my mind's eye.

"Good," he said, his breath hot on my cheek as he spoke. Had he moved closer to me? "I can sense that you've found the spark. Now just tug it free."

Nodding, I redoubled my focus on the *ofuda* and mentally reached out to it. I grabbed hold of the ends of the ribbon holding the power at bay and tugged firmly. The binding on the spell came away surprisingly easily with a loud pop. My heart leapt in my chest, and I snapped my eyes open, excited to see what I'd created.

"Whoa." My jaw dropped at the sight of a colorful bouquet of flowers in my hand. "This wasn't what I expected."

"They come in handy on dates," Shota said with a smirk. "Care to trade?" he asked, holding it out to me. "Because we're gonna do this a couple dozen more times, until you can summon flowers in your sleep."

20

After summoning so many bouquets of flowers I felt like we'd booked a room in a flower shop, the three of us packed up and caught a cab to the Nezu Shrine in Bunkyo. I was a little disappointed that we hadn't had time for me to learn how to actually make *ofudas*, but it was what it was. I knew enough that I was confident I could use Ryujin's spell on Kai, and that was what mattered.

By the time we arrived at the shrine it was early afternoon, so there weren't many visitors. Even so, I found myself glancing around nervously as we approached the *suzu* hanging from the shrine's eaves.

"Aren't people going to notice if we suddenly disappear?" I hissed as Raiden clapped his hands. He'd taken the sword out of his bag and strapped it to his belt, and we were already getting weird looks from people.

"No," Shota said as Raiden grasped the rope. "They're Muggles, so they won't see anything out of the ordinary. They'll forget they ever saw us."

"Did you just make a Harry Po—" I began, but Raiden cut me off with a mighty tug of the bell. It rang once, twice, and we joined arms just in time for the flash of light to engulf us. Like before, the light twisted into a psychedelic spread of colors, and this time I closed my eyes against it. Maybe if I couldn't see it, I wouldn't feel sick to my stomach when we arrived.

A few seconds later, my feet slammed into hard ground, and I stumbled into Raiden. He grasped my arms, steadying me, and even though I could only see blackness when I opened my eyes, the feel of his arms around me and his incense-laced scent reassured me that everything was fine. Taking in slow breaths, I waited for my vision to clear.

"Hey!" a male voice shouted. I turned toward the sound of footsteps crunching against rocky ground, and the fog from my vision finally lifted to reveal a lushly wooded mountain forest. A man about thirty years of age, dressed in a black and white gi decorated with *kanji*, was running toward us. "Who are you?"

"I'm Takaoka Raiden. This is Hayakawa Shota, my cousin, and Fujiwara Aika, our friend," Raiden said, stepping between me and the irate shaman. "We're here to enter the tomb."

"Raiden?" the shaman exclaimed. "You can't go in there. Your parents have expressly ordered—"

Raiden whirled around, drawing the dragon blade in one smooth motion. He slammed the *katana* into the temporary shrine we'd used to teleport here, and a bolt of lightning burst from the cloudless sky and slammed into the shrine in a flash of light and sound.

"Shit!" Shota tackled me to the ground, covering my body with his as debris flew everywhere. The smell of ozone filled my nose as power crackled in the air from the lightning strike. As the smoke cleared, a chunk of rock bounced off my shoulder blade, sending a small but sharp burst of pain through me.

"A little warning would have been nice!" I snapped, peering up at Raiden from beneath Shota's arm.

"Sorry." Raiden blushed. "I've never actually used this thing before."

"Are you all right?" Shota asked, rolling me onto my back beneath him. His worried gaze searched my face. "Did you get hit anywhere?"

"No." I pushed myself up into a sitting position so I could take stock of myself. I was a bit dusty, and covered in snow, but fine otherwise. "I'm okay."

"Good." Shota offered me a hand and pulled me to my feet. For once, he didn't attempt to pull away, but wrapped his fingers a bit tighter around mine. Normally I would have been annoyed, but his face was pale, and there was a cut on his forehead from where a piece of shrapnel had hit him.

Discreetly, I sent a bit of healing energy into Shota to ease the pain from the wound. His eyes flew wide as color returned to his face, and I grinned up at him as his shocked gaze met mine.

You're not the only one with tricks up your sleeve.

"Why did you do that!" the shaman shrieked, interrupting our moment. He scrambled to his feet, his face deathly pale now. "You've ruined our only way out of here!"

"I'm sure there are other ways to get down this mountain," Raiden said dryly, sheathing the sword. "I just didn't want you forcing us back out. Besides, the shrine-maker can make another one, can't he?"

"Our shrine-maker is inside the tomb," the shaman said sharply, jabbing a finger behind him. A path had been cleared through the trees. It led to a cavern entrance flanked by two enormous stone statues of a man and a woman. A strange, shimmery haze hung in front of the entrance that reminded me of an oil slick on pavement, and I assumed that was the barrier keeping Kai inside. "As is every other shaman who has attempted to go in there. They all went in, and never came out. I heard some terrible screams, but..." His voice shook a little, and he swallowed. "We have no idea whether or not they're still alive."

"How many people went in?" Raiden demanded as my stomach turned leaden. "Were my parents amongst them?"

The shaman shook his head. "Your parents are safely back at headquarters. We've retreated for now, until we can figure out how to safely reseal Kai without getting killed."

Raiden nodded curtly. "Very well. Is there a path that leads to the water?"

The shaman blinked. "There is, just through there." He pointed to a path to our left. "But why would you go there?"

"There's a way to get into the tomb," Raiden said. He stalked in the direction the shaman had pointed. "Come on, guys."

"You can't go in there!" the shaman protested as we started toward the path. "You'll die, just like the others!"

"We're going to rescue the others," Raiden called, not bothering to look back. "Stay here and guard the entrance. Don't let anyone else through. We'll be back soon."

He stalked through the trees, leaving the shaman gaping after him.

Shota and I hurried to catch up with Raiden. "You sound pretty confident," I said as I came abreast of Raiden. "Considering that we have no idea what we're doing."

"Someone has to be," Raiden said, shaking his head. "That guy looked like he was about to piss himself. I'm nervous as hell, but that doesn't mean I'm going to cower in the corner like a scared puppy. Not after we've come all this way."

I nodded, understanding. Raiden was putting his game face on —not just for that shaman's benefit, or for mine, but to show Kai that he was unafraid to face him. Show an enemy weakness, and you've already given him half the battle. I read that in a book somewhere, and it seemed more appropriate now than it ever had in my life.

Taking a deep breath, I dispelled the anxiety in my chest and forced myself to stand taller.

No matter what lay in store for us, I would not show fear. It was time to fight.

The sound of ocean waves crashing against the cliffside reached my ears, along with the tang of sea salt. A few moments later, we emerged from the trees at the edge of a cliff. We peered over the edge, and my stomach flip-flopped at the sight of the sheer drop —it had to be at least two hundred feet.

"Well, shit." Shota scrubbed a hand over his lower jaw. "I thought we'd use a feather *ofuda* to get down, but the drop is too high. The winds would blow us way off course."

"Hang on." I lifted the wrist that had my bracelet on it, where I'd attached the rest of the charms Raiden had brought. "We haven't tried this bird one yet," I said, tapping the tiny wooden bird. It flared to life beneath my touch, as if begging to be summoned. "Maybe whatever this is can fly us down."

Raiden glanced warily at it. "It's worth a shot. Let's hope it's big enough."

"*Maji,*" I said, willing the *yokai* to appear. *Yoki* blazed from the tiny charm, and I held my breath as the familiar blue ball of flame burst into life in front of us. A shrill bird call raised the hair on my arms, and the ball swirled into the form of an enormous, red-skinned man wearing a black *kimono* and a pair of *geta*—Japanese-style clogs. He stood at least ten feet tall, with a gigantic nose that protruded about a foot from his weathered face and a bushy, mad-scientist-like mane of hair. A sword and fan were tucked into his belt, and he sported a huge pair of blue-gray wings on his back. Like an ugly, red-skinned angel.

"Holy crap," Raiden breathed, his eyes wide. "That's a *tengu!*"

"A whoziwhatsit?"

"Indeed I am." The *tengu* inclined his head, regarding me from beneath his bushy brows. "You are the one who summoned me?"

I nodded. "My friends and I need to get to the bottom of this cliff. We were hoping you might fly us down."

The *yokai* looked surprised. "You merely want a ride down to the cliffs?"

"Well, yeah." I bit my lip in confusion. "Are we supposed to ask for something else?"

The *tengu* puffed out his chest. "The last time I was summoned by a *yokai* shaman, I fought in battle with him. I am not merely a form of transport—I am a fierce warrior, and I punish those who are impure." His face contorted into a fierce scowl as he looked toward the cliffs. "I am aware of Amatsu's great, evil presence down in those cliffs. I would be honored to fight by your side against him."

"And *we* would be honored to have your help," Shota said as I blinked up at the *tengu*. "But before we can fight, we must get down to the cliffs."

"Of course." The *tengu* flapped his wings, and his form blurred, as if he was vibrating on high speed. He shifted into a gigantic bird with a yellow beak and silver-blue feathers, then settled onto his belly. "Climb onto my back," he instructed.

We did as he asked, which was no mean feat—the feathers were slippery, and I had to grip great handfuls of them to keep from falling off. Somehow, we managed to find the middle of his back, and settled there as comfortably as we could. Since there was no harness, we lay flat on our bellies and grabbed fistfuls of his plumage.

"Hold on tight," the *tengu* instructed right before he flapped his wings. I tucked my face into his feathers as he kicked up dust and twigs. My stomach shot straight into my throat as the huge bird launched himself off the cliff's edge, tucking his wings tight against his body.

"Woohoo!" Raiden and Shota yelled in unison as we plummeted straight down. Their faces were shining, and they sported identical grins, as if this was the best thing that had ever happened to them.

A few seconds later, the *tengu* snapped its wings out, catching an updraft, and we began to soar toward the bottom of the cliff.

"Wow." I let out a relieved breath, my stomach sinking back down to my abdomen as it realized we were not, in fact, going to die. "I thought I was going to pass out for a second there."

Raiden snorted. "You afraid of heights or something?"

"No," I snapped defensively. "I'm just not used to diving off cliffs on the backs of mythical birds."

The *tengu* laughed, apparently able to hear us even over the whistling wind. "I would not let you fall," he said. "You have nothing to fear so long as you are on my back."

That's easy for you to say, I grumbled silently as we banked toward the cliff edge. The *tengu* landed in the sea, spraying us with salt water, and I groaned. It seemed like I was going to spend the rest of my life smelling like the sea.

"So now what?" I asked, reaching into the pouch and pulling out the stone of ebbing tide. I handed it to Raiden, then pulled out the other stone. "How do we find the entrance?"

"Well, since I don't see it, I'm guessing it's below us," Raiden said, gripping the stone in his hand. White sparks shot from between his fingers as he shut his eyes and exhaled slowly, and the wind around us whipped violently.

"I'm not sure—"

My words were cut off as the water beneath us lurched downward like someone had jerked the plug free in a full bathtub. The water began to swirl downward, and as it did, a cave in the cliff in front of us was slowly revealed.

Sharp outcroppings of stone clung to its mouth, making it appear like the maw of some great beast. As I stared, cool mist began to drift out from it. I shivered instinctively. Something inside felt dark and, well, evil. It was like staring at your closet at night when you were a kid and knowing there was a monster inside ready to eat you. But unlike then, there really was a monster waiting for us. Probably more than one monster, if Amatsu and Kai were summoning *yokai* to do their bidding.

"In there!" I said, directing the *tengu* toward the cave. It nodded once and flapped its wings, lifting from the sea and moving toward the cave. As we breached the entryway, the temperature dropped twenty degrees. My breath came out in a cloud of dark mist as the light from outside faded to a pinprick.

"Now where?" the *tengu* asked as it landed on a hard rock wall. We all looked around, but try as I might, I couldn't see anything.

"Maybe we need to make the water go back up?" I said, glancing at Raiden. He still had his eyes shut, and his face was taut with strain.

"Try it," he said, taking in a breath and opening his eyes. The stone in his hand stopped glowing, but the water didn't rise either. "I guess you don't have to maintain the spell. I thought if I stopped concentrating, the water might rise. That must be why there were two jewels."

"Okay," I said, gripping the jewel of rising tide and shutting my eyes. "I'll try to make the water rise, then."

As I concentrated on the stone in my hand, I felt its power just like it was an *ofuda*. It made me instantly glad I'd learned how to use them—I was able to direct the water to rise almost effort-lessly. My eyes snapped open a second later, and triumph filled me as I saw we were rising upward toward a cavern. As the water touched the stone inside our tunnel, it began to glow with effer-vescent algae that reminded me of Ryujin's palace, illuminating a pathway that the *tengu* followed.

A moment later, we found ourselves staring at a small cavern in a wall a few meters to our left.

"Guess that's where we're going," Raiden said, hopping off the *tengu* and jumping onto the outcropping in front of the cave. He offered me his hand.

"Right." I took Raiden's hand and jumped onto the rock, Shota right behind me. "Whoa," I said as we followed him into the cavern, the *tengu* bringing up the rear. He'd shrunk into a smaller version of his natural form so he could fit through. "Check out this mural."

I plucked one of the bamboo torches hanging on the wall and lifted it higher so I could see the painting better. It stretched all the way around the circular cavern room, a progression of scenes, and as I looked closer, I realized the woman who appeared most often was the same woman the *kami* back at the café had been drawing. A princess who wore my face.

"It's the story of Kai, Haruki, Kaga, and Fumiko," the *tengu* said. His gravelly voice was sad, and I turned around to see him gazing at the mural with a grave look on his face. "It looks like someone blacked out Haruki and Kaga's faces on all of these."

Shocked, I turned back. Sure enough, two of the four characters depicted in the murals had their faces completely blotted out.

"Why would someone do that?" I asked, moving closer to the paintings.

"Because they're trying to cover up history," Raiden said tightly. His dark eyes blazed with anger, and he snatched a torch off the wall. "Come on, Aika. We already know the story."

"Raiden, I think there's more here that the dragon king didn't tell us!" Shota called. His eyes were shining with excitement as they scanned the mural. "Just wait a moment!"

But Raiden was already stalking off, and I didn't want to stay here in the cavern without him.

Shota and I exchanged frustrated glances. "We'll have to look at this later," I said with a sigh, even though I agreed with Shota. "We can't let him go on ahead by himself."

"Fine," Shota grumbled. We hurried after Raiden, down a hall that split off the cavern entrance. I tried not to think about the way the narrow walls pressed in against us, leaving very little room to walk. I wasn't claustrophobic, but the fact that we were miles and miles below the surface, with no real map, and the sure knowledge that an evil god and shaman were waiting up ahead, was enough to freak anyone out.

No fear, I reminded myself, and lifted my chin a little higher.

We caught up with Raiden only a few steps away, just beyond a corner. He was standing stone-still and had one hand on the hilt of his *katana*. He took a deep breath and turned to look at me. Then he mouthed one word.

"Run."

21

R *un.*

The word echoed in my brain as Raiden took a step backward. As he did, his shoes squeaked on the tile floor, drawing the attention of two large shadows across the room. They stood before a massive ornate wooden shrine I instinctively recognized as a *butsudan.*

The shadows spun around, and I instantly realized they weren't shadows at all. No, they were hideous, disgusting creatures with distended guts and skin like coal. Huge eyes burned in their heads, and as their long, black tongues licked hungrily over their yellowed teeth, saliva dripped from the corners of their mouths. As the left one took a lumbering step toward us, Shota stepped in front of me, one hand pulling his *kusarigama* free while the other grabbed a tablet from his keychain.

"Stay behind me," he said, right before he invoked the tablet. "*Mezame*, Baiken!"

A *hitodama* exploded from the mortuary tablet, lighting up the interior of the cave with its blue glow. Shota snatched it out of the air, and as he shoved it into his chest, a fiery light exploded from his body. The outline of a samurai coalesced around him, and Shota's eyes blazed with otherworldly light.

"It's about time you got a real weapon. Always playing with swords like a fool," he said in a deep voice that was both Shota and the spirit he'd taken in. He hefted the *kusarigama*, a delighted grin on his face. "Let me show you how to put these flames to good use." He spun on his heel and dashed toward one of the monsters, his hand swinging around in an arc as he spun the spiked ball on the end of the chain attached to the sickle. As flames crawled across the chain, Shota sent the spiked ball flying through the air with a flick of his wrist. The flaming steel ball smashed into the charging monster with a sickening thud, knocking it off its feet in a flurry of sparks.

As the creature screamed, Shota jerked the chain back and spun it once more, only this time, flames began to crawl over the ball as well, making him look like a fire dancer as he prepared to attack again.

The creature on the right began to dance from foot to foot, its huge hands waving above its head in a motion that would have seemed carefree if it hadn't been so sinister.

"Damn *nuribotokes*," Raiden said, bringing the dragon scale *katana* to bear as he moved to my side. "Normally you can get rid of them by trapping them within a circle of salt until morning, at which point they'll evaporate along with the sun's rays. But I'm guessing that won't work now."

"Not unless you have salt and a lot of time," Shota said, his hands tightening on the grip of his weapon and swinging it even faster, causing it to whirl through the air in a blur of motion. "Have any other ideas?" He took a deep breath, eyes flicking between the two monsters. "Baiken and I can keep knocking them down, but we'll definitely have to do something fast."

"Are they dangerous?" I asked as the *nuribotoke* Shota had knocked down scrambled to its feet.

Its lips broke out into a huge, grotesque smile, and it lumbered toward us once more, but this time the movement was so quick I could barely follow it. The creature's long arms trailed behind it, and its head fell backward as its legs propelled it forward like one of those disgusting creatures in *Attack on Titan*.

"Yes, which is why I told you to run!" Raiden said as Shota intercepted the creature, wrapping up its legs with his chain and pulling them out from under it. As the creature hit the ground with a thud, its comrade charged, and this time, Shota's weapon was too bound with the first *nuribotoke* for him to stop it. Worse, I wasn't sure I wanted him to.

"Raiden," Shota cried, muscles straining as he fought to keep the creature from escaping. "You have to get that one. If I let go of this one, it'll get free."

"Right!" Raiden took a step forward and slashed at the *nuribotoke* with his *katana*. But instead of slicing through the monster, the blade slammed into it with a hard clang.

The thrum of the impact rang in my ears as the *nuribotoke* kept coming, barely slowed by Raiden's attacks.

As Raiden stumbled backward, the creature's hands snapped out with whip-like speed, grabbing hold of him by the shirt and hauling him in between the *nuribotoke* and the *tengu*.

My *yokai* pulled up short, its blade glinting in the air as Raiden stumbled, falling off balance. His arms shot out to the side, and the *katana* in his hands went flying across the room and clattering uselessly onto the stone.

"Raiden!" I cried, reaching for my own power and instinctively drawing upon the *kyuubi*, since her flames had proven to be pretty unstoppable. As I felt her presence in my mind's eye, I called her forth. She exploded into being in front of me in fireball form, and as Raiden tried vainly to free himself from his *nuribotoke's* grasp, it dragged him back toward the wooden shrine.

I grabbed hold of the *kyuubi's* spirit and slammed it into me. Fire came to my call as I sprinted forward and threw a handful of it at the *nuribotoke*. The blast caught it full in the face, tearing it free of Raiden and flinging it backward across the room.

"Little help here!" Shota called, and as I swung my eyes back toward him, the *nuribotoke* grabbed hold of the chain with its hands and jerked on it. Shota instinctively released the weapon, and as it left his hands, the creature fell on its ass.

"Get the shrine—that's the source of its power!" Raiden cried, scrambling toward his dropped *katana* as the *tengu* rushed in to help Shota, leaving me a precious moment to act.

"On it!" I yelled as the *nuribotoke* I'd blasted leapt to its feet like it was some kind of kung fu god.

It snarled, spraying spittle in every direction, but before it could do much, the *tengu* was between us, throwing the monster backward with his powerful muscles. The other *nuribotoke* was in pieces on the ground, torn apart by the *tengu's* powerful claws. To my horror, I saw that the pieces were slowly inching back toward each other, like some kind of zombie trying to reform.

"I'll hold it," he said, and I nodded, calling upon the *kyuubi's* flames. Her fire surged through my veins and coalesced in my hands as I flung it forward at the shrine.

The fireball slammed into the wooden shrine like a nuclear blast, blowing it to pieces and charring the stone beneath it. The *nuribotoke* screamed in agony, staggering backward as its skin began to catch fire. The smell of burning flesh hit my nose as it fell to the ground, writhing next to the flaming pieces of his brethren, and I had to swallow back a wave of bile as my stomach heaved.

A moment later, I felt Raiden's hand on my shoulder. "Good job," he said, steering me away from the burning *yokai*. "Now let's get out of here."

"I agree," the *tengu* said, loping over to us, and somehow its creepy smile seemed a little sadder than it had before. "We still have much darkness to face."

"Yeah, all right," I said, nodding as I released the *kyuubi* back to her charm. She went without a word, and as her power left me, I felt a little bit worse. We'd barely stepped into the place and had nearly been undone by a pretty weak monster. What would happen if we found something way worse?

Either way, I couldn't focus on it. I had to keep moving forward.

"Mom?" I called, walking into the room. It was completely unlit. Faint, pained moans filled the air, sending a shiver down my spine. Oh God, was she hurt? I lifted my torch to try to see better, and nearly dropped it at the sight of a badger hanging from a rope attached to the ceiling.

"What the hell is *that* thing doing here?" I squeaked as Raiden and Shota came up beside me.

"Help me!" the badger squeaked. Its back feet were tied together by the rope, and it spun in a slow circle in the center of the room. All along the walls were steel cages, with humans curled up inside them in various states of unconsciousness. The smell of old blood marred the air, and my heart twisted in sympathy. How many of them were wounded? "I've been stuck up here forever. You have to get me down!"

"Ignore it," Raiden said, edging warily toward the cages. "Badgers are tricksters. They can't be trusted. The moment we take him down, he's going to attack us."

"Okay..." I said dubiously as Raiden crouched down in front of one of the cages. He reached in to touch the forehead of the unconscious man inside.

"These shamans have all been drained of their *ki*," he growled. "That bastard Kai has been taking their power."

"What?" My stomach twisted in horror and disgust. I dropped to my knees in front of one of the other cages, where a woman with a blood-stained bandage wrapped around her head lay prone.

Her face was deathly pale, her skin icy to the touch, and she was barely breathing. "How are they still alive?"

"He didn't take it all," Shota said, circling the room so he could study the prisoners. "These shamans have all been left with just enough to stay alive. I imagine that Kai is waiting for them to regain their strength so he can take more power from them. That is why he kept them alive."

"That asshole." Anger burned hot in my veins as I shot to my feet. "We have to get them out of here. Where is my mother?" I whirled around, scanning all the cages, but I didn't see her. "Mom, are you in here?"

"Kai must be keeping her somewhere else," Raiden said, his voice brimming with frustration as he glanced through the other cages. "And there are no key holes on any of these cages for us to pick. I don't know how to get them out without accidentally hurting the people inside."

"If you let me down, I can free them," the badger said in a singsong tone. We glanced up to see him swinging back and forth gaily from his rope. "I know how to get the humans out of their cages."

Raiden crossed his arms over his chest. "Fine. Then why don't you tell us how to do it? If it works, we'll release you."

The badger shook his head. "It's not something a human like you can do," he scoffed. "I have to do it myself. You have to let me down." His whiskers twitched, and he gave me the most adorable puppy dog look. "Please. My ankles are in so much pain!"

"I can tell you're lying," Raiden growled, glancing from the badger to the cages and back again. "But I'm going to trust you anyway. If you fail me, I will cut out your liver and feed it to a sea dragon."

"He'll do it. My friend is crazy that way," Shota added, drawing his thumb over his throat and making a *skkrt* noise.

"That's just a myth. Sea dragons don't eat livers," the badger replied, crossing his arms over his chest as he hung there. "Now let me down. I'll do a great job, you'll see. You'll be so impressed with my work you won't know what to do. Greatly impressed. I'm a really great badger, you'll see."

"Amazing," Raiden muttered, shaking his head in disbelief. "You're like a politician."

"I guess we need to try," I said, glancing at Raiden. "But if he does anything silly, gut him like a fish."

"Works for me," Raiden said as he lifted the dragon blade. He swung it, slicing through the rope in one smooth motion. The badger plummeted to the ground, striking the dungeon floor with a thwack. He lay there dazed for a moment before hopping to his feet and scowling.

"Well, that was quite rude!" the badger snapped, shrugging out of the ropes and moving forward. "Still, because I have promised to help you, I won't smite you from the face of the Earth. Instead, I will perform a great feat of magnificence the likes of which you have never seen before." He clapped his paws together as he sauntered toward the nearest cage. "Prepare to be amazed."

He flicked the cage with his paw.

Nothing happened.

The badger tried again.

Still, nothing happened.

"I'm starting to think you don't know how to open the cages," Raiden said, taking a step forward. The badger scurried backward and threw his paws up in response.

"You don't understand. That should have worked." The badger nodded furiously before hopping from foot to foot anxiously. Then he smacked himself on the head. "Oh, I know. I forgot the magic words... It was, um... orangutan? No... orange?" He shook his head.

"Don't tell me you forgot the magic word," I said, unable to keep the exasperation out of my voice. It was hard to believe this was really our only hope.

"I didn't!" the badger cried, touching his tongue with one hand. "It's right here, right on the tip of my tongue. I promise."

"Well, we don't have all day—" Raiden started.

"*Akeru!*" the badger shouted. Scintillating magic surrounded the cages, making them flare like the sun, and for a moment, I thought they were going to burst open. But after a moment, the glow faded, and the cages remained stubbornly closed, as if nothing had happened.

"That was supposed to work!" the badger cried, wringing his paws anxiously. His big eyes darted back and forth between

Raiden and the *tengu*, and I couldn't blame him—they both looked like they wanted to murder him.

"It doesn't seem like it did," I said, shaking my head. Part of me wondered if I was going to just have to give up and try to melt the cages away. I was betting the *kyuubi* could do it, but I didn't want to risk barbecuing everyone inside. Much as I hated to admit it, the badger was our best bet.

"I think we just kill the badger and be done with it," the *tengu* said, nodding furiously. "He'll taste great in a soup."

"I agree—"

"That's it!" the badger said, cutting off Raiden. "I know the magic words." His lips settled into a mischievous smile. "You should count yourselves lucky."

"Is this where you betray us?" Raiden asked, gripping his sword. "Because if it is..."

"Look, let's assume I betray you," the badger said, holding his paws out in front of himself. "We'll fight, and the pretty shaman lady"—he pointed at me—"will summon her *kyuubi* to burn me. That will hurt so much, I'll beg for help in exchange for opening the cages, and you'll agree because that's what you want anyway. With all due respect, I'd rather just skip to the part where I help you and save all of us, but mostly me, some pain and anguish."

"That sounds like a great idea," I said, before Raiden could argue. I was tired of standing around in here—we needed to free these people and get to Kai.

"Excellent." A cold smile flitted across the badger's face. "I hope cold doesn't bother you, 'cause it's about to get downright frozen in here."

As the badger lifted his paws into the air, snow and sleet began to rain down from the sky and hoarfrost snaked over the cage bars. I was just about to ask him how this was supposed to help open the cages when he brought his paws down sharply. An earsplitting crack rent the air as a flurry of ice slammed into the cage bars. I shrieked as they shattered into a billion frozen fractals, instinctively flinching away as shards of glass and metal went flying.

The badger folded his arms across his chest and smirked. "See? I just had to let it go."

Raiden groaned. "I thought you guys were supposed to be tricksters."

"Like I said, just let it go," the badger said, shaking his head. "That was a long time ago. The past is in the past, right?"

And with that, the creature vanished in a flurry of frozen wind, leaving the three of us standing there amidst a bunch of unconscious shamans.

22

With the badger gone, there was no one to stop us from taking those poor shamans out of the cages. There were about fifteen people total, and we laid them out on the floor and triaged them as best as we could.

"It doesn't seem like any of them have serious wounds," Shota said. "A couple of flesh wounds here and there, and it looks like one got a hard knock on the head. The rest of them are just unconscious."

"So, what, do you think we should just leave them here?" I asked. "I mean, there isn't anywhere we can really take them, but still..."

Raiden's eyes lit up. "Why don't you see if your *kamaitachi* can heal them?"

"Oh! I hadn't thought of that." I glanced down at the charm hanging from my wrist. "Do you think it can?"

"The *kamaitachi* won't be able to replenish their *ki*," the *tengu* said. "But he should be able to heal any physical wounds."

Nodding, I summoned the *kamaitachi*. The weasel-like *yokai* appeared at my elbow in a flash of blue fire.

"More healing, mistress?" he asked, his nose twitching excitedly.

"Yes, please." I stroked the top of his head, unable to help myself. He was just so damned cute, and if not for those scythe-like forelegs, I'd be tempted to cuddle him. "I don't know if you'll be able to help them all, but please try."

Raiden and the others stood guard at the entrance while the *kamaitachi* and I went around and healed each of the shamans. Many of them didn't wake up, even after I'd flowed my *ki* into them, but a few groaned and stirred a little before rolling over and snoring again. My heart sank—I strongly suspected that most of them were too weak.

But just when I was about to give up hope, one man groaned louder than the others. "W-where am I?" he asked, his voice weak. He opened bleary eyes that widened when he saw the *kamaitachi* licking his arm. "Hey, get away!" He flung his arm out, and the *kamaitachi* scurried back.

"Be nice!" I scolded the shaman. The *kamaitachi* chittered angrily at him, then disappeared in another flash of light. I felt bad—I hadn't even gotten a chance to say thank you—but I didn't see any point in calling him back. Instead, I touched the charm and said a silent prayer of thanks, hoping the *yokai* would hear it.

"He was helping you," I said, kneeling next to the shaman. He was a middle-aged man, in his late fifties, with weathered skin and salt-and-pepper hair.

"I'm sorry," he said, relaxing back onto the ground. "It's just...I was startled. Were you controlling that *yokai*?"

I nodded, checking his temperature with my hand. His forehead was a little cooler than I'd have liked, but it was much improved from the icy skin I'd felt earlier when we'd first found the prisoners.

"But how is that possible..." The old man trailed off, eyes drifting to the charms hanging from my wrist.

My shoulders tensed. "I'm a *yokai* shaman. We're here to defeat Kai."

The man's eyes widened in alarm. "You must not confront him. He is too powerful. We tried to defeat him, and he...he..."

"He drained you of your *ki*," Raiden finished, coming over. He knelt by the old man's other side and took his hand. "I know it's dangerous, elder, but we have to do this. Aika and I have the means to stop him. "What is your name?"

"I am Watanabe Sojiro," he said, attempting to sit up. Raiden immediately slid his arm beneath the shaman's back to assist him. "The shrine-maker."

"Thank the gods," Shota said. "Do you think you can get the rest of our people out of here?"

The shrine-maker's eyes narrowed as he looked around the

room. "I believe I can construct another shrine and get these shamans out, but I will need help to gather the right materials." He pulled in a long breath. "I am much too weak to manage it on my own."

I nodded, then rose and went over to where the *tengu* was standing guard. "*Tengu*, stay here and assist Sojiro-san while we go ahead. I want you to help him, then guard the shrine once he's taken everyone through."

"But mistress," the *tengu* protested, "I want to come with you to fight Kai! He must be punished for his actions!"

"I understand," I said, laying a hand on the *yokai's* huge forearm. "But I am worried Kai may send someone to destroy the shrine, and we will need it to escape this place. It's very important that you stay behind and guard it."

The glower cleared from the *tengu's* face, and he nodded. "I will guard it with my life," he said solemnly.

"Good." I patted him one more time, then turned to Raiden and Shota. "Come on. We need to go."

We bid the shrine-maker farewell, then exited the dungeon and continued along the path. My senses were on high alert as we walked, ears and eyes straining for any sign of an approaching enemy, and I knew Raiden and Shota were doing the same. The two men had their weapons out, and I fingered my bracelet, ready to summon a *yokai*. But the seconds turned to minutes as we made our way forward through the darkened hallways, and even though the flickering torchlight caused shadows to dance along the walls, no monsters jumped out at us. The only sound accompanying our footsteps was the drip, drip of water from the cavern walls and the hissing of torches.

Finally, after about fifteen minutes, the path flowed into a steep staircase. The three of us climbed to the top and found ourselves standing at the threshold of a huge room with another mural of the Kai-Haruki-Kaga-Fumiko story painted on the walls. In the center were four *kofun*—megalithic Japanese tombs made of rectangular slabs of stone and stacked on top of the deceased's cremated remains. A *tori* gate and shrine, about the size of a tool shack, stood just behind the *kofun*—the first tomb was completely unadorned, the second one covered in flowers, and the third one broken into several pieces. A ragged crater sat on the ground beneath it, and from the look of things, it seemed like someone or something had torn its way out of it.

"This must have been Kai's," I said, wandering over to it. Sure enough, a large black stone box was buried in the ground, its broken lid flung to the ground beside it. "And these other three...?"

"Fumiko, Haruki, and Kaga," Raiden said tightly, crouching to look at the *kanji* characters written in the stone. "This one is Fumiko's," he said, pointing to the tombstone with the flowers on it. "And this shrine..." He trailed off and stepped past the tombs toward it.

"What is it?" I asked, hurrying beneath the *tori* gate with him. There was a small purification trough and a pair of lion-dogs guarding the entrance, but to my surprise, Raiden ignored them both. He ducked beneath the eaves of the shrine itself, where the statue of a female goddess sat, and knelt before her. She was cordoned off by a *shime-*

nawa, the sacred straw rope that marked holy spaces, and her pedestal was surrounded by piles of flowers and small bags of rice.

"It's Amaterasu," Shota said in a hushed voice filled with awe. We knelt in front of the shrine next to Raiden. "Someone built a shrine to her here."

I stared up into the face of the sun goddess who had joined forces with Himiko to seal Kai away all those years ago. And an epiphany struck me. "Do you think Kai built this shrine? And that these offerings are to her?"

Raiden frowned. "How would Kai have been able to build this while trapped in here? It's been less than two days since he was freed. Besides, I don't see why he'd worship the goddess who locked him away."

I shrugged. "Maybe he's been praying for forgiveness from her. And maybe he got the *yokai* he's been using to help him. After all, he built those dungeons somehow, didn't he?"

Raiden was silent for a long moment. "I suppose it's possible," he finally said, standing up. "There's no point in staying in this room—Kai isn't here. I don't know how, but he's made some upgrades to the tomb. Maybe Amatsu's powers have allowed him to create new rooms, like the dungeon down below that we saw. I don't know much about the dark god," he admitted.

Silently, we retreated from Amaterasu's shrine, then followed another staircase leading out of the tomb. As we left, I glanced back toward the tombs, my gaze lingering on Fumiko's for a moment. Those flowers meant something, and despite what Kai had done to those poor shamans, I felt a tug on my heart. He clearly still loved Fumiko, despite the choice she'd made in the end.

"Greetings, travelers," said a voice from the shadows as we reached the final step. The room was too dark for me to see, but as I turned my eyes toward the sound of the voice, I readied my charms anyway.

"Greetings," Raiden called back, edging forward. He had one hand on the hilt of his dragon blade, but so far he hadn't drawn it nor invoked Katsu. Part of me wondered why he hadn't done it yet, but then it was a strain every time I used the *kyuubi*. Maybe using the samurai was similar?

"If you wish to pass, you must answer my riddle," the voice said. As it spoke, torches lining the walls began to blaze with ethereal green light. "Do you wish to try?"

I bit back a scream as the speaker was finally revealed in the light. It was a gnarled tree about twenty feet tall with peeling bark and swaying weeping willow branches. Only... instead of fruit, human heads hung from those branches. Their faces writhed in anguish as they tried to scream without voices. The largest head leered at us, and the urge to turn and run struck me hard. Unlike the others, which were sallow and unhealthy-looking, this head looked perfectly fine.

"What the hell is that?" I hissed, shrinking back.

"A *jinmenju*," Shota whispered, looking fascinated. "Despite their horrific appearance they're mostly harmless. They pretty much just block the way and ask for their riddles to be solved. If you get it right, you can pass."

"What happens if you get it wrong?" I asked, eyeing the *jinmenju* suspiciously.

"You die!" the demonic tree cackled, its branches rustling in unseen wind. The lips on all its faces curled into Cheshire cat grins, and it leaned forward. "But no one ever won anything by not trying, eh?"

"Fine," Raiden said impatiently. "Let's hear the riddle."

The massive tree cackled again. "Very well," it said, holding up three severed heads on a single branch. "Riddle me this, shamans."

The three heads turned so that the one on the far left stared at the back of the middle head, the middle head stared at the right head, and the right head stared off into nothingness.

"The head on the left is named Ken, and he is married." Ken, the head on the left, opened his mouth in a low moan as he was addressed. "Pan, the head on the right, is not married." Pan began to moan then, leaving only the middle head unnamed.

"Um... okay, so what's the riddle?" I asked, and as I spoke, the tree's laughter boomed like a bass drum.

"It is simply this. Is a married person looking at an unmarried person?"

I gritted my teeth as a headache began to throb at my temples. I had no idea what the answer was, and I really didn't have time for this. I wanted to rescue my mother, not ponder useless riddles with stupid talking trees full of severed heads!

"Any ideas?" Raiden asked, glancing at me. The look on his face let me know he was just as stumped as I was. Great. Just freaking great.

"Well, do you know?" The tree grinned evilly. "Or are you going to join my friends here?" His branches rustled, eliciting moans from the severed heads.

"Sure, I've got it," I said sweetly, calling upon my *kyuubi's* power. Her spirit popped free of the charm, and I grabbed it and shoved it in my chest. "The answer is get the hell out of my way."

The *jinmenju's* eyes widened in horror as I flung a massive fireball at it. The ball of flame slammed straight into the trunk, and the tree exploded into a swirling cloud of flaming debris. The severed heads all shrieked with pain as debris rained down around the room, and we ducked for cover.

"Well..." Raiden muttered when the air had finally cleared. He glanced at me warily out of the corner of his eye as I pulled the *kyuubi* out of my chest and allowed her to regain her form. "That wasn't exactly what I expected."

"I'll say." Shota grinned at me. "You don't mess around, Aika."

I shrugged. "I don't negotiate with terrorists."

"It's about time you grew a spine," the *kyuubi* huffed. She curled her tails around her and immediately began grooming her paw.

I snorted. "I think I'm doing pretty well considering that I've only just started this shaman thing."

"You might want to save the grooming for later," Raiden said to the *kyuubi* as the tree finally withered into ash. We all turned toward it just as a doorway appeared where the tree had been. A strange silver glow seeped from the cracks around it, and a cool sensation rippled across my skin in response.

"Umm." I glanced uneasily at Raiden and Shota. "You think it's safe to go in there?"

Shota frowned thoughtfully. "It's not *yoki*," he said, moving closer to the door. "In fact, I think it might be a *kami*."

"It is," the *kyuubi* said. She strutted toward the door, completely unconcerned. "Open it, human."

Raiden scowled at her imperious tone, but he did as she asked. I threw up a hand to shield my eyes as a wave of silver light burst from the door, and Raiden cried out in surprise, his hand going to the hilt of his sword.

"Relax, children," a smooth male voice that was like rippling water said. It sounded vaguely amused. "The moonlight will not hurt you. It is already fading."

Cautiously, I opened my eyes. Standing in the center of a small room was a tall man with long, silver hair. He was clad in a dark purple *kimono* with tiny moons embroidered in the fabric, and he carried a silver staff topped with a crescent moon. He regarded us with eyes the color of molten steel in a way that should have made me nervous, except that he radiated an aura of tranquility that instantly smoothed my nerves.

While I was standing there, gawking like a slack-jawed yokel, Raiden, Shota, and the *kyuubi* dropped to the ground, prostrating themselves.

"Tsukuyomi-sama," Shota said gravely, pressing his forehead into the dirt. "It is an honor."

Tsukuyomi? Alarmed, I dropped to the ground next to my friends, despite the *kami's* non-threatening presence. Hell, I'd never seen the *kyuubi* bow to *anyone*. Tsukuyomi was Amaterasu's brother-husband, the god of the moon. He wasn't as powerful as the sun goddess, since he had to borrow some of her light, but he was one of the oldest gods around, and I was pretty sure that he could turn us into a smudge on the floor if he wanted to.

"Rise, children," the moon god said calmly. "There is no need for such ceremony here."

Warily, we got to our feet.

"Are you here to help us, Tsukuyomi-sama?" I asked. "Or are you on Kai's side?" I didn't remember the old stories very well, but I vaguely recalled that Amaterasu and Tsukuyomi weren't on speaking terms. Was the moon god an enemy?

The moon god shook his head. "I am no friend of Amatsu Mika-boshi," he said gravely, the silver light around him flickering. "I come here asking for a favor, and in exchange, I will give you a tool you may find useful when you meet Kai."

"What is the favor?" Raiden asked warily.

Tsukuyomi sighed, pulling a letter from the sleeve of his robe. "I have been trying to apologize to Amaterasu for centuries about the old misunderstanding between us, but she will not hear me. I beseech you to read this letter to her for me." His silver eyes bore into mine as he thrust the letter in my direction. "She will not be expecting the words to come from your mouth, and so will not have time to close her ears before you give her my message."

"I see." I reached for the letter, but paused, my fingers a millimeter away from it. "Do you want me to go to one of her shrines and read it to her?"

"No. There will be a time when you speak to the sun goddess directly. That is when you will give her the message." Tsukuyomi pressed the letter into my hand. "Do you agree?"

I swallowed, painfully aware of the weight of the god's stare. This letter was very important, and I had a feeling that if I failed to deliver the message, bad things would happen to me. But what choice did I have? We needed to defeat Kai, and any help I could get was welcome.

"I promise," I said, taking the letter.

"Good." Tsukuyomi waved his hand. A crescent-shaped object that looked like it was crafted from pure moonlight appeared in his palm, and he handed it to me. "This sliver of moonlight will pulse when someone is telling a lie."

Whoa. So it really *was* made of pure moonlight. "How is this supposed to help us defeat Kai?" I asked as I took it from him. The sliver was cold in my hand, but even still, it hummed with power.

"That is for you to discover," the moon god said. He waved a hand and disappeared in a flash of silver light.

"Huh." I turned back to Raiden and Shota, who both looked nonplussed. "Why do I feel like I just got bilked?"

"Shhh!" Raiden hissed, scowling at me. "He might be listening. You don't want to piss him off, not after he gave you such a valuable gift."

"Shit." I hadn't thought about that. "You know, I've spent my entire life believing that gods don't exist. It's going to take a bit of getting used to that there might be *kami* watching my every move." The idea sent an unpleasant shiver down my spine, and my shoulders hunched instinctively. It was bad enough that Big Brother was taking over the country—did I really need gods butting into my life all the time too?

Shota gave me a gentle smile, as if he could tell exactly what I was thinking. "It's part of being a shaman, Aika. The responsibility of being able to bridge the gap between the *Reikai* and the human world means we don't get to live normal lives like other people."

"Really? After getting attacked by a human-sized frog, riding the back of a giant sea turtle, stealing a monkey king's liver, and attending an undersea ball, I would never have guessed."

Raiden chuckled. "Don't forget fighting off animated corpses, talking to gods, and preparing to take down the most evil god in the Japanese pantheon."

That sobered us up. "Right. We should probably get going with that."

I pulled the *kyuubi* back inside my body, then turned toward the door. Alongside the fire burning in my veins from my *yokai* were fear and anticipation—Kai was on the other side. I knew it in my soul.

"Aika," Raiden said as I began to walk toward the door. There was a warning note in his voice. "You should let me go first." He tried to move in front of me, but I pushed him aside, my feet moving as if of their own accord. I didn't know why, but something told me I had to be the one to open this door. I had to go through first.

The moment my hand curled around the brass doorknob, a feeling of peace and contentment swept through me. It felt like coming home, like I was on the verge of entering a paradise, a safe haven. As if fate had been leading me to this door since I was born, and that the beginning of my life waited beyond the threshold.

But how could that be? My enemy, the man who had killed innocents, and who had stolen my mother away, was waiting beyond that door.

I half-expected the handle to be locked. But it gave easily, and the door swung open into a grand hall, the kind you might find in a *daimyo's* castle. Thousands of paper lanterns hung from the ceiling, shining light onto the glossy, dark wood floor where *yokai* dressed in beautiful *kimonos* danced and performed tricks with fire and illusion magic. The walls were *shoji* screens, with beautiful artwork of pastoral scenes painted on them.

And toward the back of the room, sitting on a dais, was Kai.

Even if I hadn't recognized him from the murals on the walls, I would have known it was Kai. Something deep inside me flared to life in recognition, and I felt a surprising surge of affection. He was dressed like a *daimyo*, with gorgeous gold, black, and red armor, his long black hair pulled back from a sternly handsome face and tied into a samurai topknot. But what surprised me the most were his eyes—they were a golden-brown, with laugh lines branching out from the corners. The eyes of a human man, not a power-hungry shaman possessed by a dark god.

Those warm eyes met mine from across the room, and the whole world stopped. The dancers froze in their positions, the lanterns stopped flickering, and I stopped breathing. An intense longing filled my chest, followed on its heels by bitter sadness and disappointment. Part of me wanted to run to this man and throw myself into his arms, part of me wanted to grab him by the shoulders and shake sense into him.

And the rest of me was confused as hell.

"Fumiko." Kai rose from his seat, joy blazing in his eyes. The dancers parted, and shock rippled through me as I finally saw my mother. She was sitting next to Kai, dressed in a silk white robe, staring numbly into space as if in a trance. "You came back to me!"

"I didn't come back for you," I spat, ignoring the fact that he'd called me Fumiko. I was vibrating with rage now, the fuzzy feelings gone. "I came for my mother. What have you done to her?"

But Kai wasn't listening. His gaze had moved to Raiden. "You," he hissed, paling with anger. "It wasn't enough for you to take her away to the afterlife, you had to come back with her too? I should have known you couldn't leave well enough alone."

"How typical," Raiden growled, grasping his dragon blade in both hands. He sounded different, his face a diamond-hard mask of anger. "It's always about you, isn't it? I see that being stuck in a cave for two thousand years hasn't made you any less selfish, Kai."

"What are you two talking about?" I cried, stepping between them. My heart was pounding hard now as animosity crackled in the air between them, and for some reason, it tore at me. I didn't want these two to fight.

Which was absurd, because the entire reason Raiden and I had come here *was* to fight.

"You're trying to tell me that you don't know what you've done?" Kai sneered, looking at me. There was so much rage and betrayal in his eyes, it stole my breath. "You didn't just bring any shaman into my tomb with you, Fumiko. You brought Haruki and Kaga!"

23

"Wait just a damn minute!" I yelled, jumping in front of Raiden and Shota as Kai drew his sword. "You can't just throw stuff out there like that and then attack us!"

Kai glowered at me, his hands tightening on the hilt of his *katana*. "I'm not attacking you," he said. "It's Haruki that I want to fight!"

"What am I, chopped liver?" Shota scoffed. He brandished his *kusarigama*.

Kai scoffed. "You never were a match for me, Kaga. I could kill you without breaking a sweat."

"Kaga?" Shota repeated, blinking in confusion. "Are...are you saying...?"

"This is ridiculous," I snapped. "Raiden is not Haruki, and Shota is not Kaga!"

Tears burned at the corners of my eyes, and I felt the sudden, irrational need to stomp my foot and engage in a full-on temper tantrum. "I'm not Fumiko, and none of this is real! You're just using your magic to manipulate us, aren't you!" I accused, jabbing a finger at him.

Kai's face slackened with shock. "You really have no idea, do you?" He glared at Raiden over my shoulder. "Did you deliberately keep this from her? And you say *I'm* selfish!"

"Wait a damn second." Raiden held up his hands. His gaze darted between us, and he looked as if someone had just dropped an anvil on him. "I knew about you and me, but I had no idea Shota was Kaga!"

I whirled around to face Raiden. "What is that supposed to mean?" I demanded. "Were you lying to me this whole time?"

"No." Raiden clenched his jaw. "I wasn't certain it was true, so I didn't push it. But I did warn you back at Ryujin's palace that there was a strong possibility you might be Fumiko reincarnated. That's why I didn't want to come here, but you dismissed my concerns."

"Yeah, well, you didn't exactly give me specifics, and you *definitely* didn't tell me about *you* being Haruki's reincarnation." I crossed my arms over my chest. "Is Kai telling the truth about that?"

"You already know that I am," Kai said. "The moonlight in your hand is proof."

I frowned. I'd completely forgotten about the sliver of moonlight. My heart sank as I realized it hadn't pulsed in my hand, not once during this entire conversation. Either Kai was telling the truth, or...

"You could be mistaken," I said, my voice tinged with desperation. "Just because you believe I'm Fumiko doesn't mean it's true. And Raiden and Shota..."

"Aika." Raiden's voice was heavy with defeat. "I had strange dreams when I was small, dreams in which I saw both your face and Kai's. And when I was fourteen, a fortune teller told me I would meet a woman who would help me reunite the clans."

"Raiden told me all about the dreams," Shota said. "When he first met you, he said the memories came rushing back, and that he was confident you were the person the fortune teller had mentioned."

"So *that's* why you've been pushing me away." My mind whirled with the implications of all this, even as relief at finally knowing the truth swept through me. "Because some fortune teller told you guys that Raiden and I are supposed to be together?"

"Ridiculous," Kai scoffed. "That fortune teller is obviously a charlatan. Haruki is the wrong man for you, Fumiko. He will only bring you ruin and disappointment."

"I think you've got me confused with yourself," Raiden snarled, his face reddening with anger. "*You* are the one who brought ruin and disappointment on us all when you killed Kaga!"

Kai flinched. "I admit that killing Kaga was a mistake," he said. "Amatsu whispered lies in my ear and convinced me that Kaga was going to kill Fumiko once the four of us completed the marriage ritual."

"Wait a damn second." Shota held up a hand. "The *four* of us? What does that mean? I thought she was marrying Haruki!"

Kai shook his head. "You really don't remember anything, do you?" His gaze locked with mine. "Do you truly recall nothing of our time together, Fumiko?"

"I..." I wracked my brain for something, *anything,* that linked me to him. But though I felt that same tug in my heart I felt for Raiden and Shota, I was drawing a blank. How was all of this possible? Was I somehow imprinting on every male shaman I ran across? But then again, I'd felt no connection at all when I'd first met Mamoru, and he was a shaman.

Thank the gods for that. The very idea of being forcibly attracted to that old man made me shudder.

"I can see you are familiar with all the players in our story," Kai said silkily, "but clearly you all have the wrong version. Fumiko did not choose Haruki. She chose *all* of us."

"All?" Raiden said in a strangled voice. "She was going to marry all three clan leaders?"

"Well that explains a lot," Shota said weakly. He was staring at me as if he'd never seen me before. "A shaman queen with three husbands. That has to be a first."

"There were some who protested, but Queen Himiko approved of Fumiko's decision," Kai said. He smiled proudly at me. "You were strong like your mother, Fumiko, but you did not have her head or passion for battle. You knew that choosing only one of us for your husband would not be enough to quell the hostilities, so you decided to bind yourself to all of us."

"You're lying," Raiden growled. He took a step toward Kai, gripping his *katana* tighter. "There is no way she was meant to marry all of us."

"For once, you and I are in agreement," Kai said, raising his sword. "Fumiko is mine, and I shall complete the marriage ritual once and for all and break this curse!"

"Stop it!" I shrieked as the two of them charged at each other. Raiden's dragon blade flashed with white-hot energy, and he launched a lightning bolt at Kai.

Kai stepped back, his sword arcing up in a flash to catch the crackling blast of energy. It slammed into the flat edge of his blade in a flurry of sparks, and as he stepped sideways, deflecting it harmlessly, Shota attacked.

Fire sprang from his *kusarigama* and shot through the air like a white-hot comet. Kai's other hand came up, a scrap of paper in it.

The paper flared like the sun, the symbols on it exploding with light as a nearly translucent shield of energy appeared just as the fireball would have hit him. Fire washed over the shield, but it didn't matter. Shota was already charging in.

The chain of his *kusarigama* whipped through the air, and as Kai brought his sword up to block it, the chain wrapped around the sword. Shota tugged on the weapon, and as Kai stumbled forward, Raiden launched another volley of electricity at him.

As Kai tried to react, releasing his sword and going for more paper magic, the lightning bolt slammed into his chest, lifting him from his feet and flinging him backward. He crashed into the dais, right next to my mother, in a flash of light and sound that shook the room.

"No! My mom is too close!" My heart leapt into my throat.

"Get her," Shota said, his voice icily calm as he watched Kai lay there, his robes smoking.

"Yeah, we'll keep you safe," Raiden promised as my mother shook her head, the fog clearing from her eyes.

"W-what's happening?" she asked in a trembling voice as she looked around.

"Mom!" I sprinted across the room to her, desperate to get to her before Kai recovered or the boys decided to fling around more elemental power. Either could result in her getting hurt by proximity, and I couldn't let that happen.

"Aika?" my mom asked, eyes flitting toward me as I pulled her frail body into my arms.

"Mom, I'm so glad you're okay!" My voice cracked, and relief rushed through me as I pulled her away from Kai, trying my best to shield her and hug her at the same time.

"Aika, you shouldn't have come," she said, her voice full of worry. Her body sagged against mine, and I was alarmed at how cold her skin was. "Kai is not going to let you go now that he is here. He needs—"

"Be silent," Kai snarled, his voice laced with pain and anger. Gasping, I twisted around to see him staggering to his feet. "Did you think that was enough to kill me?" A small smile flitted across his lips. "You're both so much weaker than before, and you couldn't stop me then."

"Trust me, Kai. If I wanted you dead, you'd be dead," Raiden snarled. Katsu's red aura flared out all around him, making him look even more deadly. "I was just trying to knock some sense into you."

"Then you are more foolish than I thought possible, Haruki." Darkness swirled around the wound in Kai's chest as he spoke, and my mouth dropped in horror as I realized the darkness was healing him. "Amaterasu's curse has ensured I will never die. There is no way for you to defeat me, even with that impressive weapon of yours. Despite how much help you have." A twisted smile filled his face as his eyes flicked to Shota.

"Dammit, will you all stop fighting already!" I cried as Kai took a step forward, all traces of damage gone.

"No," Kai replied, his eyes twisted with darkness and hatred as they settled back on me. "Know that I do this for you. For us. Once they are gone, you'll see that."

He leapt forward, charging across the distance in a flash of concentrated darkness. His fist leapt like a striking serpent, smashing into the underside of Shota's chin, and as he staggered backward, his *kusarigama* slipped from his hand.

Kai snatched it from the air as he pivoted, blocking Raiden's sword strike with the chain. Then, before the lightning shaman could recover, Kai twisted the chain, binding up the sword and ripping it from Raiden's grip.

As the weapon clattered uselessly to the ground, Kai slammed his knee into Raiden's gut, doubling him over. Breath exploded from Raiden's lips in a cry of pain right before Kai grabbed him by the hair and flung him into the still-recovering Shota.

Both men went down in a heap, crashing to the ground like a pair of broken mannequins as Kai calmly scooped up his fallen sword. Darkness rippled off him in waves as he turned to face me.

"I know it seems harsh, Fumiko, but once they are gone, you'll realize the truth." He turned back to them and raised his sword, rage and anger flashing in his dark eyes.

There is no point in trying to reason with him, the *kyuubi* growled in my head. *Let me out, and we shall finish this the old-fashioned way.*

She was right. If I didn't stop Kai, he'd kill them, and if the only way to do that was with brute force, then so be it. Gently, I pushed my mother aside and summoned the *kyuubi* from my body. The fire fox appeared in a flash of sapphire flame, towering over us all in her true form, causing Kai to stop mid-step.

"What are you doing?" he asked, turning to look at me, brows drawn in confusion.

"Attack Kai!" I ordered her.

"Wait—"

The *kyuubi* cut off the rest of his words with a surge of flame that hit him like a nuclear blast. Flame swirled around him, engulfing him in an inferno that melted the stones beneath his feet... only that was all it did.

Smoky darkness burst out of his hands as the flames raged around him, wrapping him in a protective layer of...something. He stood there, fire seething all around him as the darkness pouring from him exploded outward in a rage of wind and chaos, snuffing out the fire and leaving Kai standing there completely unharmed.

"As I said," he said, looking at me, and if anything he just seemed annoyed. "Your attacks will not hurt me. The cursed sun goddess saw to that." He snorted. "It's funny, in a way," he added, turning back to look at Shota and Raiden, who had done little more than disentangle themselves. "By cursing me, she has ensured their destruction."

"That may be true," Raiden growled, finally getting to his feet. "But I still have to try."

Shota nodded, his hands outstretched as he tried to summon fire. It snapped and popped around his palms and fingers, but Kai merely laughed.

"Should I let you strike me just to prove how weak you are?" He spread his arms wide, giving his chest. "Go on. Hit me with everything you have." His lips curled into a satisfied smile. "And when you have exhausted every last effort, I will break your legs so that you can only crawl like the treacherous dogs you both are."

"Stop!" I threw up my hands as I stepped between them. I might not be able to hurt Kai, but I still couldn't let him hurt Shota or Raiden. "Don't you want to be free, Kai?"

His eyes flicked to me, and his features softened.

"Aika, what are you—"

I cut off Shota's words with a wave of one hand as I met Kai's gaze.

"Well?" I raised an eyebrow at the dark shaman.

"I do." He nodded once, voice strained with emotion.

"So how do you expect us to set you free?" I put my hands on my hips. "You are a tool of Amatsu Mikaboshi. If we free you, what is to stop you from draining the power from every last shaman and allowing Amatsu Mikaboshi to take over the world?"

Kai looked as though I'd struck him in the face. "Is that why you thought I brought you here?"

I put my hands on my hips. "Is there another reason?"

"I do not wish for Amatsu Mikaboshi to rule the world." Kai finally lowered his sword. "I brought you here to help me break Amaterasu's curse," he added quietly, his voice tinged with sadness. "You're the only one who can help."

The moonbeam in my hand remained still, telling me that Kai spoke the truth.

"Are you nuts? Why would I help you?" I asked, even as I started to feel sympathetic for him. "You've hurt and killed so many innocent people."

"Yes, and now I'm trying to atone for that," Kai said desperately. "Didn't you see the shrine I made to Amaterasu? And all the flowers I left for you?"

"You think flowers are enough to make up for all the damage you've done?" I asked incredulously. "You kidnapped my *mother!*"

"You don't understand..." Kai sheathed his *katana* and moved toward me. "I just..." His throat bobbed, and he reached out and took my hands in his. "The only way to break the curse is for the two of us to marry. Please, Fumiko." He got down on his knees. "Take me as your husband, just as we were meant to do all those years ago. The gods will take that as a sign that you have forgiven me, and I will finally be free of Amatsu."

Raiden let out an incredulous laugh, and the sound of it wrenched my gaze away from Kai.

"Are you kidding me?" he snarled, hands clenched into a white-knuckled grip on his dragon blade. "You think that forcing Aika to marry you by holding her mother hostage will motivate Amaterasu to break the curse?" He shook his head. "You really haven't learned anything at all."

"Be silent!" Kai snapped, his eyes flaring with anger again. "You shouldn't even be here, Haruki."

"No, he's right." I tugged my hands free from Kai's, stepping back. "You've done evil things, Kai. Even if I did marry you, it wouldn't be enough to absolve you."

"And you're still draining shamans," Shota added, nodding his head toward the way we'd come. "If we hadn't saved them, they'd all be dead now."

"I didn't drain those shamans," Kai protested, his eyes flicking between the three of us. "Amatsu did. And I haven't hurt your mother at all. She's been well taken care of. I didn't even put her in the dungeon with all the others."

"My mother is dying from an incurable disease!" I snapped. "You put her in danger just by taking her!" I glanced toward where my mother was still sitting, and my stomach dropped at the sight of her shivering, clutching her arms around her body. "If I really was Fumiko, I don't know how I could have ever trusted you."

Kai's eyes flickered, as if a light bulb had gone off in his head. "*Ogama*," he snapped. The giant frog appeared at his side in a puff of purple smoke. "Take Fumiko's mother back to her home."

"No!" my mom cried, reaching for me. But it was too late—the *ogama* pounced on her, and the two of them disappeared in another puff of smoke.

"There," Kai said, a satisfied look on his face. "Your mother is out of danger. I no longer hold any leverage over you."

"You mean except for the fact that you won't let her leave," Shota said dryly. "Real class act, you are."

"You are incorrect." Kai spread his hands wide. "You are free to leave if you wish, Aika. But it is only a matter of time before

Amatsu comes back, and when he does, he will take over my body again and kill you all. We must act before that happens."

"Wait a minute," I said. "If Amatsu isn't here, where is he?"

"In the *Reikai*." Kai glowered. "Lucky bastard, such as he is, was able to dive right back through the barrier as soon as he was free. That's how he's been able to summon *yokai* here, and into the rest of the world, to do our bidding. He's in the *Reikai* right now, resting after glutting himself on all those shamans he drained." He sheathed his sword and took a step toward us. "Amaterasu bound my life to his so that he wouldn't be able to escape into the human world when she sealed us away in the tomb. That's why I can't be killed. If I died, he would be free."

Raiden, Shota, and I exchanged puzzled looks. "So, if the curse is broken, doesn't that mean you'll die?" Shota asked cautiously. "And that Amatsu will be stuck in the *Reikai*?"

Kai shook his head. "I'll live out my normal lifespan happily with Fumiko as husband and wife." He beamed at me. "Just as we were meant to be."

The moonbeam pulsed in my hand.

"You're lying about something," I said, backing away. "You're never going to be able to just live with me in peace as husband and wife, even if the curse is broken. You're too attached to Amatsu, aren't you?"

Kai opened his mouth to argue, but I shook my head. "I can't do this," I said, my gut churning with anxiety. "I can't marry you."

Kai's eyes narrowed to slits. "It's because of him, isn't it?" he hissed, turning on Raiden. "You still have feelings for this sorry excuse of a man, a man who couldn't bring himself to tell you the truth when he had the chance!" Anger poured off him in waves as he yanked his sword from its sheath. "You have always been in the way of our happiness, Haruki, and I will not stand for it any longer. Prepare yourself!"

24

Kai's sword lashed out through the air, and I instinctively cringed away as the clang of it smashing into Raiden's dragon blade filled my ears.

Kai bore down, pressing on Raiden's sword and forcing him backward a half step. The image of Katsu flared around Raiden as he swiveled, whipping his wrist around and using Kai's momentum against him. Kai's sword twisted out of his grip, and before he had a chance to react, Raiden delivered a well-placed kick to his knee.

The sickening sound of bone snapping echoed in the room, and Kai screamed. He crumpled to the ground as Raiden brought his blade back around, smashing the edge into Kai's face. The blow should have sliced straight through him, but as it struck, darkness writhed around Kai's body, absorbing the killing intent of the blow even as Kai went flying across the room.

As Kai skidded across the ground, Raiden pointed the dragon

blade at him and unleashed another blast of lightning. Electricity tore from the sky, slamming into Kai. Arcs of electricity leapt across his flesh, but as before, the darkness kept most of the damage at bay.

Raiden sucked in a breath, his chest heaving, and as he did, Shota raised his *kusarigama* and unleashed hell. Fire rained from the sky, once again engulfing Kai, but even as the stones melted and the room flared like a dying sun, I could tell it didn't matter.

As the blaze died away, Kai chuckled darkly. He got to his feet without a care in the world and then very intentionally put his weight on his ruined knee—it was already healed.

"Not good enough. Not by a longshot."

Raiden's eyes narrowed as he pointed his sword at Kai. "Stop, Kai. You aren't good enough to beat me on your own." He spat. "You never were. Not then and not now."

"You're forgetting one thing," Kai said slowly, lifting his hands. "I won last time."

Kai lifted a hand toward the sky, gathering tendrils of darkness around it. The darkness swirled into a pitch-black *katana* that seemed to suck all the light from the room into it. He whipped it through the air, and tendrils of black ink trailed from the blade as he strode forward.

"Siding with darkness isn't going to help you," Raiden said right before Kai struck again. Raiden sidestepped, moving out of the blade's reach before lunging in and jabbing Kai in the stomach with the point of his dragon blade. But the attack didn't affect Kai, and worse, it left Raiden's side exposed.

"I've got you," Kai crowed, swinging his blade back around to end the fight. But before it could connect, Shota whipped one hand up, brandishing an *ofuda*. A blast of superheated steam exploded from the paper, catching Kai in the face.

Kai staggered back, his screams mingling with the sound of searing flesh, but Shota didn't stop there. He lashed out once again with his *kusarigama*, wrapping the flaming chain around Kai's sword and jerking him forward. Despite his sword turning molten hot, Kai held it fast even as he lost his balance and toppled forward.

Raiden took a deep breath, pushing himself back into the fight and summoning more lightning to his sword. He flung the crackling energy at Kai. The bolt slammed into Kai in a burst of snapping electricity, sending him skidding across the ground.

But instead of lying there stunned, like he did last time, Kai jack-knifed to his feet as if nothing had happened.

"You just don't get it, do you, " Kai said. "You literally *cannot* defeat me. I am immortal."

"I may not be able to kill you, but that doesn't mean I can't beat you!" Raiden snarled, launching himself at Kai.

"Raiden, stop!" Shota called, but Raiden was too far gone to hear. This time, Kai didn't even bother to counter Raiden's attack. He just stood there, taking blow after blow, as Raiden unleashed the full force of his fury against him. Lightning bolts, sword strikes, punches, kicks—Raiden let him have it all. But none of it seemed to affect Kai, and my heart sank as I watched the darkness repair him over and over again.

Worse, Raiden was getting slower with each blow. Sweat poured from his face and his clothing stuck to his body. I had no idea how much power he had left, but I knew it wouldn't be enough.

"What do you want me to do?" Shota asked, looking at me. "I can help, but..."

"It won't matter," I said, swallowing hard as I realized the truth. We couldn't beat him. At least not while the darkness was healing him, anyway. Worse, if it kept up, Raiden would get himself killed. After all, Kai just had to get him once.

"Yeah." Shota tightened his grip on his weapon, and I could tell he was going to try anyway. Whether it was to stop Kai, help Raiden, or something else entirely, I couldn't tell, but either way, he was going to attack. That wouldn't help things.

"Stop!" I rushed forward, putting myself between Kai and Shota. "Both of you, please. I'm begging you."

"No," Kai said, and there was such finality in the word it stole my breath away. He met my gaze, the cold, dead look in his eyes turning my stomach to lead. "Haruki must die if we are to move forward."

"My name is not Haruki!" Raiden cried as he drove the crackling lightning blade in his hands straight into Kai's stomach. I screamed as the blade burst through Kai's back in a spray of black ichor that hit the ground before bursting into clouds of sulfur-smelling smoke.

"I did it," Raiden wheezed, his chest heaving.

But Kai only shook his head, casting a scornful glance at him. He didn't seem the least bit fazed. "No, Haruki. You only did what I let you." He lifted his black *katana*, and cold horror spilled through me as I realized Kai was about to deliver the killing blow. And with Raiden's sword stuck in Kai's guts, there wasn't a thing he could do to defend himself.

"Shit." Raiden's face paled, and he stumbled back, releasing his hold on the mythical blade. Kai laughed, following Raiden, completely unconcerned about the *katana* sticking out of his belly.

"Enjoy the afterlife, Haruki," he said, and brought the blade down.

"No!" I yelled, launching myself forward without thinking. I slammed my shoulder into Raiden, pushing him past the blade's arc and to safety moments before Kai's blade connected with my back.

"Fumiko!" Kai screamed as the blade ripped my flesh open. My knees buckled, and I collapsed to the ground, blood gushing all over me. "What have you done!"

"Aika!" Shota yelled. His footsteps pounded against the floor as he ran to my side, and his face was twisted in grief and anger as he dropped to his knees next to me. "Aika, no!" His voice was choked with tears as he pulled me into his arms.

Gasping in agony, I touched the *furi* charm on my bracelet. The *yokai's* power pulsed inside me, filling me up with its warmth and leeching the pain of the wound away. I held my breath, hoping with all my might that the *furi* wouldn't die by taking the wound in my stead. I couldn't die, not like this, but I also didn't want the *yokai* my father had given me to die either.

As Shota cradled me against his chest, the pulses of power gradually grew stronger inside me, until they finally built to a crescendo. I felt a flash within my chest, and then very slowly, the *furi* retreated back into the charm. After a moment, I let out a breath of relief. He was alive, but barely.

"You..." Kai lowered his sword, astonished. Blood spattered his clothes and skin from where he'd sliced into me with his sword, and tears shone in his dark eyes. "You're not hurt?"

"No," I said, pressing a hand against the freshly healed wound. Shota's hand covered my own, and I looked up to see him staring at me with the same astonished look as Kai.

"I've never seen anything like that in my life," he said. "You should be dead."

I gave him a lopsided smile. "I guess this *yokai* shaman gig isn't so bad after all."

"It was still foolish," Kai snapped, his gaze growing stormy.

"The only one being foolish here is *you,*" I scolded, getting to my feet. "I'm sorry, but I just can't have a repeat of history. You can't kill Raiden, Kai. You can't kill Shota either, for that matter. That isn't going to solve anything."

"So you're choosing them over me," Kai said bitterly, looking away. "You would truly damn me to this hell?"

"Kai..." I lifted my hands to his face, finally giving in to the ache to touch him. "I want to help you," I said, stroking his cheek. My fingers smeared my blood across his skin, and somehow the gesture seemed like an oath. "But marrying me isn't going to do it, not on its own. You wronged Haruki, Kaga, *and* Fumiko with your actions. If you want to be free of Amaterasu's curse, you have to atone for *all* of those sins."

Kai sucked in a shuddering breath, closing his eyes. His dark lashes fanned against his cheeks, and I ached at the tortured expression on his face. He looked both euphoric and devastated, and as I reached for the *ofuda* in my pocket, I suddenly found myself struck by misgivings.

Was sealing Kai away *really* the right thing to do?

"I can't tell you how long I've waited for you to look at me like this again," he whispered, cupping the side of my face. "But I don't know if I have it in me to forgive Haruki for what he did. I know I need to atone for what I did to you," he said, briefly looking at Shota, "but Haruki...he *took* you from me, Fumiko." His voice trembled as he spoke the words. "And I was left to suffer in this tomb for two thousand years, simply for daring to love you."

A tear slipped down my cheek at the anguish in his voice, and I suddenly knew that even though I might not be the woman Kai had loved, I *did* care about him. I couldn't let him suffer like this. He'd done terrible things, but he didn't deserve for his soul to be tortured for all of eternity, held fast in Amatsu's dark clutches.

"If you really love me like you say you do," I said as Raiden struggled to his feet behind me, "then you have to forgive all of us. We'll never be able to be together if you don't." I wasn't promising to marry Kai, not by a long shot, but I didn't want to detract from the point by mentioning that. Breaking this curse was more important, and I instinctively knew it hinged on Kai letting go of the hatred in his heart.

Some of the darkness in Kai's eyes lifted. "I would do anything for you," he said fervently. He dropped his hand from my cheek, then turned to Raiden, who was staring at us both with a shell-shocked look on his face. "Haruki, I—"

A loud *boom* echoed throughout the chamber, and I shrieked as a black hole opened behind Kai.

"Dammit!" Kai roared as a huge black arm with swirling red runes reached out of the vortex and grabbed him around the waist. He fought against his attacker as he was pulled back, slashing at the huge black arm with his sword, but the strikes were completely ineffective.

"No!" I shrieked, lunging at Kai. I grabbed for his legs, but Shota caught me around the waist and pulled me back.

"Are you crazy!" he shouted, pulling me back. "You'll get sucked in too!"

"Fumiko!" Kai shouted, his arms outstretched toward me. "I lo—"

The black hole sucked him in, cutting off the rest of his statement. But I damn well knew what he was about to say, and tears flooded my eyes. Kai and Fumiko's love had been a powerful thing—the powerful ache in my chest for a man I didn't know was testament to that.

"Let go of me," I sobbed, shoving at Shota's chest. "It's over."

Shota did as I said, backing away, but as he did I caught sight of Raiden.

The look on his face said that this was far from over. His eyes blazed with fury, and his skin was stretched taut across his face, as if he were about to explode.

"I can't believe you," Raiden snarled, his voice vibrating with rage. "You had the chance to seal him away. I saw you reaching for the *ofuda* in your pocket. Why didn't you use it?"

"Because," I said brokenly, "I wanted to save him."

Raiden flinched. "Save him? After all he's done to you? To *us?*" He gestured at Shota for emphasis.

"It's not like that—" I started to protest, my heart twisting at the betrayal in Raiden's eyes. But before I could explain, the walls around us began to shake. Several of the lanterns fell to the ground, and I gasped in horror as their flames began to lick at the wooden floorboards.

"Shit," Shota swore, grabbing my hand. "This place is collapsing. We need to get to the shrine!"

More lanterns began to rain down from the ceiling as we

sprinted from the room. Shota clutched my hand in his, and though it was a bit too tight, I didn't complain, focusing all my attention on running. The stairs began to crumble as we raced down them, and I shrieked as one gave out from beneath me. Raiden caught me as my hand slipped from Shota's, yanking me into his arms before I could fall down, and I stumbled for a second before I got my feet underneath me and kept running.

Thankfully it wasn't that far, and we managed to dodge and weave as pieces of ceiling crashed to the ground all around us.

My lungs burned and adrenaline surged in my veins as cracks opened up in the ground. By the time we made it back to the dungeon, the earth was shaking so hard we were clinging to the walls, barely able to keep upright.

To my relief, the *tengu* rushed out of the dungeon to greet us.

"Come on!" the *yokai* roared, spreading his enormous wings over us to shield us from falling debris. "Get to the shrine!"

"Take us to the Takaoka Shrine!" I shouted as Shota hastily clapped his hands. "We need to get to my mother!"

Nodding, Shota rang the bell twice. The familiar flash of light blinded me, and I held on tight as we were swept into the current of the *Reikai*, hoping against hope that my mother was okay.

25

"Mom," I yelled, bursting through the front door of our apartment. The moment we'd arrived at the Takaoka Shrine, I'd rushed down to the first floor and caught a cab at the curb. The cab ride had been filled with tension. Raiden had refused to look at me the entire time. He was still angry at me for what I'd done. Shota had stared out the window numbly, obviously still trying to process everything he'd been told. But he'd also kept my hand gripped tightly in his, as if he couldn't stand to let go of me after watching me nearly die. I was incredibly grateful he wasn't angry at me too—I wasn't sure if I could handle both of them giving me the cold shoulder at the same time.

I couldn't really blame the two of them for being out of sorts. Everything they thought they'd known had been turned on its head. Hell, *I* was struggling to wrap my head around it all. On the one hand, I was relieved that my feelings were finally vindicated. I wasn't imagining my connection to Raiden and Shota.

But on the other hand, how did we know Kai was telling the truth? Could he really be trusted? Yes, the moonlight Tsukuyomi had given me hadn't reacted, but just because Kai didn't think he was lying didn't mean he was right. What if Raiden's version of events was the real story? I didn't know how to determine which one was correct. But that was a problem for another day.

Right now, I just needed to see my mother.

"Aika?" my mother called from her bedroom as I rushed up the stairs. My heart soared—her voice sounded weaker than ever, but it was there. I dashed into her room to see her lying atop her rumpled bed sheets, still wearing the silk robe Kai had given her.

"Mom," I choked out, falling onto my knees next to the bed. I gathered her up in my arms and rocked her, my tears soaking her clammy skin. "I'm so glad Kai kept his word."

"He is not an evil man," my mother whispered, her voice barely audible. "He did not lie when he said he tried to keep me as comfortable as he could. That tea he gave me numbed the pain from my illness and made it easier to bear."

"I'm so glad to hear that," I said, my voice trembling. Gently as I could, I laid my mom back on the bed sheets. "You're way too cold, Mom, and weak. I'm going to call an ambulance."

"No," she whispered, her gaze heavy with exhaustion. "It is too late. All that travel through the *Reikai* has sapped my strength. The doctors can do nothing to help me."

Her words hit me so hard in the chest I couldn't breathe. "No," I croaked, fumbling for the cell phone that wasn't in my pocket. Panicking, I turned to Raiden and Shota. "Let me borrow one of your phones," I said frantically. "We need to call 911, now!"

Shota shook his head, his dark eyes filled with sadness. "It's already happening now. Look."

Slowly, dread weighing my motions, I turned back to my mother. A blue glow was emanating from her skin, and as I stared, her spirit gradually began to lift from her body.

"Please, Mom," I begged, grasping her cold hand. "Don't leave me."

"I will never truly leave you." My mother's spirit fully separated from her body, and she smiled down at me. Grief swelled in my throat, but on its heels was a strange sort of happiness. My mother's spirit form looked different from her body—her face was unlined by weariness, and she had long, dark hair that hung to her waist, just like it had been before the cancer. She wore one of her knee-length dresses with the cap sleeves that she loved so much, and her face glowed with an inner contentment.

"Don't despair, Aika," she said softly, reaching for me with a ghostly hand. Her fingers passed through my face, but they left a warm tingle on my skin, as if she'd really touched me. "It is my time to go. And you will not be alone, not so long as you have that young man with you." She looked at Raiden. "You will take care of my Aika, won't you?"

I turned back to Raiden, and my heart sank at the expressionless look on his face. God, did he hate me now for what I'd done? Would he reject my mother's dying wish?

But he simply inclined his head respectfully. "I will guard her with my life, Fujiwara-san."

"Good." My mother beamed, then turned her head to the sky. "I can pass on in peace. Your father will be coming soon."

"My father?" I asked, excitement banishing some of the grief. I hadn't considered that I might be able to meet his spirit, but it made sense—my mother's next of kin would come to guide her into the afterlife.

"Here he is now," my mother said as the air next to her began to shimmer. Another glowing spirit appeared, and my mouth dropped open in shock and dismay. It wasn't my father at all, but a wrinkled old man wearing ancient Japanese armor, his hair secured in a samurai topknot.

"Oh!" My mother's eyes widened. "Who are you?"

"I am your great-grandfather, Genzo," the old man said, frowning. "Were you expecting someone else?"

"My husband," she said, confusion and hurt in her voice. "Fujiwara Hidetada. Why has he not come for me?"

"Your husband!" Genzo exclaimed. "Why would he come for you? He is not dead." He reached for my mother. "Come, Hamako. We must cross over to the *Reikai* now, before it's too late."

"Wait!" I cried as he grasped her hand. "If my father isn't dead, then where is he?"

My great-great-grandfather looked me dead in the eye. "You must find that out for yourself. Before it is too late."

And with that, he disappeared, leaving me with a hole in my chest and a mountain of questions I couldn't hope to answer.

To be continued...

Aika's story will continue is Monsters and Magic, Book Two in the Shaman Queen's Harem! Amazon can be really bad about notifying readers about new releases, so be sure to subscribe to Jasmine newsletter at www.jasminewalt.com so you don't miss the next book!

GLOSSARY

This short, spoiler-free glossary will help you familiarize yourself with some of the Japanese and mythological terms in this book.

butsudan – a shrine traditionally found in Japanese Buddhist temples and homes.

daimyo – (Feudal Japan) one of the great lords who were vassals to the shogun (general).

furi – a monkey-like yokai appearing in both Chinese and Japanese legends.

gaki – the spirit of a jealous or greedy person who has been cursed with an insatiable hunger.

geisha – a Japanese hostess trained to entertain men with conversation, dance, and song.

haiden – the hall of worship at a Shinto shrine.

hakama – a form of loose trousers with many pleats in the front, worn as part of Japanese formal dress.

haori – a lightweight coat worn over a kimono.

hitodama – a floating ball of fire, said to be souls of the dead that have separated from the body. Within this story, hitodamas are the spirit form of both *yurei* and *yokai*, which a shaman can merge with in order to use their powers and abilities.

hiyaku – Japanese word for "soar."

honden – the most sacred building at a Shinto shrine, intended purely for the use of the enshrined kami, who is usually symbolized by a mirror or sometimes by a statue.

jinmenju – a yokai tree with human-faced fruits called jinmenshi, a human-faced child. The tree is said to be found in remote valleys in the south of Japan and China.

kabuki – a form of traditional Japanese drama with highly stylized song, mime, and dance, performed only by male actors using exaggerated gestures and body movements to express emotions, and including historical plays, domestic dramas, and dance pieces.

kamaitachi – a weasel-like yokai with sickle-blades for arms.

kami – a divine being, such as a god.

kanji – a form of Japanese writing using Chinese characters.

katana – a long, single-edged sword used by Japanese samurai.

konnichiwa – Japanese term for "good afternoon."

ki – Also known as *chi* or *qi*, ki is the energy that flows through all living beings, plant or animal.

kimono – a long, loose robe with wide sleeves and tied with a sash, originally worn as a formal garment in Japan.

koka suru – Japanese term for "descend."

Kuchisake-onna – Also known as the "slit-mouthed woman," the Kuchisake-onna is the ghost of a woman who was mutilated by her husband, then returned to earth as a malicious spirit.

kusarigama— also known as a "chain-sickle". A weapon that consists of a sickle (farming tool) with a weight that is attached to the end with a long chain. The wielder typically swings the weight at the enemy and uses it to coil the chain around his weapon or arm, then finishes him off with the blade. It is a very versatile weapon, as the sickle and weight can be used in a variety of combinations.

kyuubi – also known as "the fox spirit" or "nine-tailed fox," kyuubi is a well-known yokai appearing in Japanese and Chinese mythology. They are trickster yokai, known for their shape-shifting abilities and illusion magic as well as the ability to wield foxfire.

maji – Japanese word for "merge."

matcha – a powdered green tea used in Japanese tea ceremony.

makuragaeshi – a child ghost that haunts specific rooms in a house. They especially like to play pranks on guests.

mezame – Japanese word for "awaken," used by a shaman to summon yokai.

mokumokuren – a common yokai that often lives in torn shoji, tatami mats, or walls.

naginata – one of several varieties of Japanese blades, fashioned as a pole weapon similar to a spear.

ningyo – a fish-like creature in Japanese mythology, sometimes depicted as a mermaid.

nuribotoke – an animated corpse. They are typically believed to have revived due to poor care of a household's shrine.

ofuda – a type of household amulet or talisman, issued by a Shinto shrine. They are traditionally hung in the house for protection.

ogama – a giant toad yokai.

Okaa-san – a respectful Japanese term for "mother."

osuzumebachi – a Japanese giant hornet.

Reikai – Japanese term for the spirit realm.

reiki – a healing technique based on the principle that the therapist can channel energy into the patient by means of touch to activate the natural healing processes of the patient's body and restore physical and emotional well-being.

ryokan – a traditional Japanese inn featuring tatami-matted rooms, communal baths, and other public areas where visitors may wear yukata (a light cotton kimono) and talk with the owner.

Ryujin – a dragon god also known as Watatsumi or Suijin. He is the guardian deity of the sea in Japanese mythology.

sakura – Japanese word for "cherry blossom."

sanshutsu – Japanese word for "yield."

Shinto – a Japanese religion dating from the early 8th century and incorporating the worship of ancestors and nature spirits and a belief in sacred power (kami) in both animate and inanimate things. It was the state religion of Japan until 1945.

shoji – a light screen consisting of a framework of wood covered with paper or other translucent material, used originally in Japanese homes as one of a series of sliding panels between the interior and exterior or between two interior spaces.

sumanai – Japanese term for "I'm sorry."

suzu – a round, hollow Japanese bell that is often draped outside Shinto shrines. Ringing the bell is said to call the shrine's kami, allowing one to acquire positive power and authority while repelling evil.

tanto – a Japanese dagger.

tatami – a rush-covered straw mat forming a traditional Japanese floor covering.

tengu – a legendary bird of prey yokai, traditionally depicted with both human and avian characteristics. They are considered protective, if dangerous, guardians of the mountains and forests.

torii – the gateway of a Shinto shrine, with two uprights and two crosspieces.

umigame – a giant sea turtle yokai.

wakizashi – a Japanese short sword.

yokai – a class of supernatural monsters in Japanese folklore.

yoki – ki, or energy, given off by a yokai.

yurei – Japanese word for "ghost" or "spirit."

ALSO BY JASMINE WALT

The Shaman Queen's Harem:

Ghosts and Grudges

Monsters and Magic —Coming Soon!

The Dragon's Gift Trilogy:

Dragon's Gift

Dragon's Blood

Dragon's Curse—Coming Soon!

The Nia Rivers Adventures:

Dragon Bones

Demeter's Tablet

Templar Scrolls

Serpent Mound

Eden's Garden—Coming Soon!

The Baine Chronicles Series:

Burned by Magic

Bound by Magic

Hunted by Magic

Marked by Magic

Betrayed by Magic

Deceived by Magic

Scorched by Magic

Taken by Magic

Tested by Magic (Novella)

The Gatekeeper Chronicles

Marked by Sin

Hunted by Sin

Claimed by Sin

ALSO BY J.A. CIPRIANO

A Ritual of Fire

A Ritual of Death

Seized

Claimed

Hellbound

The Half-Demon Warlock

Pound of Flesh

Flesh and Blood

Blood and Treasure

The Lillim Callina Chronicles

Wardbreaker

Kill it with Magic

The Hatter is Mad

Fairy Tale

Pursuit

Hardboiled

Mind Games

Fatal Ties

Clans of Shadow

Heart of Gold

Feet of Clay

Fists of Iron

The Spellslinger Chronicles

Throne to the Wolves

Prince of Blood and Thunder

Found Magic

May Contain Magic

The Magic Within

Magic for Hire

Witching on a Starship

Maverick

Planet Breaker

ABOUT THE AUTHORS

JASMINE WALT is obsessed with books, chocolate, and sharp objects. Somehow, those three things melded together in her head and transformed into a desire to write, usually fantastical stuff with a healthy dose of action and romance. Her characters are a little (okay, a lot) on the snarky side, and they swear, but they mean well. Even the villains sometimes. When Jasmine isn't chained to her keyboard, you can find her practicing her triangle choke on the jujitsu mat, spending time with her family, or binge-watching superhero shows on Netflix. You can connect with her on Instagram at @jasmine.walt, on Facebook, or at www.jasminewalt.com.

J.A. CIPRIANO is a New York Times bestselling author of over fifty science fiction and fantasy novels. When he's not creating imaginative and spectacular tales, J.A. lives in California with his wife and son, where the weather is always nice and sky is always bright. He also has three chinchillas. Two of them are gray, and because of this, they are named Slate and Cadmium. The third is named Jet because he's black, and Jet is old English for black. See, creative. He also has a cat named Turtle. This does pose problems for his four-year-old from time to time. He one day dreams about owning the car from Supernatural, but only if it comes with Castiel. You can connect with Jason on Facebook, join his reader group, or visit his website at www.jacipriano.com